A Highlander tamed...

Laird Daniel Murray seeks adventure, battle and freedom for his countrymen. Putting off his duties as laird—with a promise to his clan he'll return come spring—Daniel sets off with his men to fight alongside William Wallace and the Bruce. But soon he stumbles across an enchanting lady in need. She tantalizes him with an offer he simply can't refuse and a desire he attempts to dismiss.

A lady's passion ignited...

Escaping near death at the treacherous hands of a nearby clan, Lady Myra must find the Bruce and relay the news of an enemy within his own camp. Alone in a world full of danger and the future of her clan at stake, she must trust the handsome, charismatic Highland laird who promises to keep her safe on her journey—and sets her heart to pounding.

Together, Daniel and Myra will risk not only their lives, but their hearts while discovering the true meaning of hope and love in a world fraught with unrest.

The Highlander's Lady

Eliza Knight

The Highlander's Lady

Book Three: The Stolen Bride Series

By
Eliza Knight

The Highlander's Lady

****
FIRST EDITION
October 2012

Copyright 2012 © Eliza Knight

THE HIGHLANDER'S LADY © 2012 Eliza Knight. ALL RIGHTS RESERVED. No part or the whole of this book may be reproduced, distributed, transmitted or utilized (other than for reading by the intended reader) in ANY form (now known or hereafter invented) without prior written permission by the author. The unauthorized reproduction or distribution of this copyrighted work is illegal, and punishable by law. The characters and events portrayed in this book are fictional and or are used fictitiously and solely the product of the author's imagination. Any similarity to real persons, living or dead, places, businesses, events or locales is purely coincidental.

Cover Design by Kimberly Killion @ Hot Damn Designs

****

Eliza Knight

Also Available by Eliza Knight

The Highlander's Reward – Book One, The Stolen Bride Series
The Highlander's Conquest – Book Two, The Stolen Bride Series
A Lady's Charade (Book 1: The Rules of Chivalry)
A Gentleman's Kiss
<u>Men of the Sea Series:</u> *Her Captain Returns, Her Captain Surrenders, Her Captain Dares All*
<u>The Highland Jewel Series:</u> *Warrior in a Box, Lady in a Box, Love in a Box*
Lady Seductress's Ball
Take it Off, Warrior
Highland Steam
A Pirate's Bounty
Highland Tryst (Something Wicked This Way Comes Volume 1)
Highlander Brawn (Sequel to *Highland Steam*)

Coming soon…
A Knight's Victory (Book 2: The Rules of Chivalry)
The Highlander's Warrior Bride (Book 4: The Stolen Bride Series)
Behind the Plaid (Book 1: Highland Bound)

Writing under the name Annabelle Weston

Wicked Woman (Desert Heat)
Scandalous Woman (Desert Heat)
Mr. Temptation
Hunting Tucker

Coming soon…
Notorious Woman (Desert Heat)

****

The Highlander's Lady

Visit Eliza Knight at www.elizaknight.com or www.historyundressed.com

Dedication

For Peepa, who used to sit me on his lap and sing me Irish ditties, would run with me through the fields, swearing there was a pot of gold at the end of the rainbow. For inspiring in me a love of all things Celtic and especially a belief in magic and make-believe. May you forever dance upon the plush clouds of dreams as you sleep in eternal bliss.

Acknowledgements

Special thanks to Lizzie, Andrea, Vonda, Kate and Kim! Thanks, my dears, for all of your help in making this book possible!

Thank you to my family for suffering a diet of grilled cheese, pizza delivery and various other take-out gastronomies while I physically attached myself to the computer—oh, wait a minute, you guys love that stuff! Lol

Chapter One

Early December
Highlands, 1297

A loud crash sounded from below stairs, startling Lady Myra from her prayers. What in all of heaven was that?

She'd been sequestered in the chapel for most of the morning—penance for her latest bout of eavesdropping.

The chapel was dark, lit only by a few candles upon the altar. A fierce winter gust blew open the shudders, causing the candle flames to waver. Myra rushed to the windows, securing the shudders once more, feeling the wood rattle against her fingertips.

Her stomach muscles tightened with unease. There were not often sounds like this at Foulis. In fact, she'd never heard such before.

The Highlander's Lady

The very floors seemed to shake. Imagination going wild, she pictured the boards beneath her feet splintering and falling through to the great hall below.

Myra kept a keen ear, waiting for a sign that would reassure her that nothing was amiss. For once she hoped to hear her older brother, Laird Munro, railing at the clumsy servant who'd dropped something, but there was nothing save an eerie silence. The hair along her neck rose and with it, her skin prickled as an acute sense of dread enveloped her.

The castle was never this silent.

"Astrid?" she called out to her maid—but there was no reply. Not even the scurrying of her servant's feet across the floor. Where had the maid gone? She was supposed to wait for Myra outside the chapel door. "Astrid!" she called a little louder this time, but still there was no reply.

'Twas as if she were alone, but that made no sense. Foulis Castle was always bustling with people. Unable to stand the silence, Myra scrambled to her feet. She lit a tallow candle by the hearth to light her way in the darkened corridor and slowly crept toward the door of the family chapel. Nothing but a whisper of a breeze from her gown disturbed the areas where she passed—'twas how she was able to eavesdrop so often. Locked away, supposedly for her own good, since she was a girl, she learned an important lesson. If she were to find out anything of import, she had to be secretive and slick, so she learned to creep.

She did so now with practiced ease, sidestepping boards known to creak and pausing every few moments to listen for sounds. She strained to hear a whisper, someone's breathing, anything that would assure her that she had in fact let her imagination get the best of her. But there was nothing.

Fighting hard to keep the fear from suffocating her, she reached the door, and with tortured slowness gripped the cool iron handle. She wanted to throw it open, and ignore the dread that held her hand still. But she had to trust her instincts. Something was terribly wrong. She could feel it. Myra leaned in close, pressing her ear to the frozen wood. She remained motionless, listening. Again silence. Satisfied there was no imminent threat, she began to open the door. An earth shattering shriek and another loud crash broke the silence. Myra slammed the door. Was that...? She shook her head. It couldn't be. Scrambling away from the door, she dropped her candle which snuffed itself out. God's teeth! Was that a battle cry? Granted, she'd never heard one before, but 'twas not just any shout. Nay, this sound was terrifying. A cry that sent her knees to shaking and her lip to bleeding from biting it so hard.

She could barely see, the candles at the altar weren't putting off enough light. What in blazes was she supposed to do? How would she protect herself? Damn those guards. Why hadn't there been any warning? Shouts of caution. Why hadn't the gates been closed?

Was it possible that she'd just not heard the warnings? She had been deep in prayer, worrying about her sore knees, and to add insult to injury she'd needed to use the privy for hours. Had she been that preoccupied? Angered? So distracted that if someone had shouted in her ear she probably wouldn't have heard it? She took a deep breath to figure out her next course of action.

The secret stairways! Lucky for her, the chapel was located in a tiny corridor off the gallery above the great hall. A hidden stair, inside the chapel, led up to the master's chamber. Embarrassed after her penances—which were often, Myra chose not to venture into the great hall, instead she preferred to use the hidden stairs. She knew them well. All of them. When she was just a girl, her father had shown her where they were located, and when she'd once found them fun, she now found comfort in their obscurity. Now they

The Highlander's Lady

would not only help hide her embarrassment but they might even save her life.

Myra did regret being sent to Father Holden for having listened in on a very private and political conversation. Her ears burned from hearing all the things he and his allies had said. Worry consumed her.

But this was no time to think back on that conversation. Or was it?

There'd been a warning. Rumors of an impending attack. But who would attack Foulis? Any why? Such an act was foolish. They had excellent fortifications. A stone gate tower was built at the front of the castle walls, with at least a half dozen guards on watch at a time. Her brother Byron made sure the gate was always closed, and most often barred. Their walls were thick and she'd thought impenetrable. If they were being attacked, there should have been fair warning. The guards could see all around the castle. No hidden spots for an enemy to hide. Her brother's retainers kept guard upon the walls and the lands. This she knew — so how?

Then Myra remembered — from a neighboring clan, Laird Magnus Sutherland had told her brother that they suspected an attack would come from a trusted ally. There would be no warning. Anyone could be the enemy. Except Magnus had warned of one.

Ross.

Upon her father's deathbed this past spring, he'd signed a betrothal contract between Myra and Laird Ross — despite Ross being old enough to be her father. Myra and Ross' daughter, Ina — who made Myra want to pull her own hair out — were the same age. Myra crinkled her nose. Wasn't it wrong to be the stepmother of a woman who shared her birth year?

Myra's reaction to the news of her betrothal had garnered her a penance too — three days in a hair shirt and her skin had been so irritated she'd not been comfortable in even the softest linen chemise Astrid could find for her for nearly a fortnight.

Could it be him? Was that how the enemy had gained entrance without warning? If 'twas Ross, the he probably tricked everyone into thinking he'd come to discuss the impending alliance between their two clans. Byron wouldn't have suspected an attack—despite the warning—he was too trustworthy.

Myra backed toward the center of the room. Faint cries of pain floated through the floorboards. Fear snaked its way around her spine and threatened to take away her mobility. She grabbed the wooden slat leaning against the wall to bar the door. The candles flickered. Whoever was downstairs was not here for a friendly visit. Heaven help her. They would leave no room unturned. Myra prayed her brother and his wife, Rose who was heavy with child, were safe. That Astrid was hunkered down somewhere with the other servants. She covered her ears from the cries of pain and anger. There was little doubt the enemy was causing great destruction.

"Zounds!" Myra tamped the candles on the altar, putting the chapel into shadows and stalked toward the tapestry of a great wildcat on the hunt. She flipped back the covering, not even a speck of dust to make her sneeze since she used it so often. Pressing on the rock that opened the hidden door, she slipped into the black, closing the door behind her. Silent, she welcomed the comfort of nothingness as she slid her feet along the landing until she reached the first step. Finally something positive had come from her many penances, after using this particular staircase at least a thousand times, she knew the exact measurements of each step. The depth, the height. They fit her feet perfectly now.

Fingers trailing over the dusty, crumbling stone walls, she made her way carefully but briskly down the stairs until she reached the wall behind her brother's study. She peered through the imperceptible crack in the wall where she often stood to listen—as she had just the day before. The room was lit by a few candles as though her brother had been there, but he was not now. The room was empty and undisturbed.

Where was he? And Rose?

Myra's unease was slowly turning into an acute fear. She refused to let her nerves take over. There had to be another explanation. They *couldn't* be under attack. She refused to believe it. Her mind skipped over every other possibility. Perhaps the men were involved in another round of betting. Fighting each other to see who could best who. That made sense. All the servants would be crowded in the minstrel's gallery above to watch, and the great hall would be a raucous room full of shouting, sweating, swearing warriors.

That had to be it. A mock battle of some sort.

Yet, this felt different. Every nerve in her body strained and her teeth chattered with fear. Why was she reacting so physically when it might possibly be nothing more than a bit of rowdy warrior fun? Her overactive imagination? Probably. But, she would have to see for herself. Myra continued along her path, winding down and nearly to the great hall when she heard a distant whimpering. Nothing more than a whisper of a sound, but in the complete and silent dark, it was telling. Recalling the number of steps she'd taken, she calculated that she must be just outside Rose's solar. She ran her hand along the wall searching for the small metal handle, then nudged the door an inch ajar. It was indeed Rose's solar, and the whimpering was coming from inside, but she couldn't see who it was, since the doorway was hidden behind a bureau that was pushed against it.

Myra listened for a few moments longer to discern if there was only one person in the room. It had to be Bryon's wife. "Rose?" she whispered.

The whimpering stopped.

"Hello?" came the tentative voice of her sister-by-marriage.

She called to her softly, "Rose, 'tis Myra."

A scuffling, like shoes scooting across the floor sounded within the room. Within moments Rose's tear-stained face peered through the crack. Her brown eyes were red rimmed and her fiery curls jutted in frantic wisps from her head.

"Myra!" she whispered frantically. "Ye must help me. They've come. I think they killed Byron. Everyone."

"Who? Wait, help me push this door open, ye must come in here."

Rose shook her head. "They are tearing the castle apart as we speak. If I come in there, then they will too."

Myra's sister-by-marriage was right. It would be impossible for them to put the bureau back in place. They had to escape unnoticed. The secret passages were the only way — and they had to remain concealed. "Can ye get to Byron's library? There's a passage through the hearth."

Rose looked about frantically, as if expecting the door to her solar to bang open at any moment. She nodded, fear filling her eyes.

"I will meet ye there. Go. Quickly." Myra reached her fingers through the door and gripped Rose's, hoping to give her some measure of comfort. "I will be there waiting."

Rose nodded again, squeezing Myra's hand with trembling fingers.

"I'm going now, Myra."

There was silence and then a creak as Rose opened the door. For several agonizing heartbeats, Myra waited. Waited for Rose to be struck down. Waited for the sound of shouts as she made her escape. Waited for something horrifying to happen. But there was nothing.

Myra counted to thirty, slowly, with even breaths, and then she ran back up the dark winding stair until she reached

The Highlander's Lady

Byron's library. Peeking through the crack, she determined the room was still empty. With trembling fingers she found the hook in the wall, and slid her finger through it yanking and twisting until the lock unlatched and the wall opened behind the hearth. The library's hidden door was heavy, but not as heavy as it could be. Made from plaster to look like stone, it was a perfect disguise within the wall. Ashes from the grate stirred and made her cough. She hid her face in her cloak to stifle the sound, and muttered a prayer of thanks for no fire being in the hearth.

Her heart felt as though it would explode, racing like sheep hunted by wolves. Myra crouched low to wait for Rose, hoping that should the enemy enter she'd have time to shut the hidden door without their notice.

Dear God, let Rose make it here safely.

Now she knew for certain, the castle was under attack. None of it seemed real. Fear prickled her skin. Why would anyone want to attack her home? And Byron couldn't possibly be... "Nay," Myra whispered with a shake of her head. Byron couldn't be dead. Just couldn't.

Her breath hitched and panic threatened to take over, but she willed herself to calm. Willed herself to stay strong for Rose and her unborn niece or nephew's sake.

What felt like hours later, but in reality was probably only minutes, the door to the library crept open. Myra bit her lip hard, expecting to hear the scrape of booted heels on the wooden planks, but there was only a whisper of slippers. Rose.

"Myra?" her sister-by-marriage called softly.

"I'm here." Myra scrambled out of the hidden door in the hearth, bumping her head on the oak mantel. "Come, we must hurry."

Rose didn't hesitate. They were through the secret door, the last inch closing when the main door to the library crashed open. Rose jumped beside her, letting out a strangled squeak. Myra reached up, finding Rose's lips in the dark and pinched them, indicating silence.

Rose nodded, and gripped Myra's hand with deathlike force.

Myra did not want to wait and see if those who'd entered happened to notice the wall shift when she'd closed it the remainder of the way, and so squeezing Rose's hand, she urged her down the steps.

Where she'd been able to fly in the dark before, she now had to tread lightly. Rose was already off balance with her huge belly, and not being used to the darkened stairs was made all the more unstable.

Myra prayed constantly, a litany in her mind, for the enemy to not follow, and luck must have been on their side because they made it to the door leading into the dungeon without one of the evil villains following.

She stopped and gripped Rose's shoulders. Although she couldn't see her face, Myra stared in that direction.

"Listen now, sister. Ye must hide in here. They willna find ye. I promise."

"Where?"

"The dungeon."

From the shudder of Rose's shoulders, Myra imagined her shaking her head hard.

"Ye must. If they find these tunnels, all is lost. But within the dungeon, they'd not find ye there."

"Where are ye going?"

"I have to find Byron."

"Nay! Ye canna! He's dead!" Panic seized Rose's voice, and she appeared to be on the very verge of hysterics.

"Shh... Ye dinna want them to hear us. I willna tarry long. But I must see if he lives."

Rose sobbed quietly and pulled Myra in for a hug. They stood for as long as Myra would allow, which wasn't nearly long enough, before she pushed the dungeon door open and guided Rose inside.

"Hurry back," Rose said, her voice cracking.

"I will."

Myra wasted no time rushing back up the stairs to the great hall. Peering through the hole, she saw nothing but destruction.

Bodies with blood flowing. Furniture turned and tossed. Food and wine mingled with the blood upon the floors and tables. Even a few of the dogs had been slaughtered. The dogs. Why would anyone slaughter an innocent animal? Tears pricked her eyes, but she willed them away. What did the enemy have to gain? She kept asking herself that question over and over and still didn't have an answer.

The enemy still lurked within the room. A few warriors she didn't recognize boasted of their heinous glory while another maniacally abused the body of a dead servant.

Bile rose, burning the back of her throat. There was no way she could get inside without being seen.

"Myra." Someone grabbed her ankle, tugging.

A scream bubbled up her throat, threatening to wrench free, when logic filled her mind with the sound of her brother's voice. Weak and pain-filled.

Myra crouched before she collapsed to the ground, patting the stone stairs until she felt the slightly cold flesh of her brother's hand. She scooted close, her knees pressing against his side, feeling his shuddering breaths keenly.

"Byron, what's happened? How did ye get in here?" she whispered.

His breathing was labored and she was surprised she hadn't heard him before.

"Ross attacked..." He breathed deep, his lungs rattling. "Just as Sutherland said he would. I crawled into the tunnels...hoped you'd taken Rose...was trying to find...her."

Part of the conversation she'd overheard... Myra squeezed her eyes shut, trying not to cry, wishing this nightmare away. Her brother was badly injured. Her people slaughtered. The enemy waiting with glee for her to show her face.

"Why did he attack?" she asked.

Byron squeezed her fingers, but even his grasp was feeble.

"They are not our allies. They are allies of England."

Myra's stomach turned. She swallowed hard as her worst fears came true. And she was supposed to marry the bastard. Shaking her head, she gripped Byron's hand hard. There was no time for her to dwell on it now. She had to help him.

"Come, let me help ye. We must patch up your wounds. Where are ye hurt?"

"There's no use for it, sister. I'm going to die..."

For what seemed like a lifetime, there was silence. Her heart felt like it'd been ripped from her chest, and the fear of her brother passing before she could say goodbye collided with her senses.

"Nay. Nay, we will bring ye down to the dungeon with Rose. She'll help me."

Byron chuckled softly. "Ye're a good woman, Myra. As much as ye're a pain in the arse. But ye must leave me here. I need ye to do something for me."

Tears stung her eyes, and if she could see, her vision would be blurred. "What? Anything, tell me."

"I need ye to see Rose safely to the Sutherlands. And then I need ye to deliver a message."

The Sutherlands were their allies, and to be trusted. The chief himself had been involved with William Wallace at Stirling Bridge, a major reason for their victory. He'd been the one to warn of the Ross treachery. Rose would be safe within their walls.

The Highlander's Lady

"I will."

"Ye must find Robert the Bruce. He is..." Byron's voice trailed off again. Time was running short. She could only pray he would last long enough to give her the full message. "He is at Eilean Donan... Not safe. He'll never be king if... Ye must tell him about Ross. Tell him that there is an enemy within his camp...tell him Ross is in league with the English and plans to kill him."

Myra shuddered. King Edward, better known as Longshanks by her kin, was responsible for this war. He wanted to scour the Scots from their own land, the greedy bastard. She'd lived in fear nearly her entire life. The Sassenachs were monsters that lived under her bed, crept in the shadows of her nursery as a child, and even now when she felt as though she was being watched it was by one of the demon English.

With William Wallace fighting alongside the Bruce, they'd won the Battle of Stirling Bridge—a major victory for the Scots—and it emerged that her country might indeed gain their freedom from English oppressors. But not if they were being undermined from within. Not if Ross gave away their secrets and whereabouts.

Damn him!

"Tell Rose I love..." Byron's voice trailed off and Myra felt him shudder against her knees.

Myra shoved her anger to the back of her mind, concentrating on her brother's last ragged breaths. A sob slipped from her throat and she collapsed onto his chest, hugging him, trying to push her warmth into him, trying to bring him back from death. All around her on the floor, his warm sticky blood flowed.

But 'twas no use. Byron was gone—and at the hands of a man she despised. An enemy of her country. An enemy of her family. A man she vowed to never marry. Not in this lifetime, nor in the next. She would see Rose to safety and then she would see to the demise of Ross—tell the Bruce of the traitor's existence.

Myra slipped her brother's ring from his finger, the one made of gold and onyx, a symbol of the Munro clan chief and shoved the ring into her boot. With a start she realized what Byron's death meant.

Myra was chief.

"Dear Rose, please birth a son."

She didn't want to be chief. Had no idea how to run a clan.

Cradling her brother's head, she laid him down gently, giving him one last kiss on the cheek. She swallowed her fear, clear on what had to be done. Conviction straightened her spine as she stood. As chief of Munro—for hopefully only a month or so longer—she would see this deed done.

Myra raced down the steps to the dungeon, finding Rose where she'd left her.

"We must make haste." Her voice came out harsher than she intended, but Rose made no comment on it.

Pulling Rose back into the darkened corridor, they made their way farther down the stairs.

"We will have to crawl through here. Think ye can manage?"

"Aye," Rose said. She didn't ask what Myra had found and her voice too grew harder as though she knew her husband was dead.

Myra could not imagine how Rose felt. To be left so soon by her husband and a bairn on the way.

They crawled through the last tunnel, the weight of the castle above them. The stones were slick and bits of debris littering the floor jabbed into her palms.

Ye can do this. Myra repeated the words in her mind a thousand times, and with each recitation, she felt a little stronger.

The Highlander's Lady

When they neared the end of the tunnel, a bright light slipped through a crack of stone, beckoning them forward. A breeze whistled through the crack sending wintry chills up and down her limbs. 'Twas cold outside... Traveling would not be easy.

"We're almost there," she called to Rose who crawled behind her.

Rose let out a little grunt.

"Keep that bairn inside ye." Myra had the sudden horrific thought that Rose might go into labor from all the stress of the day on her mind and body.

"He's to stay put," Rose panted from the exertion of crawling.

"Let us pray 'tis a boy."

They at last reached the end where there was room to stand. Myra helped Rose up, her legs wobbly.

"When we leave this cave, we will have to keep close to the walls, and ye'll need to stay hidden while I fetch us a horse."

"Nay!" Rose shook her head vehemently. "The attackers are sure to be out there."

"Aye. But what choice do we have? We canna stay here and wait for them to find us."

In the sliver of light coming from the hidden entrance, Myra could make out Rose's eyes shifting about in thought.

"We shall walk into the village and get a horse from there," Rose offered.

Myra shook her head. "Most likely they've burned the village, or at the very least are looting it. I'll not have us stuck there." Myra pressed a steady hand to Rose's belly, feeling the child kick within. A surge of protectiveness filled her. "Or be killed. We will see my brother's heir to safety. Ye and I together."

"I trust ye." Rose nodded, her eyes wide. "I do."

"All right, then, ye stay here. If I'm not back within a quarter hour, run."

Chapter Two

"My son, ye must marry!"

Laird Daniel Murray looked at his mother, irritated, and tried like hell not to shout at the daft woman. Please, not this again. 'Twas the same conversation — if one could call it that since he did not utter a word — each time he graced Blair Castle's entrance, his home. He'd only just returned with the dawn, and already, she was making his head ache. He was sure she wouldn't be pleased that he planned to leave within the hour.

"Aye, your mother is correct," his uncle Artair said with a great sigh. They all sat at the great table in the hall, bowls of lukewarm porridge and hunks of freshly baked bread before them. Uncle Artair's grey, bushy brows sagged over his eyelids, and the wrinkles in his face were a map to his past. "Ye must have an heir, Danny, ye must."

Daniel cringed inwardly. He despised being called Danny, for it brought out images of a lad still dressing in bairn gowns, racing and tripping through the bailey. He glanced around the room, taking in the tapestries of Murrays of the past. They depicted strength, pure raw power. Battle scenes, treaties signed. Every image pounded the one thing into his head he couldn't escape from—he wasn't leader material. And yet, he was their laird. Daniel knew how to fight. Hell, he was an expert in combat. He could negotiate a treaty or a farmer's dispute with the best of them. But here, in Blair's great hall, he'd always felt lacking.

"Listen to your uncle, he is an elder of the clan and speaks the truth." His mother pushed from her chair and rushed toward him, still beautiful even with a few crinkles at her eyes and greying hair. "We've presented ye with nigh on a dozen brides and yet ye've tossed them all to the wind. What will become of the Murrays without an heir?"

Daniel stood and trudged toward the wide hearth filled with a roaring fire, not because he sought heat, but because he wished to put some distance between himself and his *loving* family. He took a long gulp of his ale. The brides, as his mother called them, were ridiculous half-wits. Not one of them wanted to be with him for him. They wanted to be mistress of Blair. They wanted his wealth. His name. Not one of them had been blessed with an intelligent thought, nor could they hold a meaningful conversation. Daniel had been bored within moments of being introduced. He was not stupid. He realized that all the *assets* he had would garner interest, and instead that was what would draw a woman to him. Even still, he would also like for his wife to like *him*. At least enough to smile when he walked through the door. His mother and uncle meant the best for him, but he found their tireless efforts to see him wed taxing. He was not ready to marry.

Settling down when he was in the prime of his bachelorhood did not appeal to him. He wanted to sow those oats before pledging his life to another. Daniel was not the

The Highlander's Lady

type of man who would leave his wife to entertain himself elsewhere. At least, that's what he believed since he'd never been married before. His cousin Magnus, Laird Sutherland, was a good man, a man he saw himself much like. Magnus loved his wife.

Daniel couldn't imagine that he would feel the same way about love, as Magnus. Especially since he unsure what love was, or that he felt any interest in perhaps being on the receiving end of it, but he did want companionship. Someone he could share things with, enjoy an evening of dancing and even the pleasure of bedding. Making love was a superb way to let the nights pass.

All of that however, seemed an impossible feat. 'Twas luck that brought Magnus to his bride, Arbella de Mowbray. 'Twas that same luck that brought Magnus' brother Blane to his wife Aliah, for she was Arbella's sister.

There were no sisters left in the De Mowbray family. Daniel was out of luck.

"Are ye listening to your mother?" Artair's voice was heavy with weariness.

Daniel turned to face his mother, trying not to let his frustration show. Artair was his father's brother—and his mother the sister to his Sutherland cousins' father. When his mother, Fiona, married the old Laird Murray—his father, grey as a storm cloud—she'd been young and he already on his third wife. The laird had passed the year before in a clan battle. Died like a warrior—although before Daniel was ready to take on the duties expected of him.

"I was not pleased with the brides ye showed me. I willna tie myself to a woman who does not satisfy me."

"What are ye looking for then?" his mother asked. Her eyes were dark green like his own, and shone with her own bit of annoyance. "Ye must marry, Danny. Everything is at stake. 'Tis best—"

"I know what's best for the clan," Daniel said, his voice coming out harsher than he intended. He was tired of everyone thinking him not fit. Whether they believed it, or he did, there was no other way for it. Daniel was laird. He had to do what was best for his people. And as much as it pained him, he had to reveal the terms he'd agree too, his terms, else they nag him to an early grave. "I will marry come spring."

"Spring? This spring?" Fiona's eyes were wide flashing between speculation and hope.

"Aye, this spring."

His mother was so moved, she clapped with joy, and his uncle breathed such a heavy sigh of relief, the ale in his cup rippled.

"Until that time, I leave the clan in your hands, Uncle."

"What?" His mother's exasperated shout rattled the rafters.

Artair raised his brows and sat heavily back in his chair, placing his ale on the table, no doubt getting ready to calm Fiona.

"I've decided to join William Wallace and the Bruce."

Artair sat forward at that, whatever relief he'd experienced completely wiped from his face. "Are ye insane, Danny?"

And here they went…

"Nay, quite the opposite." Daniel tried to keep his voice calm, even placed his ale on the mantel and crossed his arms over his chest, trying for casual. "'Tis a known fact the English plan an attack on our people come the spring. When Wallace and his eight thousand men took Stirling castle, 'twas a blow to Longshank's Sassenach pride. The English king is a bastard and willna let a prime stronghold easily slip from his fingers. Rumor has it he's already recalling troops from abroad to aid in his cause against us. He willna stop until he's seen to it that every last Scot is bled from this world. Wallace needs my help

The Highlander's Lady

to train the men. The Bruce needs the support of all the leaders in Scotland. We must show that we stand behind him, that the Murrays dinna want to be ruled by English."

"Aye, but did ye not say your cousin Ronan was going?"

Ronan was Magnus' and Blane Sutherland's youngest brother. The man was a force to be reckoned with when it came to a sword, a man Daniel was not only proud to call blood, but proud to call a Scot. He'd have Ronan guard his back any day.

Daniel took a few steps toward the great table, his lips thin. Mother rushed to sit, ringing her hands. He'd known this would not be easy. "That he is, and I plan to help him."

"But what of your other cousin Angus Moray, who fought beside Wallace at Stirling Bridge and was mortally wounded?" Fiona gripped the edge of the table, her voice low and smooth as though she fought to keep her temper in check. "Should ye like that to be your fate?"

Daniel was sure his mother hoped to scare him from going. But his cousin's death only further made him want to join the fight. Her reminder of it only upped his keenness to leave Blair.

He crossed his arms over his chest and stared down at her.

Blood drained from his mother's face and her mouth opened and closed a few times before she spoke. "Ye will not back down." 'Twas a statement not a question. Despite how much she badgered him, Daniel's mother was well aware when he would not falter from his course.

"Nay."

Artair let out a long breath, placed his gnarled hands on his knees and pushed to stand. Taking a moment to gain his bearings, the old man hobbled toward him. He placed a firm hand on Daniel's shoulder—having to reach up considerably high given that Daniel took after the Sutherland side of the family and was easily a foot taller.

"I give ye my blessing. I will support ye. But ye must come back alive. 'Tis a dangerous thing ye're planning to do, and ye'll put the clan in danger should ye get yourself killed."

Daniel gave his uncle a small smile of appreciation. The older man's support meant a lot more than Daniel was willing to let on. 'Twas something he'd not ever received from his own father. "Thank ye." Turning to face his mother he said, "Will ye give me your blessing?"

She contemplated, her fingers dancing over her skirts as if she counted how many things could go wrong. Her gaze was fixed on her hands, and if he wasn't used to such behavior from her, he might have thought she'd not heard him. Finally, she nodded. "I will support ye, Danny, but I dinna like it."

He stepped forward and pulled his mother into his embrace. Citrus and cloves. She smelled as she always had since he was a small helpless thing. 'Twas a smell he'd forever associate with comfort. For however prickly she was, Fiona had a tender heart at her center. Daniel knew that was as good as he was going to get.

"Thank ye."

She nodded against his chest, patted his back. "Ye'd best go so ye can come back. I've a list of brides to prepare. Not sure who is left." She pulled back a bit and gave him a challenging lift of her brow. "Might have to marry ye to Heather."

"Dear Lord, nay!" he teased back. He'd not ever marry Magnus' youngest sister. Not only was she too closely blood related for his tastes, she was only fifteen summers. Far too young for him. Daniel liked a woman fully grown and ripe.

"Well, it was a good try. The lass is going to have a hard time finding a husband that will take her on."

Too true. Heather was a hellion of the highest order. Magnus often sent her to Blair Castle for the guidance of

The Highlander's Lady

Daniel's mother. Not that Daniel was sure any of her guidance was heeded.

He shrugged. Heather was the least of his problems. "'Haps she'll settle in time."

"As I hope ye will."

"Spring."

Mother nodded, then gave him a stern look. "Will ye bring Heather home to Dunrobin afore ye set off for the Bruce?"

"Aye." He agreed, even though it was completely out of his way. Dunrobin was a week's travel north and the Bruce's camp at Eilean Donan was that much to the west. He'd essentially be doubling his travel time, but nevertheless, if that was his mother's price for supporting him, then he'd take it.

Daniel disengaged from his mother's arms and excused himself. He had much to speak to his men about—they'd probably balk that he did not plan to bring any of them with him. No doubt, they'd wonder why, and he'd have to assure them that this was nothing to do with their own skills, but with his need to seek out one last adventure. He frowned. They'd likely not understand that. Best to come up with some other excuse.

When he spotted his second in command, Leo was leaning against the rails of the horse ring watching a new stallion being broken.

"My laird." Leo nodded.

"I'm to leave Blair for a time."

"Where will ye go, my laird?"

Daniel did not miss the faint, but noticeable flash of irritation in Leo's eyes. The man had been his father's second in command and Daniel had not changed that when he took on duties as laird. Perhaps he should have reconsidered. For whatever reason, his father ingrained in everyone's mind that Daniel was a failure. He wasn't sure what prompted the constant reproach from his sire. All he knew was that it was never-ending.

"I'm going to help the Bruce and Wallace train their men."

"And why are ye leaving us behind? Are we of no use to the Bruce? Have ye no pride in your men?"

Ballocks! Daniel had an idea the man would not be pleased, and when he put it that way, it certainly sounded much worse than it had in his own mind. He'd have to bring them with him. Perhaps an opportunity to bond with the men and gain their respect as a leader.

"I didna say ye weren't coming. Prepare a dozen of our best men. The rest stay behind to guard the castle. Blair is a strategic location Longshanks will surely want."

Leo nodded, his eyes narrowed as if trying to assess him. Daniel frowned. "What are ye waiting for? Snow?" he growled.

His second in command whirled around and headed toward the fields where the men trained.

Maybe when he found a wife, he'd find a new second too. He needed a man he could trust, someone who would not second guess him at every turn. Even though he wasn't happy about it, it probably was best if he took a few men with him, because despite it being winter, there was no telling whether or not he'd be attacked on the road. Plenty of outlaws roamed around, just waiting for a chance to strike. 'Twas a shame there were men starving and freezing, or just plain evil enough, to try and steal his cloak and supplies. A few men Daniel could fight off, but when food was scarce, outlaws tended to band together into small armies of their own.

Damn... He should have spent more time listening to his father, paying attention. Then maybe being laird wouldn't seem so daunting. He would have been better prepared for the life he was born into, less apt to run away from the things

The Highlander's Lady

he felt were to restricting. A wife. A family. A laird's duties. All of it, made him imagine a noose tightening around his neck. If only he'd been a better study. But no. Instead he'd been too interested in fighting, in making sure his sword gleamed and the point drew blood just from staring at it. He'd been too preoccupied with lifting every skirt that passed—as long as she was willing to engage in a carnal romp, he was game. No wonder his father had always rolled his eyes and given a disgusted grunt when he'd come into the great hall and seen Daniel dancing with lassies, wrestling with his men or playing cards.

Daniel had always assumed his father was too stiff, didn't like to enjoy life. But since the lairdship had been thrust upon his shoulders... Well, it wasn't a fun responsibility. That was as much as he was willing to admit right now.

He'd make the most of this winter. Come spring, he was resigning himself to a lifetime of drudgery.

Glancing over the fence, he watched as the handler trained the horse. The stallion kicked, bucked, didn't want to be tamed. Much like himself. He and the warhorse had a lot in common. Hands trying to tame their ways, make them fall in line. So many people demanding they follow the rules, making them bend to the will of those who would see them take a certain path. It was all too much. Daniel couldn't get away fast enough. He stared at the horse. Soon they would both relent, and be forever changed.

He had the urge to whip open the gate and let the beast run free. But if he had any chance of his people taking him seriously, that was not the right choice.

Daniel walked with heavy shoulders back to the keep to see about his cook preparing several bags of supplies. The sooner they left, the better. They could hunt for fresh meat— but at this time of year most of the animals would be hibernating or laying low in their warm dens. It made more sense to take as many provisions from the castle as they could spare, else they could starve before he reached his destination. If the weather had anything to do with it—they'd best hurry. Judging from the grey sky, snow would be coming soon. The last thing he wanted was to be stuck in a storm. They needed to make considerable ground and seek shelter as soon as possible. The ride would be slower with Heather in tow, but the quicker they dropped her at Dunrobin, the quicker he could be about his way.

Daniel's blood surged. God's teeth, he loved a good adventure.

Chapter Three

Myra hid among the pine trees upon a rise and watched as Rose approached Dunrobin Castle across the flat valley below. The cold wind whipped inside her cloak, numbing her skin. *Lord, please let her arrive safely.* She repeated her prayer a hundred times or more until the gates opened and Rose disappeared within its depths. Her sister-by-marriage would be safe—and Myra wouldn't have to worry about the Sutherlands insisting she remain with them.

Myra couldn't allow for such. She had a promise to keep. A Scottish king to save. Even knowing Rose was safe didn't cause her muscles to relax. If anything, she was even more on edge, for now she was all alone.

The loud grumbling of her stomach reminded her of how little food she'd consumed over the past several days, and how unlikely it was she'd get more before reaching her destination. She had to keep reminding herself of her promise, or else she might run through the gates of Dunrobin and throw herself on the mercy of their cook. Instead she focused on her journey, ignoring her persistent stomach, and kept telling herself that once she was far enough away from Dunrobin, with no fear of the Sutherlands chasing her down, she would forage for mushrooms or nuts *if* she could find any. There wasn't much else to be found. Winters in Scotland were harsh and what little could be foraged was most likely already gone.

Closing her eyes, she breathed in the crisp air. She was well and truly alone now. Her head felt heavy. Filled with the weight of the tears she'd left unshed, the strain of being chief to a clan she'd never expected to inherit. The death of Byron…

Her eyes stung, but she willed away the tears. She'd already been through so much, she refused to give in to her grief now. Pulling the Munro ring from within her gown where she'd tied it on a leather strip, she kissed the onyx and then tucked it away.

"Come now, Coney."

Her horse, which she'd named for his color so much like a pinecone, nickered and obliged her turning him around. His soft mane swayed in the gentle breeze, both of their breaths came out in puffs of steam. 'Twas cold. Frigid cold, and tonight she'd not have the warm body of Rose to sleep beside. Perhaps she'd sleep on the horse.

Getting Coney out of the stables, and the horse for Rose had been easier than she'd thought. No one, not even her own people, had been in the stables. The place looked deserted. If it weren't for the occasional shout or scream, she wouldn't have known they were in the thick of an attack. Even still, she knew how lucky she was to have gotten away. They'd climbed onto the horses, leaving at a fast pace, so scared, they didn't dare look back. Only when they were miles away from Foulis did she turn back. Black smoke billowed, curling and mixing with the low-hanging clouds. Fire. The bastards had set her home on fire. She prayed that some of the villagers and

The Highlander's Lady

the servants had escaped. The devastation Ross had wreaked on her clan was unthinkable. Boiling rage burned within her. She would have revenge. Ross would not get away with this. Not as long as she was alive!

At the pace they'd had to take with Rose's condition, it'd been five days since they escaped. After their initial burst, their horses had to maintain a slow pace, and frequent stops for Rose's bladder had been unavoidable. Myra was not capable of delivering a child in the wild, cold Highlands. She frequently checked to make sure Rose still held the bairn tight within her womb. At least now, she'd be able to let her horse fly.

Byron must have been looking down on them, protecting them along their journey, for they did not run into any trouble, though she'd had difficulty in hunting for them. After spending hours fashioning a spear from a long, thick stick she found and using the dirk at her hip, she'd finally killed a squirrel. Not an easy task, especially since she felt so out of practice. As a young girl she'd often hunted with her father. But after mother had been abducted… She had not been allowed to do so again.

The only supplies she'd been able to gather from inside the stables were a plaid blanket, water skin and, she was sorry for it, the rest of the horse master's luncheon. She'd given all the food to Rose and her unborn bairn, and waited over a day before hunting to feed herself, else she faint and not be able to protect her sister-by-marriage and her brother's heir.

Myra needed that bairn to be born. Needed it to be a boy. She couldn't possibly take on the responsibilities of laird. Not now. Not when she felt so uncertain of herself. When she'd be made to marry all the sooner. She'd murder the Ross before she married him.

And she might just murder him anyway for revenge.

She supposed it was utterly selfish to imagine a bairn taking away her burden. Were there any elders left? Surely some of them had escaped who could decide clan matters and train the bairn until he was ready to do so himself.

Myra frowned and stopped Coney a moment to assess her direction. What was she thinking? She wasn't that horrid of a woman to expect an innocent child to take on the duties with only the elders. She would have to be involved somehow. As much as she didn't want to. Byron was dead. 'Twas her duty. Enough of her time had been spent behind the walls watching Byron work on tasks, handle disputes. Myra could do it. And probably well. But she couldn't think on that now.

She had to head south-west to get to Eilean Donan. A castle she'd never been to but heard much of its beauty, mystique and defense. Situated in the middle of a loch she'd been told. Surrounded by mist nearly all day and protected by fairies.

The Bruce was there. Harbored within the enemies own camp and he had no idea. She prayed she could make it in time before another tragedy struck. As it was, she would need reinforcements to come back to Foulis to reclaim her castle. After murdering everyone within, the Ross clan would surely claim the lands for themselves. And when they found Rose and Myra had disappeared, they would come looking.

Rose was safe. Nestled within Dunrobin with one of the fiercest warriors Myra had ever heard of. Magnus Sutherland. Byron had trusted him and she would too.

Myra, however, was not so safe.

Alone in the forest, winter upon them with only a makeshift spear and dirk to protect herself.

Zounds! An impossible task had been given to her.

Keeping her groan of frustration within, Myra gritted her teeth and pushed her horse forward. She needed to make haste. It would take her nearly a week to reach Eilean Donan, and success was likely not on her side.

Daniel glanced up as a haggard, overly pregnant woman was brought into Dunrobin's great hall.

Daniel sat with Magnus and Blane talking strategy. His cousin Ronan had already joined Wallace and his men—where Daniel wished to be.

"My God," Magnus muttered under his breath as he stood to greet the woman.

Her fiery hair stood on end and her gown was torn and dirty. Her face smeared with grime, tears streaking down her cheeks. The woman looked ready to collapse.

"Are ye Laird Sutherland?" she asked Magnus, her weary eyes darting guardedly, her lower lip quivering.

"Aye."

She glanced with unease at the rest of the men.

"Ye are safe. What is your name?" Magnus said, walking toward her.

"Lady Rose of Foulis."

That got Daniel's attention and he too stood. "I know Laird Munro." Munro was an ally of his. A damned good card player too. And he had a beautiful, clever, fascinating, younger sister who…completely despised him.

Rose burst into tears, her hands gripping her swollen belly and she swayed on her feet.

"What has happened?" Magnus' wife, Arbella rushed into the great hall toward the woman, taking her by the elbow.

Lady Munro sank into the equally pregnant arms of Lady Sutherland.

"My husband… There was an attack. Everyone is dead."

Daniel's blood ran cold. "Everyone?"

Rose nodded through sobs. "Except for Myra."

"Myra?" Daniel asked, the familiar name sending sparks through his veins.

"Aye. Byron's sister. She brought me here."

He recalled well who Myra was, from several years before when he'd visited Foulis. She'd danced with abandon, laughed until tears came into her eyes, and then simply vanished. Daniel had found her utterly charming, but obviously the feeling was not mutual. She'd told him she'd be back in a moment and he'd waited and waited... Daniel shook his head. Now was not the time to feel sorry for himself or try to figure out why the only woman who'd ever spurned him disliked him so much—for if she hadn't she would have come back to him.

"Where is she?" he glanced behind Lady Munro, the doorway completely empty.

Rose shook her head. "She is gone."

"Gone?" Magnus looked sharply at Daniel.

"Aye. She had to deliver a message for my husband."

"To whom?"

Rose shook her head. "I dinna know. She wouldna tell me. Only that 'twas life or death. And death if she didna."

That didn't sound right. Myra could be in danger. While he had a few moments in her arms several years before, he knew not of her mind other than she lied to him. He didn't know many women who could defend themselves, or keep themselves alive in the wild—especially a spoiled heiress. Lady Arbella and Lady Aliah were the only women he'd ever met who could hold their own.

Despite his bruised ego, he couldn't let Lady Myra just go off alone in the wilds of the Highlands. His stomach soured thinking what could have happened to her already. Especially with an enemy on her tail.

"I will go and retrieve her," Daniel said, surprised at the hard tone in his own voice.

"Nay!" Rose shouted, her wide eyes connecting with his. She looked like a feral animal, ready to pounce on him, save for the unsteadiness of her legs. "You canna. Byron died giving her the message. She must be allowed to deliver it."

"Has she any men with her?" Magnus asked.

"Aye. Two dozen," Rose said quickly before falling into another fit of tears.

Well at least the Munro woman was protected. If she hadn't been he would have insisted, message or no. In any case, he'd keep an eye out for her. Soon he'd cut off toward Eilean Donan and who knew where she was headed.

"Come, let me attend to you," Arbella said to Rose.

"Nay, wife, I must speak with her regarding the attack," Magnus interjected.

Daniel and Blane both nodded their agreement. An attack on an ally meant an attack could be forthcoming.

Arbella sent Magnus a frown that Daniel had witnessed on more than one occasion—it meant she would get her way. He did not want to be caught in the middle of it. He started toward the main door.

"I will let you speak to her after I've cleaned her up and gotten her something to eat. I'd hope for nothing less if I were in her shoes. She is with child."

Daniel stopped, a sick sense of curiosity making him turn to see how Magnus reacted. He would enjoy ribbing his cousin later over this. The last statement seemed to be what garnered Magnus' agreement. In fact, it would have gained any man's, for no man wanted to press matters onto a woman liable to either break into a fit of tears or a rage that could cow a seasoned warrior.

Daniel hadn't had much experience with pregnant women other than a few of the servants who did their best to remain emotionless. Arbella was another story, and judging from the fit of tears and defiance Rose waffled between, he was willing to bet most females were a bit on the mad side when carrying a child.

Blane sat quiet at the table, his face a little pale.

"What is it?" Daniel asked.

Blane shook his head. Daniel groaned, unable to leave his cousin looking so odd.

"Come now, tell me."

Daniel sat down and watched as Rose was led away with Arbella. Magnus rejoined them at the table.

"Just ye wait, brother," Magnus said.

"Ah, so that is what has ye worried," Daniel said, putting the clues together. "Aliah is with child."

"Aye." Blane looked ready to lose his last meal.

Daniel laughed.

Both of his cousins glared at him. Daniel shrugged. "I feel for ye both. 'Tis something I'll not have to deal with for a little while longer."

"And then ye'll have a hellion on your hands."

"Not if I can help it," Daniel said. "My wife will be sophisticated yet obedient."

Both Blane and Magnus snickered and glanced at each other in a knowing way that made Daniel's blood burn.

Daniel glared at them. "Just ye wait and see then. Ye'll be mighty jealous of my bride."

That only made them laugh and Magnus slapped his large hand on the polished wood table.

"To hell with ye both. I'm for Eilean Donan. I need to warn the Bruce of the attack on Foulis. Ye send word there if ye find out anymore."

Daniel left Dunrobin's great hall with the sounds of his cousins' laughter burning an irritating path up his spine. He supposed he deserved their laughter. He'd made plenty of fun of them when they both married. 'Twas only fitting they'd return the favor.

His men were gathered outside, and when he approached they shifted slightly in manner, as though they were keeping something from him. Daniel had grown tired of their allegiance to a dead man—even if it was his sire. The men were fiercely loyal to the late laird, and had not as yet grown quite so with Daniel—even if they had fought with him before in battle, had his back and likewise. They knew he was their leader now, and yet they clung to the memory of his father and the black words his father had spewed.

Frowning, Daniel approached Leo, locking on the man's countenance. When he spoke his voice was low, deadly serious. "I've grown tired of your attitude."

"I know not what ye mean," Leo said with a smirk.

Daniel replied with the answer he knew best—he reared back and punched Leo in the jaw. The man's head snapped to the left and his feet left the ground, landing him squarely on his arse.

Daniel turned to the other men who stood, eyes wide. He shook out his hand. The skin split over the middle knuckle stung like the devil, but the sheer pleasure that raced through his veins made it worth it.

"The lot of ye have not been showing me the respect I deserve. I'm your laird, your chieftain. If ye canna bow here and now and offer me your complete loyalty then be gone with ye. I'll not tolerate another slight."

The men glanced from Leo to Daniel, which only served to make Daniel's anger hotter. Leo was still sprawled on the ground, looking about himself deliriously.

"Dinna look to him for your answer. If ye canna answer for yourself while looking at me, then ye are not man enough to belong in my guard. Murrays are not flaccid cocks. Kneel or run."

One by one the men knelt before him, swords drawn and stabbed deep into the earth, hands over their hearts. Even Leo, arse that he was, knelt and gave his loyalty. A tightness filled Daniel's chest. Pride. Power. Daniel's jaw muscles flexed, his breaths deep and slow.

"Better. Now up with ye. We must make haste to reach the Wallace camp before the first snow."

Several hours later, Myra pulled Coney to a halt beside a shallow, trickling burn. The water gleamed crisp and clean over rocks covered in algae. Her muscles were stiff as boards. So painful she could cry. With a groan, she dismounted and stretched, feeling the ache from the top of her head to the tip of her toes.

Judging from the particularly bright spot behind the clouds, the sun was high in the sky, meaning it was midday. Myra knelt before the water, filled her water skin, and then cupping her hands stuck them in the water to get a drink. Cold! Holy Heavens! She jerked back without taking a sip. With a deep breath of fortitude, she plunged her hands back into the near frozen stream and took a long sip of the cold water. It trailed a soothing path down her throat and filled her hungry stomach, quelling some of the hunger pains. But she needed food. Real food. 'Twas probably a good idea to look for something to eat while she was here as there might not be another opportunity.

With no coin, she'd not be able to buy anything from a tavern or even a vegetable cart, and she was safer not calling attention to herself. A woman alone was a woman likely to be a victim. That much she'd learned.

Myra had no interest in being a victim today. Coney dipped his head down to the water, taking long sips. She pulled her makeshift spear from where she'd secured it along the side of the horse.

Glancing into the burn, she spied no fish, only the occasional floating leaf passed by. She waited several more

The Highlander's Lady

minutes, begging even a small fish to appear. But there was nothing.

Rabbit perhaps? She crept along the brush, shaking limbs, but not one animal ran out. She would have settled for eating a mouse at this point. Her legs were starting to shake and pains shot through her belly like knives.

If there were no rabbits or mice offering themselves up to her, at least she could use the spear to dig or knock a few chestnuts from the trees. Judging from the trees, the only nut she was likely to eat was an acorn… *Damn*.

Myra checked around the ground, but found not one mushroom she could eat. She shrugged, disappointed but not defeated, and gathered several handfuls of acorns and two rocks she could crush them with. She went back to Coney, sat heavily on the ground and began to crush an acorn. Her first bite was bitter and she cringed, but chewed anyway. She'd no time to light a fire to roast the acorns, and if she didn't eat something, she'd never be able to make it as far as she wanted to before making camp for the night. After the sixth acorn, she could take it no longer. She drank several more handfuls of water, hoping the cool liquid would fill her up. She even thought briefly of eating the algae but wasn't sure about whether it would harm her or not.

"We'd best be on our way, Coney."

The horse glanced up from the small patch of grass he was munching and nodded. Or at least, it appeared that he was nodding. Was he nodding? She rubbed her eyes and blinked. Or was she overcome with delirium? This couldn't be good, she needed to get moving while she still could. Myra tucked the leftover acorns into the pouch attached to her saddle. If it came down to it, she supposed she could choke down a few more tonight. Sliding her spear in place, she mounted and urged Coney to walk along the burn. She'd follow it for a pace to keep herself on course. Myra had only a brief idea of where to go. But she couldn't let that thought linger. A case of nerves was not something she needed to deal with now.

Coney had much more strength that she did—having been able to munch freely on grass and clover. Myra would have, but she'd heard it had to be cooked first, else she'd get sick. Lighting a fire would only draw unwanted attention, so she left the grass to her horse.

Thank goodness for Coney. She'd never be able to walk all the way to Eilean Donan—and not because of starvation. There was just simply no way she'd make it there alive on foot. She was bound to be accosted, or at the very least someone would want to steal her horse. With Coney's speed, she had the chance of escape.

If her brother had made sure she knew one thing, it was that the world was not safe for a woman. She was vulnerable. Weaker. And men took advantage of that all the time. No one knew that better than Byron and Myra. Their father had drilled it into their heads before he passed, and then Byron had taken up the litany.

Their mother, God rest her soul, had been assaulted. She survived it, but was never the same again. Myra scarcely remembered her mother, as she'd taken her own life when Myra was barely seven summers.

'Twas then her father showed her the secret passageways, and never let her out of the castle walls again. She wasn't even allowed to greet guests. Became like a ghost herself. And now, here she was, completely alone, with barely a means to protect herself, set about on a treacherous journey. The wide open space set her on edge. She longed for the confinement of Foulis as much as she yearned to not crave it. The English were bound to be teaming around Wallace's camp, waiting for the moment they could attack. She'd be lucky to make it.

Byron wouldn't have tasked her with the impossible. She had to tell herself that again and again. He had to have

The Highlander's Lady

believed she could make it. He'd taught her well to defend herself—although she lacked for weapons. If he believed in her, then she needed to believe too.

Myra closed her eyes and sent up a prayer to the heavens, to God, to her brother, to see her safely to Eilean Donan.

Promised to speak and think more like a lady—no more curse words.

The horse's feet clopped on the ground, kicking up tufts of grass where the earth was moist from the water. As much as she wanted to stay near the water, Myra was aware that Coney's lone footprints would lead an assailant straight toward her. A lone rider was ripe for the picking—a female even more so.

She veered away from the burn and stopped. *Satan's ballocks!* A group of haggard looking horsemen came out of the trees to her left their gazes directed at her. Evil grins curled their nasty lips, showing rotten teeth and a few vulgar tongues waggled in her direction. Myra only looked at them for a moment before kicking Coney into a gallop. Not today. She would not be a victim.

Barely a day had gone by since leaving Rose and already she was done for. Nay, she'd not let them take her.

"Go!" she shouted to her horse, leaning low over his mane, and hanging on for dear life. Coney raced along the burn, his hooves digging deep into the moist earth and flinging rocks, grass and mud with them.

The men gave chase, shouting indiscernible threats behind her.

Myra had no idea where she was, or where she should go. There was bound to be a village or hut or something along the length of the burn. Where there was a stream, there was bound to be someone nearby.

"Help!" she screamed at the top of her lungs. "Help me!"

There were no answering calls besides the barbs behind her. No one rushed to her aid, not even God struck down those who would see her removed from her task of saving Robert the Bruce. *Ballocks! Ballocks! Ballocks!* A lot of good her promise of using more ladylike words in exchange for protection did.

There was no one to help her, she was sure of it, and she was probably only gaining the attention of more vagrants who would see her for their supper.

If it came down to it, she would fight these men with every last breath she had. If they were going to take her, at least one of them was going down with her.

Myra turned back for a split second to see they gained on her. That split second was all it took.

Pain splintered her head and she felt herself falling backward, away from her horse. She hit the ground—breath forced painfully from her lungs. Through dazed, blurry eyes, she made out the low-hanging branch of a tree.

"Zounds…" she muttered. Myra gripped the dirk from her hip, forcing her eyes to focus. Forcing the pain in her head to go away. She squeezed her eyes shut. "Och…"

Her head hurt like the devil. Nausea gripped her. She rolled to the side in time to see how close they were. The men reined in their mounts and the animals whinnied at such abrupt treatment. Coney meandered somewhere nearby, she hoped.

"Well, well, well. Would ye look at that?" One of the disgusting men chuckled as he dismounted.

His steps, slow and measured, scared the piss out of her. His boots came into view, and she forced herself to glance up as he bent toward her.

Chapter Four

The hilt of Myra's dirk dug deep into her palm. Her jaw hurt from clenching it so tight. She watched as the man moved toward her with nightmarish slowness. Almost like she watched the whole episode occur from afar as it happened to someone else. His knees hit the ground beside her, spraying dirt onto her face but luckily not into her eyes.

"Nay!" Her ear piercing shriek rent the air, and she wasn't even aware of the force she put behind it until it came out.

The man, slick with his own grease, paused a moment, his hands outstretched. In that moment of hesitation, Myra took action.

She ripped the dirk from her belt loop, raised it over her head and without a moment's thought or uncertainty, she struck out. Her arm vibrated as her blade sank home. Myra opened her eyes not realizing she'd closed them, and at the same time pulled her blade out to strike again. The only sound the man made was a gurgle, and she could see why as ribbons of liquid red flowed with eerie elegance from his neck.

His hands clutched to his wounded throat, eyes bulging in her direction, although they were so clouded, she didn't think he truly saw her. Myra scooted away from him, up onto her knees, her dagger still poised to hit its mark should any of his friends follow.

"Stay away from me!"

The men looked with horror at their leader and again at her as the man fell completely to the ground, the life gone from him. Myra moved to crouch on her feet, her legs, filled with such tension, she was ready to spring up and run for miles if she had to.

"We only wanted a bit of fun," one of them grumbled. "And ye killed him."

Myra took note of their dirty, ripped plaids, all differing in color from one another. Whether they were outlaws, from the same clans or differing clans, it mattered little.

"I'm not of a mind to have any form of fun with ye." Her voice was gravelly, strained. Her blood surged with some kind of power, which she'd heard her brother mention sometimes happened in battle. He called it the battle rush, and she certainly felt that way.

The men looked to each other, mumbling. Myra prayed they contemplated leaving. The three of them could easily overpower her if they decided to. They probably knew it too. If they had any true love for their fallen leader they may indeed seek revenge on her person. She would fight them with every last breath she had. If she was going to go down, she wasn't going alone. *Please…go away.*

Myra's feet tingled, and her knees were starting to shake. She loosed her grip on the dagger in an effort to stretch her fingers and repositioned her hold, elbows out, ready to strike.

The Highlander's Lady

"Get out of here, lass," the one who'd spoken before said. He glanced at his men and then back at her, murder in his eyes. But at least he'd had the forethought to send her away.

Myra backed away, one excruciating step at a time. From the corner of her eye she spied Coney munching on grass. Damn horse! Didn't he know his mistress' life was in danger? Not a warhorse at all, but, lucky for her, he was fast as lightning.

"We'll not harm ye, ye have my word. And we hope ye'll not harm us," he said.

They were lying. Waiting for her to run so they could chase her again. These men liked to the chase, she could tell. Myra didn't respond, only kept her gaze on them as she found Coney's reins with her free hand. She lifted her leg, blindly searching with her foot for the stirrup—she dare not take her eyes off the group. Could be a ploy, a trick they had in mind to take her guard down a notch.

Myra was not going to be fooled today. She'd not be a victim.

She'd killed a man.

A fact she was full aware of, but it was then the realization struck and her belly burned, recoiled and threatened to return the acorns to the earth.

At last her boot hooked inside the stirrup and Myra thrust her foot through, making quick work of yanking herself up and flinging her leg over the side. The horse was calm beneath her, his warmth sinking into her trembling limbs.

"Dinna follow me," she shouted.

The men ignored her as they tended to the dead man.

Myra wasted no time urging Coney into a gallop—this time away from the water's edge. She burst along the moors, the woods to her left, wanting desperately to surge into the darkness, but knowing she'd have to slow her pace, and right now she needed speed. Needed to be away from those who'd threatened her life.

Miles later, she realized she still clutched the dagger in her hands, blood caked to her hands and arms. She reined Coney in and trotted over to the woods. As soon as she was covered with the shadows of the forest, she pushed the dagger back into the loop, struggling until it finally was in place.

A clicking sound had her swirling around in her saddle to see what in the world it was until she realized it was her own teeth chattering.

In fact, her entire body shuddered and trembled.

"Oh, God... I dinna think I can do this."

On her own for less than a day and she'd had to kill a man with her bare hands.

Why couldn't she go back to the way things were? When she was in her home, sitting before a fire, wondering how she could entice her brother to hold a great feast, just so she could sneak in to dance. She'd give up freedom forever, doom herself to haunt the secret passageways the rest of her life if only things went back to normal.

A swift breeze blew, whipping her unkempt hair into her face, swirling her skirts around her ankles. Myra shivered. She'd never get to go back to that carefree time. Life for her was forever changed.

She climbed from the horse, positive she was alone. Her knees buckled and she knelt upon the solid ground, her hands sinking into the leaves that covered the earth. Her lips tingled, and her throat burned. Tears filled her eyes and fell in great drops to the ground. Her shoulders shook as she sobbed. Sitting back on her heels, she closed her eyes, her face toward heaven.

"Help me," she whispered.

The Highlander's Lady

'Twas surprising how much a punch in the face changed a man.

Daniel was completely awed with how his men transformed. They listened to his direction without complaint. They went about their duties—none trying to shirk what responsibilities were theirs. They even *looked* at him differently.

Perhaps the biggest change though, was the respect his men now showed him. The same deference they'd shown his father. Daniel had long ago proven himself a man when it came to fighting. Many of the dozen with him now had been in training with him as a boy. Many of whom he'd knocked down repeatedly. Many he'd saved in battle. There was no doubt that Daniel was the best of his father's men. In that arena, he'd already gained the warriors' nod.

What Daniel had struggled with over the past year was gaining their respect as a leader.

Truth be told, he hadn't done anything about it either. Shouting and seething hadn't done any good. It only made things worse. They respected him even less, and it was his own fault. He just hadn't realized it until now. What an idiot he'd been. It was so simple. The key to peace among his men. He'd never asserted his power. Once he took that first step, grabbed the reins, punched Leo in the face, he proved he wouldn't stand for their disrespect. No one thought he had it in him. And Daniel didn't blame them. He'd not proven himself. Until now. The dark, slightly swollen shadow on Leo's chin and the red, split knuckles on Daniel's right hand had proved it. And also served as a reminder.

While he'd gained their respect—in the same fashion his father had, physical force, the bunch of fighting boors—he was still cautious enough not to trust them completely. He'd made it clear they needed to prove themselves to him, that he was no longer going to tolerate their derision.

They'd been upon the road for several, uneventful hours, passing pastures of sheep and small farms with thatched-roof crofts. Smoke swirled through their makeshift chimneys and he longed for just a moment to be inside, warming his hands by the fire. 'Twas freezing outside. Judging from the position of the sun, only a few hours of daylight were left, near winter making the days shorter. Daniel itched to reach the Wallace camp. He'd left Blair over a week ago, and it was about time he finally reached his destination. They had a few more days to go if they rode hard each day. Not only was Daniel eager to begin helping in the training of men, but he was also keen on any news of the English.

A shout sounded to his right. Somewhere in the forest?

Daniel held up his hand, halting his men in place. They drew their weapons, turned as one in a circle to face the woods and listened. Another—a scream this time. Sounded feminine.

"A family being attacked?" Leo asked, his gaze shifting from the woods to Daniel.

"Could be." He listened a moment longer, hearing another female scream. "Let us investigate."

In a long line, they rode at a steady pace into the trees. They were riding blind. No one had any idea what was going on. It could be a band of thieves, or a lone man, so it made more sense to go in slow to see what they were up against. For all they knew, whoever screamed was being chased by a wildcat or boar. Or maybe even fell while fetching...something. He shook his head. That didn't make sense.

Several birds flew in zigzags, as though they tried to escape the sounds of the woman in distress. Daniel took in the forest sounds, heard the chirping of birds, the occasional scurry of a small animal, feeling the slight breeze upon his face.

The Highlander's Lady

The woods here were thin, only several hundred feet between the road they'd been on, toward the trickling burn he spied ahead. The forest was dark from the clouded sky and the thick needled firs mixed in with the oak trees.

A whirl of movement fled past his line of vision beyond the trees.

"What in hell?" he muttered. It looked to be a horse and rider, cloak flying out behind.

The assailant?

"I'll chase him down, ye check on the woman," Daniel ordered.

He spurred Demon forward, breaking away from his men. His eyes narrowed on the black cape that whirled with fury behind the break-neck pace of its rider. As he cleared the trees, surging forward, he was surprised with how fast the rider was able to get ahead. Hell.

A long, wild mass of raven-colored hair grasped at the air.

The rider looked decidedly like a woman…

She was bent low over the horse—a very dexterous horse. One used to running fast, slimmer in body and longer of leg than his own massive horse.

Demon would have a hard time catching her, but Daniel was determined.

He spurred Demon on, shouting out for the rider to stop, but his own words whipped back toward him, not carrying over the wind. The rider was a good quarter mile ahead of him and with each passing moment growing further away.

Suddenly, she stopped and veered to the left into the trees. Had she seen him behind her? She hadn't bothered to turn—not that he could see anyway. But what other reason would she have to go into the trees? Perhaps she had a shelter there. Or worse.

This was an ambush.

Damn. That thought hadn't come to mind until now.

The devil had coerced them into the woods and then taken flight, hoping he would follow. And now he was a good mile or two away from his men.

Hopefully they'd already realized it was a trap and were hastening toward the direction Daniel had taken. He pulled on the reins, slowing Demon's pace and turned into the woods too. Daniel was good at walking silently through the woods and had trained his warhorse to do the same. 'Twas an important skill to have ever since he'd become a man—the English were always afoot.

Daniel wanted to groan aloud, but kept silent. What if the lass was leading him straight into an English camp?

He stopped Demon altogether.

Following her was not worth the risk.

He had a mission. A plan. He was going to the Wallace camp. There was no time for an ambush. While he was in the mood to fight, and could use a little sport, 'twas probably not for the best.

Reluctantly, Daniel whirled his horse around, intent on returning to his men, when a loud sob stopped him.

'Twas faint, but sobbing all the same. Heart-wrenching sobs. And decidedly female.

He glanced with weariness from the direction of the cries and longingly back toward his men. Was it possible he'd gotten it all wrong and this was no ambush at all?

Mo creach! His ballocks were stuffed between a rock and a mountain rise. What the hell was he supposed to do? If the person weeping—a woman—was in need, could he truly leave her to her own defenses? And if it was a trap, surely he could hold them off until his men arrived.

Decision made, he uttered an oath under his breath and forged ahead, broadsword in one hand and *sgian dubh* in another. Weapons readied, he tensed as he edged through the trees, making sure to steer Demon with his knees in a way

The Highlander's Lady

that would make the horse's carefully placed hooves as silent as possible.

The scene he came upon made his heart twist. He clenched his jaw, gritting his teeth and peered through the trees around the woman who knelt upon the ground crying her soul to the heavens. There did not appear to be any signs of danger or of a trap. He studied the surrounding area for anything out of place, a glint of metal from the sun. Nothing. She was quite alone.

Daniel sheathed his weapons and dismounted, his boots making a soft whoosh within the leaves.

The woman gasped and he heard a shuffle and crunch of leaves and sticks as she scrambled to gain her footing. Her hands and the front of her gown where her cloak opened were covered in blood, a dagger was pointed in his direction. She must be hurt. He had to help her.

Her truffle-brown eyes were wide, wild, like that of an animal that had already been speared once and only wanted to be left in peace to lick his wounds. Beyond the blood, her gown was covered in mud making the color indiscernible. The garment looked in bad need of repairs. Her face was smeared with dirt and streaked with tears. A lot like Rose's face had been. Leaves and other debris clung to the cloak draped over her delicate shoulders. There was something familiar about her, but Daniel wasn't sure where he would have come across her. Perhaps at one of the inns while he was traveling. Judging from her gown and cape, she was not of noble stock, meaning that he could have bedded her or she may have only served him ale.

"Lass." He held out his hands, showing he bore no weapons. "I'm not here to harm ye. I'm here to help ye. I heard ye scream and followed ye."

Her throat bobbed and her eyes searched all around, assessing, weary.

He continued, speaking softly, "I am alone now, although I've a dozen men sure to follow me. Dinna be afraid, we willna harm ye."

"'Tis what the others said."

"Others?" Now Daniel glanced around. Had he missed them?

The woman nodded, her tangled hair clinging in her eyelashes. "They tried..." Her words were breathless, ending on what sounded like a choke. She flailed her arms out of a sudden, and stared at him, eyes filled with fright. "I killed him."

At her words, he started. The bloody hands made sense now. He was glad to hear she was not harmed physically. "Who, lass?"

She shrugged, looking helpless at the same time she looked utterly dangerous. "I dinna know."

"Ye killed a man ye dinna know?"

"Aye. He was going to hurt me."

Daniel wanted to pull her in to his grasp, to offer her comfort, but he had a feeling that would only gain him a knife protruding from his chest.

"'Tis all right. Ye did so out of defense. God will forgive ye."

She nodded, then stared down at her bloody hands, her face draining of what little color she had.

"I killed him. But I'm still alive." Her words were soft, not meant for him.

"What is your name, lass?"

She glanced up at him again, as if noticing him there for the first time. Daniel thought perhaps she might be in shock. "Myra."

An odd coincidence? This lass was certainly not Munro's sister. The Myra he knew was elegant. This woman was wretched. But those eyes... "I am Daniel." He didn't wish to

The Highlander's Lady

scare her by giving his title, and instead hoped by giving her his Christian name, that she would be more comfortable with him—and perhaps put that dagger away. "Can I help ye, lass? I can stand guard while ye wash up in the burn."

Her eyes met his, and again he was struck with recognition, but still baffled, she couldn't be the same Myra he knew. Had to be that he'd met her somewhere else. Myra was a common enough name wasn't it? Damn him for being such a merrymaking fool.

"Aye," she said simply. Myra turned and headed toward the burn, tripping over her gown more than once, but catching herself each time. He noted that she did indeed stop to put the dagger away. Daniel had to keep himself from laughing at the possible thought of her being afraid she might stab herself with it if she fell. Putting it away was not for his safety, but for her own.

Daniel followed her to the burn at a safe distance, with both horses' reins. He watched how even with trembling limbs, she delicately knelt before the water and rinsed away the blood and mud from her hands and arms. After splashing and scrubbing her face clean, she took a long sip. From where he stood, he could not see her face, but heard her speak clearly.

"Have ye anything to eat?"

The poor woman had probably tossed her accounts when she'd killed the man. "Aye. Whisky too."

He didn't know why he hadn't thought of that before. Whisky always helped to settle a person's mood. Reaching into his satchel he pulled out an oatcake, a thick slice of jerky and the smaller wineskin that held his precious whisky.

Daniel dropped the reins and turned to give her the items, only to be stunned still. 'Twas indeed Munro's sister. Myra. He should have known, but she'd looked like a bar wench or a farm woman. Dirty, unkempt. Not the sister of the Munro Laird. She was a lady. Born and bred. And she hadn't identified herself as a lady. He didn't miss that part. Myra Munro had been through hell and back, he couldn't begrudge her looking a mess. A wicked bruise streaked across her forehead. Had they hit her? He was surprised to see her standing. And where was her guard that Rose spoke of? Was it possible Rose had lied, or had her guard been taken down when she killed the man?

Why hadn't she told him who she was?

Perhaps she felt she needed to protect her identity. Daniel would not press her on it—for more reasons than that. She probably wouldn't remember him at all. They'd danced, laughed, but then she'd disappeared when he went to get her another mug of ale. He'd not seen her the rest of his visit. Likely he'd bored her to death and she'd felt the need to escape him—mayhap that was why she didn't like him, he was boring. Hell, he'd been there for three more days after their first meeting. She didn't look as though she recognized him, and Daniel wasn't about to remind her who he was. He'd never been spurned by a woman before and he wasn't willing to relive it.

"My lady, what happened to ye?" He was aghast at what he saw.

Anger flashed in her eyes. "I told ye I was attacked." She grabbed the offered goods from his hands.

Ballocks, he was dense. Lady Munro had told them of the attack on Foulis, but he'd not been paying much attention. Instead he'd been thinking of Myra—and here she stood before him. He was aware she did not speak of the attack on her castle however, nay, she spoke of the man she'd had to kill who'd attempted to steal her virtue.

"I am very sorry for your troubles, my lady."

Myra nodded, bit into an oatcake, her eyes rolling with pleasure. Good God…

"What are ye doing in the middle of the woods?"

She flashed him a glance from her fiery eyes. "Besides killing men?"

Why did he get the feeling she wanted him to be next?

Chapter Five

Why did Daniel have to be so darn handsome? Granted he was fierce, huge, immensely frightening, but still... There was something so insanely attractive in the shadow of stubble along his jaw, the slightly imperfect nose, and intelligent hazel eyes. He wore his dark hair long and wild, and she had the sudden urge to thread her fingers through it, to try and tame it.

"Do ye plan to kill me?" he asked.

Despite the situation, the stress of the day and the fact she was fairly certain she was in shock, Myra did laugh.

"Nay, I willna kill ye, Daniel."

He smiled, further improving his handsome face. His smile was crooked, roguish, and showed off his wide, full mouth and the one tooth that faintly overlapped another. Dear Lord, why was she all the sudden thinking of kissing that mouth? She'd never kissed a man before. Perhaps it was the shock...

Myra glanced away, pretending to dry her wet hands on her gown, realizing too late, she ended up smudging more dirt back onto her palms.

"Ye can trust me. I'll help ye if ye allow it."

Myra could attempt to finish this journey on her own, but she wasn't stupid enough to think she'd make it another few days without running into more brutes. Her best bet to deliver the message to the Bruce was to take advantage of Daniel's offer of help.

She nodded and met his gaze. He stole her breath and she took a moment to gain it back. She'd never been a shallow lass, but the way she craved looking at his face, how she wanted to devour every dip and line, made her feel... Delicious and wicked.

She'd be wearing a hair shirt for months at this rate. What the hell was happening to her?

"I think I do need your help," she managed to say without looking at him.

"Ye have it."

"I am traveling to Eilean Donan."

"As am I. I'd be happy to escort ye."

Why did he have to be so agreeable? And answer her so quickly. She didn't like it. "I'm likely to have an enemy following," she warned.

Daniel crossed his arms over his broad chest bringing attention to the area. Myra frowned all the more and forced her gaze to his boots. Soft leather boots encasing overlarge feet. The man was a giant. Did he realize that? His feet were easily twice as long as her own.

"I will keep ye safe. May I ask why ye're traveling to the Wallace camp?"

Myra shook her head, chancing a glance at his face. "Nay." The least he knew the better.

Daniel raised a dark brow. "Nay?"

"I canna tell ye. If ye are set on knowing then I'll be on my way without your help."

Myra turned, ready to climb back on Coney and somehow brave the wilds of the Highlands on her own again. If she'd been able to make it this far, she could power through it. She could try to survive. For a few hours.

At least she was no longer hungry. The food Daniel had provided her filled her belly and the whisky had burned a pleasant path down her throat, making her feel warm though her fingertips felt cold. There'd been no time to grab her gloves before escaping and she'd not found any in the stables.

"I canna leave ye to fare on your own. We are both traveling the same way. If your purpose is private, I shall not keep ye from it." Daniel's voice was even, steady.

Myra paused, her hands on Coney's withers. Could she trust him?

"Ye will provide me escort then?"

"Aye."

"And protect me, no matter what?" She stroked over Coney's mane, still not turning around.

"Aye."

He was too agreeable. She had to offer him up a real challenge. "What if I am attacked by one of your own men?"

"I will see ye protected. Ye have my word."

"What if the Bruce does not like my…reason for visiting Eilean Donan, will ye protect me when he threatens to toss me into the dungeons?"

Daniel chuckled. "Is your purpose so nefarious, lass?"

Myra laughed at his easy nature. He teased her and offered her comfort at the same time.

"Nay, but ye must swear it all the same." She turned around this time, her eyes meeting his. They were a sharp green, intense.

"I swear it."

The Highlander's Lady

"What of yourself? How will ye protect me from yourself?"

Daniel laughed at that, spreading his arms outward. "Have some faith, Lady Myra, I wouldna harm ye. I do possess a certain amount of self-control."

Myra studied her escort for several moments, taking in his towering height, the breadth of his shoulders, strength of his legs. He was a man built for warring. Despite his considerable bulk, he moved with ease and grace, giving credence to his control of his body—but his mind was another matter.

"Ye'll pardon me for being skeptical. 'Tis not a man's tendency to contain himself when alone with a female."

"Truly? Ye think all men beasts?" He stepped closer to her and she imagined heat coming off his large frame in waves.

"Those I've come to meet."

"Ah…"

Was there a twinge of hurt in his words? Had she offended him?

"I mean no offense, Daniel. 'Tis only my experience that I speak of."

"I take no affront, Lady Myra. Ye've been through quite a trauma today."

He glanced up at the sky, assessing the whitish-grey clouds and she did the same, wondering at his thoughts.

"I will see ye safely to Eilean Donan, so ye might be about your business." He paused, considering her. She felt more exposed than she'd ever been in her life, and she couldn't be sure why. She was completely clothed. He had no idea who she truly was. "On one condition."

Myra swallowed, feeling her nerves prickle. He was indeed a man. "What is your price?"

Daniel nodded his chin in her direction, a challenging glint entering his eyes. "Ye must agree to marry me."

She gasped, stepped back, her mouth agape in horror. She fisted her hands into the folds of her gown and cloak. "Marry ye?" Shaking her head vehemently, she tried to keep her throat from closing in panic.

"Aye." He didn't sound even a quarter as nervous as she did. Almost like he asked lasses to wed with him on a daily basis.

Was the notion of being forever tied to another so mundane to him? Of so little value? What kind of a man was he?

Miraculously, she was able to recover her voice and was pleased when her reply came out in steady, even tones, "Why would I do that?"

"Because ye want to reach the Bruce in one piece. Because your reason for getting there is of such importance ye will not tell me why. Because I will keep ye safe and ye've already had the misfortune of meeting one of the many vagrants upon the road. Next time ye may not be so lucky — even with your swift hand."

He had a point… Myra didn't want to die. She didn't want to leave this earth without having completed her mission. She'd given Byron her word. She would deliver to the Bruce the news of his enemy. Pray that the Bruce hadn't already found out the hard way. Then she'd have to return to her clan. *Her* clan. They were her responsibility now.

Taking a deep breath, Myra asked, "If I agree, when would the ceremony take place?"

"Spring." Daniel reached for the wineskin of whisky, their fingers brushing as he took it.

She glanced down, not even realizing she'd still been holding his drink. A slight shiver passed through her. His fingers were rough against her softer skin, scraping. She bit her lip, and watched him take an extra-long gulp of the whisky. Perhaps she was not the only nervous one. He was

The Highlander's Lady

just better at hiding his feelings. Drowning himself with whisky. The idea had merit. When he finished she took it back for another long gulp.

There was one thing Myra had not known before meeting Daniel—she liked whisky. And apparently, whisky liked her. She felt warm, giddy almost. Happy. Hmm... Maybe she should give it back...

Married come spring. That was several months from now. She could certainly agree today and then disappear. By the time he found her, she could join the church, or perhaps beg the Bruce to let her arrange her own marriage, for she was essentially Laird Munro. Theoretically, she could make that decision on her own.

Myra glanced again at Daniel. His eyes were warm, but cautious. She got the feeling he was hiding something from her. Something he knew and didn't wish to share. Well, what did it matter? They all had secrets, she certainly had hers. Keeping this man around so she made it safely to Eilean Donan was better than going at it alone.

There was also the... No. She couldn't possibly consider it. Or could she?

Marrying him—or at least pretending to—would get her out of marrying Ross completely. Not that the bastard having attacked Foulis wouldn't cancel out their betrothal, but just so there was no doubt their marriage contract was voided. To be safe. Ross wouldn't be the first man to force an unwilling bride into a lifetime of misery. Marrying someone else would be a deep wound to his pride—one she was more than happy to inflict. But that meant she would have to go through with the marriage with Daniel and...the bedding. Additionally, Daniel would become the chief of her clan unless Rose birthed a male bairn. That was sure to prick Ross' pride. Judging from his clothes, horse and weaponry, Daniel was wealthy. He didn't offer her a surname or the name of a clan. At the moment, with men surely fast on her heels, she didn't want to delve into it either. In the end, did it matter? If she was planning on returning to her own clan, the man she pretended to wed was insignificant.

Nevertheless, being married to Daniel, though she knew so little about him, would still be better than marrying the man who'd massacred nearly her entire clan. If it came to actual nuptials, she'd discuss his clan with him then. 'Twould be the part of her revenge on Ross.

Taking a deep breath, she said, "All right."

Daniel raised his brows as if he'd been expecting her to say no. He reached again for the whisky.

Myra tried not to laugh aloud, and instead bit the inside of her cheek. Hard. Aye, he was good at hiding his emotions, and certainly used the whisky to aid him.

She'd shocked him. There was an odd power in that realization. But it was swiftly gone with the knowledge that by agreeing to marry him she was essentially giving up her own freedom.

"Then ye are now under my protection." Daniel's voice wasn't as strong as it was before.

"Ye were hoping I'd say nay?" Her words came out before she could pull them back, and Myra felt heat suffuse her cheeks. Being so sheltered within Foulis she'd often spoken her mind, however it got her a paddling from her father or from her nursemaid, and as she got older, penance from the priest.

Daniel chuckled, though the smile barely reached his eyes. "Nay, 'tis glad I am ye said aye."

Myra narrowed her eyes, watching as beads of sweat formed on his brow and trickled down over his temples. His reaction was not only priceless considering he was the one who laid it out on the table, but also moved to ease her sense of weariness. Daniel was human after all, and genuine.

The Highlander's Lady

"I promise not to kill ye on our wedding night," she offered in half humor, her lip quirking up slightly.

Too late she realized what her reference brought to mind as Daniel's eyes darkened a little and his gaze roved over her. He grunted, as if accepting her at her word, but his mind was far this present moment. Nay, he was where she was—thinking ceaselessly and with abandon about… The wedding night. A bedding. One she was not entirely opposed to. What would it be like to feel his large, strong, coarse hands on her? To have his lips brush over hers, brand her flesh as he claimed her? Myra's heart pounded and sweat formed in beads along her spine. Goodness she felt hot of a sudden.

Myra was completely and utterly aware of what went on between a man and a woman. Not only because she'd been told—and she'd been warned that it was not pleasant at all for a woman, but being that one of her favorite pastimes was to sneak about in the hidden passageways, she'd seen more than one occasion of lovemaking. And it didn't look unpleasant at all.

Quite the opposite.

Zounds! Why was she even thinking about making love to Daniel? She was not really going to marry him. She was going to go along with it until she'd kept her word to her brother, then she'd go back to Foulis and take on the responsibilities of laird. Rebuild their castle, reinforce their clan. Until the day her nephew could do so himself—*pray, be a nephew*!

Daniel stepped toward her, and she stared down at his booted feet, taking note once more how much larger they were than her own. What was it she'd heard the vulgar warriors shout out on more than one occasion? The bigger a man's feet, the bigger his… She gasped. Slowly, she allowed her gaze to travel upward over his well-shaped, muscular legs, the plush wool plaid, leine shirt that clung to his broad chest, thick arms, then finally back to his ruggedly handsome, chiseled face.

Myra swallowed at what she saw there. Desire. And it only intensified her own. Suddenly her mouth was dry, and she was afraid if she spoke only a choking sound would come out.

"How shall we insure our agreement is set?" His voice was lower than before and sent a shiver racing through her.

"What do ye mean?"

"I canna have ye back away from this."

Why did he suddenly seem so much closer?

"Why do ye need a wife?" For there was no other reason for him to have made that the condition. The man was in need. She had to know why before she agreed to anything further.

He smiled, his eyes dancing at her having figured him out. "Ye are astute, my little lass."

"And ye are not answering the question."

He grinned wider. "'Tis a promise I made to my clan. I've not yet married and they hound me at every waking moment."

She nodded, completely understanding that. Her clan had hounded her too, and thank goodness her marriage had yet to take place. Daniel needing to marry only further proved his importance to his clan. Was it possible a powerful chief stood before her?

Myra cocked her head, more questions filling her mind. "Why are ye going to the Bruce?"

Daniel shrugged. "I like to fight."

Myra laughed. "At least ye're honest. I'll be a widow before long."

He grinned and winked, thrilling her to her toes. How could he do that by simply shutting one eye? Myra didn't know, but she certainly wouldn't mind him doing it again.

"Now ye are avoiding the question."

The Highlander's Lady

"What was the question?" she asked, hoping he wouldn't make her do some sort of pagan blood oath.

"How can I ensure ye will not run away once I've seen ye safely to the Bruce?"

She had no idea... For she planned to go back to Foulis upon relaying her message. Myra shrugged. "Trust?"

"A Highlander never trusts anyone completely."

"Then ye are without many friends."

Daniel frowned. "Enough playing games. I must have a guarantee that ye'll marry me come spring."

"Or else ye'll have hell to pay from your clan?"

"Nay. My mother and uncle will only make sure I'm married to someone else."

"Then why not do that?"

"I want to marry ye."

His confession took her breath away. She took a step back, unsure of herself and the worth he thrust onto her. "Why?"

Daniel shrugged. "Ye are fair bonny, lass. Ye're brave and I like my women strong in mind as well as body."

She was flattered that he'd noticed those things about her and that he liked them. Most were turned off by how *not* simperish she was. Myra was no Rose. She was not likely to do what her husband told her, and she was likely to get into trouble with the gust of the wind.

"Thank ye."

"No thanks required. I didna say it to flatter ye, simply stating facts."

How could he make the nice things he'd said sound so horrid? Myra frowned, whatever warmth she'd gained from his praise dissipating.

He was a man after all. 'Twasn't like she could expect much. Why was she trying to make him out to be better than the others she'd known and met along the path of her life? He was exponentially better than the vagrants, but was he up to par with some of the other nobles that had visited Foulis?

Her frown deepened and her fingers played distractedly with a string along the wrist of her once beautiful gown. She couldn't understand why, but she did find him better. And he was ruining it by scowling and being so matter of fact.

Refusing to let him dampen her mood, Myra decided she would take the higher road. "Nonetheless, I thank ye. What did ye have in mind? I've no parchment paper, have ye? 'Haps when we arrive at Eilean Donan, or at an inn along the way, we could write up a contract of marriage."

Daniel shook his head. "Nay. Must be now."

"Now?"

She glanced around. They had no way of getting parchment paper anywhere near here.

"So ye've something in your sporran then or in your satchel on that warhorse?"

Daniel snickered, and Myra narrowed her eyes.

"I'm of a mind to handfast, lass."

She took a step back. "Handfast?" Now she was the one shaking her head. That was not good. Handfasting wasn't permanent, but it could be made so. If he bedded her and she were to become with child…

"Then ye did plan to run." His voice hardened sending a chill through her.

"Nay!" Myra shook her head vehemently, keenly aware of how alone she was with this man.

"Why would ye deny a handfast then? 'Tis the best solution to our dilemma."

Myra didn't see it that way. Nay, handfasting was as good as a wedding ceremony in her eyes. Would be harder to get out of too.

"Who are ye?"

"I told ye, I'm Daniel."

"Aye, but what of your clan?"

The Highlander's Lady

Daniel stepped closer, and the air around her grew warmer. She had the urge to snuggle closer, to pull some of that heat off of him and onto herself. He was distracting her from what she needed to know.

She took another step back.

Daniel followed her, his toes nearly touching her own.

"I am a relation to Andrew Moray—William Wallace's leader until he passed. Does that satisfy your curiosity?"

She nodded, although it only assuaged it somewhat.

"Then we shall handfast."

Her face was so hot now, she swore it was going to burst into flames. He wouldn't take no for an answer and she was fast running out of options.

He gripped her hands, those large calloused fingers scraping over overs. Myra forced her fingers not to tremble which only made her knees knock together. The intent look in his eyes scared her more than when she and Rose had come to the end of the tunnel and she had to go in search of horses. This was frightening in an entirely different way, for it looked like he would kiss her and she'd never been kissed before. Worse still, she wanted him to kiss her. No, nay, she didn't!

Myra swallowed, trying to catch her breath as his boots nudged into her feet.

"I would handfast with ye, Myra, if ye're to be my wife come spring."

She found herself nodding in agreement. Oh, wayward neck!

Then he did bend down, eyes slightly closed, his black hair falling in virile wisps against his stubbled cheeks. Myra was not going to close her eyes. She was going to watch every moment of this. Feel every touch, breath.

Daniel's lips met hers. They were warm, soft and rough at the same time. They brushed back and forth as if he wanted to feel every last trace of her lips.

His lashes were dark, long, thick, and pressed to his cheeks. Little blue veins were etched over his lids, and his brows were arched, full. A tiny scar graced the space between his brows. As his lips tenderly touched hers, making her heart race, her palms sweat and legs tremble, Myra found she could no longer concentrate on his features.

She closed her eyes.

Chapter Six

*H*oly Mary Mother of God...

Myra's lips were the sweetest of sins. Soft, plush, warm, wet where she'd flicked her tongue over them. Daniel couldn't get enough of her sweet kiss. Couldn't get enough of *her*.

She was tempting, seductive. Her cheek was warm as his nose bumped against it. Daniel wanted to tuck her tight against him, to feel the entire length of her body pressed to his. But he couldn't.

Not yet.

She was so innocent. He didn't want to scare her. Handfasting was important. Must be done, and now.

Gently, he pulled away from her, took in the dazed look in her eyes. She gazed at him with wonder, surprise, and there was a bit of fear dancing in there as well.

He gripped her hands in his, feeling them tremble slightly at his touch.

"Why did ye do that?" she asked.

"Kiss ye?"

"Aye." She kept pressing her lips firmly together, only to move them around a little, like she could still feel him kissing her.

Daniel tried hard not to laugh a little at that. He'd kiss her again if she didn't stop.

"I couldna help myself."

"I told ye, ye had little control." She frowned in the most adorable way.

Daniel grinned. "Ye tempt me. Did ye not enjoy it?"

Myra's face flushed a pretty shade of red and she flicked her gaze toward the ground. "Nay." She bit her lip.

"Interesting."

Her head snapped up. "Why do ye say that?"

"Well, from the way ye kissed me back, and the feel of your quickened breath upon my cheek I would have thought ye did. Ye didna pull away either. 'Twas I who ended the kiss."

At this she met his eyes, fire dancing in their depths. "Are ye saying that ye didna enjoy it?"

Oh, saints, this woman was a pleasure to tease.

"Well, I could tell 'twas either your first, or ye've been with some lousy kissers."

She gasped, her blush deepening, spreading down her neck, and he wished to rip open her cloak and spy if that blush caressed her breasts. She wiggled her fingers at him and too late he realized where he'd been staring. And she'd caught him.

"What was it ye were saying about self-control? Ye have none?" Myra gave a disgusted snort and rolled her eyes.

Daniel had to remember that she was a lady. A virgin. An innocent. Not one of the women he'd likely take up with at a tavern or one of the more promiscuous widows he enjoyed

The Highlander's Lady

well into the night. Myra may not even know exactly what went on between a man and a woman.

He was suddenly contrite.

"Apologies, my lady. I seem to have forgotten myself."

She grunted in a very unladylike way. "I'd say so. Shall we get on with it?"

"With what?"

At this, she rolled her eyes once more. What the hell was happening? Daniel always had the upper hand. How was it that this slip of a woman had made him lose his mind? How had she taken over control of him so quickly and easily? 'Twas only a kiss, and not even a very good one. There'd not even been one tongue involved.

Daniel glowered down at her, sickened when he noted that slight streaks of natural red twisted through her otherwise black hair. Why should he notice such a fine detail?

"The handfasting, ye brute. 'Twill not be long before the man's friends come along, hoping to catch me off guard. They've not taken kindly to me killing their leader."

"My men will have likely met up with them and sent them on their way."

"Let us pray, since ye do not appear to have your wits. Does kissing always affect ye so?"

The little twit… Daniel gripped her hands harder, stared at her with sudden seriousness and watched her eyes widen. "Nay, it doesna, and ye'll need to learn to treat your husband with a bit more respect." Now he realized why her brother kept her hidden away. Understood why when Daniel asked about her, Byron had claimed she was unruly. She was a spritely woman with a fiery temper and he aimed to tame her.

Come spring, she'd be the model wife, one he'd be proud to show off to his mother and cousins. But most of all, if she didn't tone down her boldness, she'd likely get herself into trouble. Which she'd already done. Been forced to kill a man, and had seemingly recovered quite well after the initial shock. Daniel was puzzled. The woman made no sense to him.

Perhaps he'd not given her enough credit.

Myra yanked her hands away. "I'll not handfast with a brute. I've come this far, I can make my way, with or without ye."

Despite her words he could see the fear in her eyes, see her lip tremble. She was scared. Perhaps most of her bravado was from fear. Daniel had no sisters and while he did spend much time with his female cousins, women still mystified him. He'd need to be gentler with her. Especially if he was going to gain her agreement.

Daniel needed a wife, and Myra offered up the perfect opportunity. She would save him from certain doom. Marriage to a complete stranger.

"I'm sorry, lass. I didna mean to frighten ye. I promise ye, I'm not a brute."

She frowned. "Ye promised to control yourself too and yet ye've already kissed me."

Daniel reached for her hands once more, stroking his thumb over her knuckles. "Aye. If 'tis your wish, I'll not kiss ye again." *Until the bedding…*

The way she hesitated showed him that she wanted him to kiss her again, that she wasn't as opposed to it as she made out.

Daniel smiled, trying for sweet to keep her calm and it worked. Myra smiled back, the most beautiful smile he'd ever seen.

"Ye are beautiful, lass."

"Thank ye."

Ripping a small strip of cloth form his plaid he wrapped it around her hands. "I would take ye to be my wife. As God and his bounteous earth would be my witness, I wed with ye."

The Highlander's Lady

Myra swallowed and licked her lips several times before repeating his words.

"Come spring we'll make it official."

"Congratulations, my laird." Leo and his men rode up just then, obviously witnessing their exchange.

"And now we have witnesses," Daniel said to Myra before turning to Leo. "Allow me to introduce Lady Myra—we've handfasted until spring."

"My lady," Leo and the others said as they dismounted from their horses and knelt before her.

Myra looked as shocked as Daniel felt. She took the strip of plaid from him, shoving it into her boot. His men were so quick to show her loyalty. They knew not who she was, only that she now belonged to him. 'Twas a good sign that his men were well and truly on their way to seeing Daniel for his true self, without the veil of his father's scorn hanging between them.

"Leo, a word," Daniel said. Turning to Myra he motioned for her to remain where she was. "I'll be but a moment."

Myra winged a brow, as though she wanted to retort, but to his surprise she kept her opinion or rejoinder to herself. Daniel smiled. He'd made the right choice.

Several yards away, he came to a stop and met Leo's eyes. "What did ye find?"

"Found several men burying a dead man. We asked who he was and they said it was their leader, that a woman had killed him."

Daniel nodded. "Myra."

"Aye, we gathered that as soon as we came upon ye. There is blood covering the front of her gown."

Daniel had forgotten about that. They'd have to get her something different to wear soon. A bloody gown would only draw attention. Besides that, he wanted his wife to wear something befitting a lady. Befitting Lady Murray. His wife.

The term brought a sick twist to his gut, and Daniel for a moment thought he might toss up his meager breakfast.

"Are ye all right, laird?"

"Fine," he bit out.

"Ye look a might pale. Did ye know she killed a man?"

"Aye."

Leo nodded. "We made sure the other men headed in the opposite direction with plenty of threats to keep them well away."

Daniel nodded.

"She is verra brave," Leo said, staring off toward Myra.

"Aye."

"She'll make ye a good wife."

"Aye."

"Well, it's a good thing we joined ye when we did to provide witness."

"Aye." Seemed to be he was speechless, capable of only answering in one syllable words. He'd not expected to be so affected by taking a wife.

"Who is she?"

"She is the sister of the late Laird Munro."

"Lady Munro arrived at Blair the morning we left, no?"

"Aye. Apparently his sister dropped her off then took to the road on her own."

"Why?"

Daniel had given his word that Myra's mission was for his knowledge only. He shrugged. "Nowhere in particular, she was in a bit of shock. I told her I'd protect her."

"By marrying her?" Leo looked skeptical.

"Aye. And she doesn't know I know who she is. Keep it between us." Yet another way to test his man's loyalty.

His second-in-command shrugged, then changed the subject, obviously accepting what Daniel had said. Daniel couldn't have been more pleased. "Saw some smoke coming

The Highlander's Lady

from several places in the woods. Small swirls. Most likely camp fires. We're not alone here. Best if we were on our way, so we can make it out of these woods which are filled with rough men. Especially with a lady in tow."

Daniel nodded.

"If I may speak freely…" Leo's expression looked strained.

"Ye are free to speak your mind, Leo, but choose your words wisely."

"What will ye do with the lady at Eilean Donan? It's a training camp for soldiers."

"'Tis also a castle, and castles oft have women to help run things. I'm sure she'll find plenty to do there."

However smooth his answer sounded, Daniel wouldn't let on that he was in fact worried over what she would do there. Myra had yet to share her message with him. What if the Bruce didn't like what he heard? What if she was sent on some other errand beyond a message? She'd killed a man easily—albeit in self-defense. Was it possible she was sent to assassinate the Bruce? If so, by whom?

What better way to send in a killer. No one would ever suspect a woman, least of all a beautiful woman, sister of a laird who'd just been murdered.

Daniel looked over at Myra, watched as she stood, shoulders back, eyes straight ahead, neither staring at anyone or anything.

She puzzled him, intrigued him. He'd just have to be on his guard. And when she went to deliver her message he would insist on attending her. Even if she was spitting mad over it. There were still a few days left until they arrived at the camp, plenty of time to learn more of her secrets.

"The men and I are pleased ye found a woman to wed, my laird. We've watched your mother and your uncle bring in many from around the Highlands. None were so bonny, nor so brave as the lass ye've tied yourself to."

Daniel smiled wanly. He was right. "Thank ye, Leo."

Dismissing his man, he walked back to Myra.

"We best be on our way. The woods are filled with men like the one ye killed. Some desperate enough to try and attack a dozen Highland warriors."

Myra nodded. "My horse—"

"Ye'll ride with me."

She frowned up at him, eyes deepening in color. "I'm capable of riding myself. Have not fallen from a horse in many a year." She shifted her gaze away and touched the bruise on her head.

Putting two and two together, Daniel came to the realization that she had indeed fallen from her horse after being hit with something, or perhaps running into a branch.

"All the same, ye'll ride with me."

"Why?"

Daniel drew his brows together in a frown. He didn't like the way she looked at him as though he were resorting to trickery. He wasn't used to being questioned. Particularly not from a woman—save his mother.

"Dinna question my orders."

"There ye go again, acting like a brute. I'll ride my horse; he's fast."

That was part of the problem. How could he be sure the lass didn't race off at the first chance she got? "Ye'll ride with me, end of discussion."

Myra stared at him, an expression on her face that made Daniel wish he was a mind reader. She must be cursing him to hell and back behind those large brown eyes.

"I can see ye're in a mood to be bossy. I suppose since ye're a laird ye must be used to giving orders and having them obeyed. I'll oblige ye this once, but in future, I will continue to question ye."

The Highlander's Lady

From the corner of his eye, Daniel watched his men mount their horses and pretend not to listen, although several of them did snicker.

Damn her. He gripped her arm and yanked her close to him so that his lips brushed the shell of her ear. "Dinna *ever* question me in front of my men. *Ever*." His voice was low, threatening.

Myra simply nodded, but kept her lips pressed closed. When she looked at him there was fury in her eyes, but she did as he said and walked toward his horse, her head down. Why did he feel like such a monster? He hated watching her look so meek and dejected. One of the reasons he'd asked her to wed with him was her fiery nature.

Daniel did not want to stifle her. And yet, he did not want her to make him look a fool in front of his men. How did one balance such a thing? If he weren't on such new, precarious ground with the men then he may not have cared.

Now he'd shown her that he could be a brute, just like she'd accused him. He'd probably lost her trust.

Ballocks! He wanted to slam his head against a tree. He'd set out on this journey to enjoy the last few months of being a bachelor, and now he found himself handfasted to a woman he barely knew, whose spirit he'd just crushed and he still wasn't sure if his men truly saw him for the leader he was.

A swig of whisky would be good about now. He approached his horse and climbed up behind the stiff body of his bride.

He leaned forward and whispered, "I'm sorry," in her ear.

If possible, her back became even more rigid.

Well, he'd let her fume at him for a while. But she'd just better be over it by the time they arrived at camp. He wasn't going to sleep beside a woman with a natural ability for killing, who appeared to want to cleave his head from his shoulders.

He pushed Demon into a trot, one of his men taking the reins of her horse as they all moved back through the woods and onto the road. The next village they passed he would try to procure a new gown for her. And a bath—as an apology. She'd most likely enjoy the chance to wash the stench of death from her flesh. Not that he could smell it, but he had noted that she kept looking at her hands, as if unsure of whether she'd washed the blood completely off.

The bath would be it. He would not cater to her any more than that. He would not issue any more apologies either. Nay, the woman would have to learn her place. Daniel would welcome her fire behind closed doors, and if she wished to take him to their chamber to burn his ears that was more than fine with him. He'd enjoy the makeup part, where he was able to taste the sweet flesh of her lips again. To fully sink his tongue into her mouth and stroke over the velvet of her little pink tongue.

Damn. His cock tightened. Thank goodness for his sporran, else she'd feel the rigid length against her buttocks.

Double damn. Now he couldn't get the image of her buttocks from his mind. They would be the color of cream and rose. Smooth, silky, round. He'd take a globe in each hand, feel her supple flesh filling his palms. Massage them... Oh, God. Now his cock twitched.

The ride to Eilean Donan was going to be long—and he was going to be hard.

'Haps it might be best to bed her along the way?

Nay. He would try to hold off until spring. He'd not brought bedding into the negotiations and while he barely knew her, he was aware of one thing—she wasn't ready for the bedding. Daniel would wake up missing his cock and ballocks if he tried.

He scooted back a couple inches, trying to get away from her heat. Concentrating on something else might help. He

The Highlander's Lady

thought of training the men. Aye, that was best. Which weapons they would train with the first day. He'd teach them about combat fighting, hand-to-hand. He was good at that. One of the best. All the physical exertion would leave him tired and then he'd not want to worry about bedding her.

Save, how was he to pull this off? How could he train the men and keep an eye on her at the same time?

Daniel gritted his teeth.

What was her message? The urgency of her journey? As soon as she was done being angry with him, he was going to sit her down and have a long talk with her. See if she wouldn't agree to at least tell him a little. He needed to be assured that she wasn't actually out to kill the Bruce. Lord knew there were many who were.

Wouldn't that just be ironic if his wife ended up being an assassin to the man he'd sworn loyalty too? Oh, his mother and uncle would never let him live that down. His cousins would roast him on a spit.

His men would never respect him if that were the case. Well, ballocks, the woman had just better not be. Or she'd have hell to pay.

Chapter Seven

Myra's spine hurt like the devil. She'd never sat so straight before. Not even in church. Not even when on her knees taking her penance. The blades of her shoulders were pulled so taut they nearly touched. Her neck was a solid column.

Her muscles and back screamed for her to arch it, to stretch it, but doing so would only put her closer to Daniel and as it was she could feel the heat of him curling around her, making her feel… Hot.

Oh, dear Lord, why was she so hot? Made no sense with the frigid temperatures.

Her skin felt afire, and every time he huffed a breath she felt it all the way to her toes. Every time he shifted, she had to make her body even stiffer. 'Twas taking all the willpower she could summon to stay so taut. To not give in to her body's urge to touch him, to relax.

The Highlander's Lady

If they didn't reach camp soon, she would lean back against him and stretch like a lazy cat. Feeling every inch of his body that would come into contact with hers. Her spine curling against his muscles. Such thoughts brought imaginings of wicked things. More kisses.

She'd not expected his lips to come into contact with hers. Hadn't expected the jarring wave of heat that came along with it. Myra's entire being felt as though it were floating in a cloud, she'd been light-headed, dizzy with some unexplained feeling.

And then he'd had to ruin the wonder and joy of her first kiss by pointing out how terrible she was at it. Mortification had never run so deep. What exactly had she done wrong? To her, it seemed as though Daniel had done everything right…so right. Perhaps she was supposed to pucker her lips more. Press them more fully against his? Oh, what was the use? She had no idea what to do, and was likely never to learn since she vowed from this moment forth to never kiss another man again.

Never.

Daniel would be her first and her last kiss. Myra gritted her teeth in frustration. One moment he was sweet, sensual, completely drawing her in, and the next he was blunt, coarse and brutish. Myra never felt so out of her element. She'd never felt so at odds with her emotions, convictions. Swearing to one thing in her mind, her body changed with whatever he said or did, completely upending her promises to herself.

Daniel shifted again behind her, groaning low under his breath, as though he tried to hide his frustration. 'Twas obvious Daniel was just as uncomfortable as she was. He couldn't stop moving behind her, and every other minute an oath or curse came from his lips. A couple times Myra had to bite her cheek to keep from laughing. His mouth and obvious love of naughty words was just as bad as her own. At least, for the short term of their handfast, she'd be able to enjoy that, since she had no plans to enjoy anything else with him.

Judging from his constant movement and swearing, kissing wasn't the only thing she was terrible at. Apparently, Myra was also an awful riding companion. If he groaned one more time, she might just elbow him in the ribs, or better yet toss him from the horse just to let him out of his misery.

However uncomfortable she was, Myra did admit one thing—she felt safe. For the first time in over a week, she could let just a little bit of her guard down. She didn't have to be on constant alert. She could glance about her, watch the squirrels climb the bare trees of winter and then fly through the air as they leapt toward needled firs. Watch them gather acorns in their little mouths before darting around in a pattern meant to confuse any who would steal those acorns.

Ugh…acorns. Another reason she was grateful to have met up with Daniel. She never wanted to eat another raw acorn again. From what she'd heard, they weren't bad cooked into a stew or bread, but hadn't someone told her raw acorns were lethal for a horse? Was it possible they were lethal for her too? She supposed if she were to die in the next day or so from stomach pains, she'd know.

Myra turned her attention from the squirrels to gaze at the horizon. The Highlands were most beautiful in winter she believed. The mountains graced the landscape in jagged arches, their whitecaps visible from here. Snow had already fallen on the great rises. Wouldn't be too long before it fell upon the land in droves. She prayed they reached their destination before the snow fell. That the Bruce did not force her out into the elements as punishment for relaying words he was certainly not keen to hear.

If they were to get caught in a snow storm, they may be stuck in one spot for days at a time—or worse, perish from cold. She prayed they climbed over the mountain pass before the storm—avalanches weren't an everyday occurrence, but during a storm they weren't entirely implausible either.

They passed beyond the road that was alongside the forest which housed many who'd seek to harm her as Daniel had put it, and rode through valleys and over a marsh—the grounds not as soft due to the cold—until they came to a small village surrounded by stone rises on two sides and a darkened forest on the other. The sun had just barely begun to set, setting pink tones to caress the clouds.

When Daniel pulled his horse to stop before a tavern, Myra groaned. For certain, he and his men would seek a few pints and the company of women while she... What? Nestled down with the horses? Joined them in their debauchery?

"Bastard," she muttered as she dismounted to follow him inside. As much as she'd rather keep company with the horses, it just wasn't safe. She didn't know where she was, and quite frankly, her appearance was sure to draw a few questioning eyes. 'Haps here she could inquire about a new gown. Although she had nothing to pay for it. A bucket of hot water and lye then to scrub away the stain of her assailant's death.

"Dinna say anything," Daniel said to her under his breath. "And pull your cloak tight to hide all that blood."

Myra nodded. She disliked immensely his take charge attitude, his need to dominate everything, but she also didn't want to cause a scene or have him decide he'd no longer escort her.

From inside rowdy, boisterous noise emanated. Shouting, laughter, female squeals, cheers, and clinking of glasses. The tavern sounded as though the people inside were celebrating something. Glancing around the town, she wasn't sure what exactly it could be. The place was small, quiet, not particularly impressive. Maybe they were simply celebrating being alive. Myra would drink to that.

Daniel pushed open the door with Myra huddled close to his back, his men behind her. She felt safe, even in this place, surrounded by large, imposing warriors.

"May I help ye?"

Myra peered from behind Daniel's wide back to view the small man who greeted them at the door. He was older, red-haired with streaks of white shining through it and a matching beard halfway down his chest. His eyes were small, but only because the skin around them sagged in wrinkled folds. He looked a bit like an old elf or at least what Myra had imagined they looked like.

"My wife and I require room for the night, a new gown, a hot meal and a bath. My men also require food and lodging for the horses." Daniel's voice was commanding but amiable.

The little old man tilted his head to get a look at her. He smiled showing brown, crooked teeth. There was nothing sinister in his smile, he appeared quite cheerful.

"We've a room indeed, quite large actually. Comes with a large price."

The muscles in Daniel's back tightened and instinctively she tightened too.

"What is your price?" he asked the tavern owner.

The man gave him a number that had Myra cringing. Easily thrice the cost of a normal room.

"Done. Just see to it that price gives me all I require, and quickly."

Myra's mouth fell open. He was willing to pay that much for her? How wealthy was Daniel?

The tavern owner looked just as shocked, his eyes momentarily widening enough to show they were sky blue. "Name's Miles, sir." He stuck out his hand. "Nice to do business with ye."

"'Tis Laird."

Myra's eyes widened. He was a laird indeed.

The Highlander's Lady

Miles took a step back. "Apologies, my laird, my lady." He bowed low. "Please, if ye would wait here, I'll see that one of the maids shows ye to a room and then have a nice meal, hot bath and gown sent up."

"And my men?"

"Tavern's this way lads, we'll take mighty good care of your horses and see that not a one of ye is hungry nor thirsty by the time this night is through."

Myra rolled her eyes as Miles ambled away, intent on seeing to their every wish. She supposed he didn't see many lairds come through his doors—nor ones that simply paid the outrageous price he voiced.

Moments later, a worn-out looking woman welcomed them with a lukewarm smile and spoke directly to Daniel. "Name's Sara, I'll be helping ye with all your needs – for as long as ye stay. Right this way, my laird."

Just what did she mean by *all your needs*? Myra didn't like the hungry look in Sara's eyes. She'd be damned if she'd allow her to tend to any of Daniel's needs.

They headed through a thin corridor, the wooden planked floor creaking beneath their shoes, until they reached a narrow, uneven wooden staircase. Sara climbed the stairs, and Myra grew tired just from watching her. 'Twas obvious she'd been working a long day—if not all her life.

When they reached the second floor, a landing looked over the tavern below and Myra was only separated from it by a rickety railing. If she leaned against it she was pretty sure she'd fall to right into the men drinking and playing cards at the table beneath. A few of them looked up, tilted their mugs toward her and Daniel and shouted something she couldn't make out. Whatever the strangers said it didn't sit well with Daniel. He stiffened all the more and sent a menacing glare to the men below, all of whom only laughed.

Oh, dear Lord...

Daniel's men heard those who'd been shouting. They took threatening steps toward the locals. Weapons would be drawn, blood would be shed… And she had a feeling it was all her fault.

Placing a timid hand on Daniel's arm she said, "Call your men off, else we will sleep outside tonight."

She watched his jaw tighten, the muscle bouncing beneath his flesh. But he listened.

"Leo," he called with a shake of his head. That was all it took.

His men backed down, calling for refills of their mugs.

Sara opened the door to the chamber. "Here ye are. I'll have a bath and food sent up."

"And a gown," Daniel reminded her.

"Aye, a gown, my laird."

Myra was growing irritated with how the maid only spoke to Daniel and acted as though she were not even there. Did the man have to have so much power over everyone?

Sara scuttled away, leaving Myra quite alone with the man she had so many mixed feelings toward. The room was large — at least Miles hadn't lied about that. A decent sized bed took up most of the back of the room. A table and two chairs sat beneath a small square window which filtered in some of the waning sunlight and beside that a small brazier for a fire. Little square tables graced either side of the bed, one with a candle and flint, the other with a basin and pitcher.

'Twas cozy, quaint, and obviously made for two.

Heat suffused her cheeks.

"Ye canna stay in here with me," Myra said, staring at the bed.

She refused to kiss him ever again, let alone have him bed her.

"Ye have no choice."

At his words she whirled around, feeling the heat of her anger fill her cheeks. Hands clenched, she ground her teeth together, trying not to fly into an unladylike rage, complete with a few well-chosen words.

"I have a choice. Everyone has a choice." At least, if a person was willing to deal with the consequences, they did.

Daniel didn't flinch at her retort, he did however study her with an expression she'd never seen before. 'Twas dangerous, dark. His jaw muscles clenched, but he did not narrow his eyes in a glower, instead his gaze rested coldly on her, sending a chill up her spine.

"Choice? Nay, I disagree."

Myra's hands flew to her hips. "Would ye have everyone under your thumb?"

"Nay, 'tis not possible."

Oh, blazing baby Jesus, did the man have no sense? Myra tried to gape at him, but was finding that task to be quite difficult.

"Are ye daft?"

At that he did react quickly, stepping toward her only once but closing a distance that would have taken her many steps. His face drew close to hers, enough so that if she moved an inch closer her lips would be on his.

"How dare ye talk to me like that," he growled. Then his lips were on hers. She didn't even have time to catch her breath.

This kiss was different than the one he'd given her by the burn. This time his lips pressed demandingly to hers, taking control, ownership. And she didn't back away. Nay, Myra pressed harder, her fingers curling over the thick muscle of his shoulders, nails digging in through his leine shirt. Daniel's hands roved over her back, hauling her up against him with a shock to her senses. She gasped, her mouth opening up enough for his invasion. Hot, slick, velvety tongue swept inside her mouth. Oh, by the saints... She was delirious with pleasure, with need, wanton thoughts.

Myra swirled her own tongue around his, loving the way it sent jolts of fire through her system, made her body weak with the need for him to kiss her forever. She was not timid, didn't balk when he nibbled her lip or when his hands stroked over her arse and tucked her closer, the hardness of his arousal pressing wickedly against the apex of her thighs.

Oh, she was a bad girl, a very very bad girl. But she refused to feel regret over her actions, over her body's obvious wicked desire, over her need to see this moment fulfilled. Daniel wasn't a stranger, he was her husband for the moment and she was his wife.

This was allowed... And she was going to revel in being allowed to touch him this way, to take the pleasure he offered this once.

Save...for one little problem. Myra was angry at him. Tired of him bossing her around. If she was going to kiss him, allow him to stroke her arse, it was going to be on her terms.

She shoved against his chest and slapped his cheek—not as hard as she wanted to, but hard enough that it got her point across. Myra refused to be taken advantage of. Even if his kiss did send her body tumbling into a pleasurable abyss.

Daniel looked shocked, took a step back, his eyes filled with both passion and anger. "Do ye show no respect for your laird?"

That pushed her over the edge as flashes of Byron's shuddering breaths, his warm sticky blood, came to mind. "Ye are not my laird! My laird died!"

She clasped her hands to her lips, not having meant to reveal so much. The man had no idea who she was and she'd kept it that way on purpose.

Sorrow flashed in Daniel's eyes. And his hand came out briefly, fingers touching her knuckles before he withdrew. Even in that subtle touch she felt comfort.

"Are ye a widow?"

Myra chewed her lower lip while she contemplated lying to him. But what good would it do? If he thought she were a widow, he may not treat her so gently and insist that they bed each other since there was no maidenhead to breach. If he ever did find out the truth he'd not trust her either, and while she truly didn't care how he felt about her in the future, she needed his protection now. Needed his support until she'd at least spoken with Robert the Bruce—and the Bruce accepted her news with grateful ears.

"Nay."

Relief flowed freely in Daniel's expression. Why was that?

"I'm sorry for your loss. Your father?"

"Aye." Partly true, her father had passed a few years ago.

Daniel's lips thinned a little and he nodded.

Before they could continue their conversation a knock had Myra jumping, the tension in her body painful.

Daniel opened the door a smidge to see who it was and then let in the troop of tavern workers carrying a rickety wooden tub, a linen towel and several buckets of water.

"Set it before the brazier," Daniel ordered.

As they went about filling the tub, Daniel lit a fire within the brazier, instantly bringing warmth into the room. A sudden chill went through Myra. She hadn't realized how cold she was until now. The water they poured into the tub did not steam, and she prayed that it was at least lukewarm, else she'd die of cold before her bath was through.

"My laird," Sara came into the room, completely bypassing Myra and handed a folded bundle of cloth to Daniel. "The gown, and I managed to rummage up a clean chemise."

Daniel flicked his hand toward Myra, and irritated look on his face. "'Tis for my wife, not me."

"I but thought—"

Daniel cut the maid off. "Give them to her."

Myra tried to hide a smile when she thought of him adding, *ye daft woman*, onto the end of his sentence, for he truly did look at the maid as though she were mad.

Sara pouted as she handed the gown and chemise over to her and then quit the room. Myra unfolded the gown, pleased to see that while it was the color of lush red autumn leaves, it was clean. And soft. Looked a little smaller than her own, but she would manage.

After the servants left, Daniel sprawled in one of the chairs and gazed at her. The heat of his gaze had her tumbling back to their passionate kiss. If she wasn't careful he'd ignite her into a ball of tumultuous flames. Her nipples hardened, reminding her how much she actually wanted him to touch her.

"If ye dinna have your bath soon, the water will be colder than it already is." Daniel didn't look in any hurry to leave.

Myra winged a brow. "Then ye'd best leave the room so I may be about it."

Daniel grinned, gazing at the length of her body. Myra had to admit that she was glad their anger at each other appeared to have dissipated, even if it was replaced by desire.

"I've never seen a lady bathe."

"And ye're not likely to today."

He sighed deeply, and a might exaggeratingly. "Then I shall see if any other ladies in this tavern would oblige me."

"Ye'll not have much luck finding another lady here, but if ye do, and she does, more power to ye."

Daniel chuckled as he left, the door clicking quietly behind him.

The Highlander's Lady

Alone in the little chamber, Myra finally let her shoulders sag all the way, feeling the stretch from the base of her spine all the way up her neck. She shucked out of her cloak, gown and chemise, tore off her boots and hose, wishing for a hearth so she could burn the soiled garments. The brazier was just not large enough. The strip of fabric that had bound their hands lay beside her boots. She picked it up, rubbing her thumb over it, surprised at its softness. Had to be Sutherland wool.

Gooseflesh covered her and she was suddenly aware of how naked and vulnerable she was. She tossed the strip into the brazier. There's was not a marriage in truth. Though she was alone, she crossed her arms over her breasts and hopped over to the tub, not liking the frigid temperature of the floor on her feet.

"Zounds!" she screeched as her toes touched the cold water. 'Twas not in the least bit warm.

Myra clenched her jaw tight. Sitting was not an option. She'd stand, preferring to get her bath over with as quick as possible. She scrubbed furiously, dunked her hair and scrubbed some more. By the time she was finished — perhaps five minutes later — her teeth chattered, her fingernails were blue and she was so prickly from cold she looked like a trussed up goose.

Myra jumped from the tub, grabbed the linen towel which by luck had been set to warm beside the brazier. She wrapped herself up in the warm fabric, feeling the heat seep into her bones.

But it was soon gone as the cold turned her hair into what felt like icicles. She toweled her hair as dry as she could, then tossed on the chemise. The fabric was tight over her breasts and hips. She tried to stretch it out, but it did little. She'd have to deal with what she had, for now. Soon she'd be back at Foulis — her handfast null and void.

Daniel's tempting kisses a distant memory.

Chapter Eight

Watching other men drink until they slurred their words was not as much fun as actually joining in.

Daniel glared over the boisterous tavern. Even his own men had imbibed in more than usual. They played cards, gambling with the locals and flirting with the tavern wenches. The place reeked of dirty sex — literally filthy — stale ale, vomit and burnt meat.

But being down here in the corner, feet up on the table in front of him, hands steepled before his frown, was better than being upstairs where Myra bathed. Completely naked.

As it was, he couldn't stop imagining what her lush curves would look like. When he'd kissed her earlier in the day he'd gotten just the barest hint of plush, perky breasts and hips that were the perfect size for grabbing onto in the heat of passion.

Damn. He didn't want to be thinking about that. His cock tripled in size. Thank the saints no one could see how hot he was for his *wife*. Ballocks, *wife*! He'd not wanted a wife at least until spring... This was supposed to be his time to revel in being a bachelor. One last hurrah before he tied the knot—and yet he'd already wrapped his cloth around her tiny hands. Hands he couldn't stop imagining rubbing over his bare chest, gripping his—

No doubt, his men were wondering what he was doing down here in the tavern rather than up in the rented chamber ravaging his wife.

He was wondering the same thing.

But it wasn't as simple as that. Myra didn't realize who he was. When she hadn't recognized him he'd kept his clan name silent. If she knew he was the man she'd dismissed a few years prior, she would never have agreed to the handfast. The question was, would he have relented?

Nay. Never.

The moment he'd laid eyes on her at Foulis Castle years before, twirled her in his arms, he'd known. Perhaps not consciously, but somewhere deep inside the decision had been made. 'Twas a wonder he'd not thought of her before when his mother had presented him with one laird-hunter after another. Her body had molded to his, her rhythm had been the same as his own, as if they were made to dance together. And there he was back again to the bedding. If they danced so well, their lovemaking would be even better.

Beyond bodies though, he'd found he liked her. Genuinely. And that didn't happen so often. Most of the time he found the women he associated with to be shallow or uninteresting. 'Twas the opposite with Myra. She captivated him.

Daniel had made the right decision in not telling her they'd met before. Not telling her that he'd known the laird she lost was not just her father but her brother too. Part of him had wanted to call her out on her hiding that fragment of the truth, but he wanted her to... He didn't know. Trust him?

The Highlander's Lady

Was he embarrassed? He wasn't easy to shame, but nothing felt like it normally did when he was around her. Almost as though she brought out a side of himself he didn't know existed.

Aye, letting her retain some bit of her secrecy was a good decision for them both. He was sure of it. Now, he just had to prove to her that staying married to him was worth it.

In order to do that, he had to remain down here. Where she wanted him. When they reached the Bruce, he would talk to the man himself about Foulis. The people there were most likely without protection. Daniel could give them the protection they needed. His clan was vast, wealthy and had the means.

"More ale? Meat?" one of the tavern wenches sloshed brew from a jug into his mug and then slapped down a large leg foul on a crusty old trencher.

Daniel nodded, hoping she'd leave him be, but when he noticed it was Sara and her eyes were greedily devouring him, he was pretty sure she wouldn't just saunter away.

"Need a real woman for the night, love?"

Daniel glanced at her face, took in the pock marks and greasy brown hair. "Not today, lass." He didn't want to hurt her feelings by saying more.

Sara glared at him. Apparently denying her was just as bad.

"Suit yourself." Her hip bounced off the table upsetting his mug of ale which spilled right into his lap.

Daniel growled and jerked to standing. The woman didn't even glance around to see what happened as she marched away.

Daniel gritted his teeth, thrust aside the urge to grab her and make her clean it up. Instead he stood, sloshed off what he could and stomped up the stairs. Luckily, his plaid didn't soak in the ale, but he'd had enough watching the men carouse and he was certainly not going to wait for another wench to dump ale all over him.

Hopefully Myra was out of the tub, and if she wasn't she would just have to deal with him being in the room. He wasn't going to spend another moment in the company of anyone else.

Knocking sharply on the door he waited for the sound of Myra's voice to let him in. She didn't take long, in fact, opened the door for him with a welcoming frown.

But her frown didn't concern him. He was too busy studying the high cheekbones, arched brow, plush, pink lips. Her hair shined clean. Amazing what a little soap did. She'd grown nearly threefold in beauty. Daniel had to admit that he found her scowl charming. He was getting used to her ire. And enjoyed the play of emotions constantly running across her face.

"Ye're back awfully soon," she grumbled then turned around and walked toward the center of the room.

Daniel tried not to laugh. Most of her talk was just that — talk. She had a softer side he'd seen beneath the tough exterior. How he'd enjoy peeling away the layers.

"Got ale spilled on me."

That caught her attention. Myra whirled back, her brow raised questioningly as she glanced him over.

"Did ye…"

He had a feeling what she was going to ask — if he'd put advances on another woman — even if her words came out sounding a little strangled. Jealousy flashed in her eyes. Good. Aye, that felt really good.

"I did nothing. That wench who brought ye the gown was none too pleased when I turned down her invitation."

Myra's eyes widened, her mouth forming a sensual O that made him want to kiss her hard, toss her onto the bed and claim her once and for all.

The Highlander's Lady

"Shocked that I said nay?"

"Actually, aye," she said, her voice filled with wonder.

Daniel rolled his eyes. "I'm not as much of a brute as ye think me. Would I lay with another woman the day I handfasted? Nay. Never. I dinna plan to lay with another woman as long as I live."

"Why?"

Her taken aback expression had Daniel puzzling over many things, which he didn't realize he was saying aloud until too late. "A married man should never put his pike inside another. Did your father do so? What makes ye think I'm such a swine?" He crossed his arms over his chest and glowered at her. He'd done nothing to make her think so ill of him and yet she did.

She stepped forward, her small fingers lightly touching one of his arms. The scent of soap and woman floated up to his nose. He flared his nostrils, taking it all in. Daniel had to keep himself from closing his eyes in complete ecstasy.

"I meant no offense. I'm sorry. 'Tis just..." Her words trailed off as she sucked her lower lip in her mouth, eyes cast down.

"Aye?"

She looked back up at him and Daniel nearly took a step back.

"I was brought up to believe that not all men are honorable." Pain momentarily marred her features, but she washed them away with a couple of blinks.

What happened to her? Had someone hurt her?

"Ye would make me a sinner before ye truly know me?"

Myra flinched. "I will try not to pass judgment on ye in the future."

She said future. Did that mean she believed they had one? Aye, they were handfasted, she'd promise to marry him in truth come spring, but he had his doubts.

"Thank ye." There was really too much left unanswered between them. 'Twas driving Daniel mad.

Myra shook her head and turned around, walked toward the table and chairs and sat down in one. 'Twas then he noticed how form fitting the gown she wore was. Every notion he'd had of her curves was true. She was endowed with a supple, lush body he couldn't wait to devour.

Daniel licked his lips, then bit his tongue. Control. He needed control, else he ravaged her on the spot. He whirled around opened the door and shouted down for whisky.

The strong drink would loosen her tongue, make her warm, and hopefully help to dull the pounding in his groin.

Moments later the door was opened by Sara. Her cheeks were red and eyes blazing with anger. She carried a tray to the two of them. Daniel was pleased to see meat and bread along with the whisky and two small cups.

Thank the saints, Sara did not say anything to either of them as she placed the tray a little too hard on the table before turning to leave.

Daniel avoided meeting her gaze. He didn't know what he'd done to cause the maid to feel he'd issued an invitation, but it was clear she was not pleased he'd chosen to remain with Myra. He shook his head. Did no one respect the sanctities of marriage? Not that they'd officially married, but no one here was the wiser to that.

As soon as the door was closed, Daniel rummaged through his bag that had been brought up after the horses were bedded down. He found a clean plaid. Grabbing the end of his belt buckle, a small cough stilled his fingers and had his head shooting up.

"What are ye doing?" Myra asked in a small voice.

"I told ye the wench spilled ale on me. I'd rather not remain in it. 'Tis mostly dry but I'd rather have it dry by the brazier."

The Highlander's Lady

"But…"

"Aye?"

"Nothing." Her face was as red as an apple and she stood from her chair, whirled around and faced the wall. She waved a hand over her head. "Go about it then."

Daniel grinned. She was so prickly. He liked it. Liked the challenge of taking that frown and making it into a smile.

He made quick work of removing his plaid, rolling out the new one, pleating it, laying atop it, belting it around the middle. When he stood he whipped the extra fabric over his shoulder. The standard length of a plaid was nine yards—Daniel's was easily ten. He was that tall.

"I'm finished, lass."

Daniel had to stifle a laugh as she turned ever so slowly around, her eyes squinted nearly closed as if she expected to find him nude.

"I assure ye, I am fully covered once more."

Her face was still just as red, and the way she swallowed, her fingers curling within the folds of her too-small gown made him wonder what exactly she was thinking.

"Have ye eaten yet?" he asked.

Myra shook her head.

"Come then, the meat will fill ye up."

She nodded briskly and sat at the table picking up a piece that was burnt black as tar on the bottom. Whoever was in charge of cooking at the tavern did a horrendous job.

"Wait," he said. Daniel reached for her meat and using the dirk from the strap at his hip sliced away the burnt parts, tossing it in the brazier where it sizzled. "Ye dinna want to eat that part."

"Thank ye," she said shyly.

Daniel nodded and picked up the jug of whisky, the scent of it making his mouth water. He poured them each a healthy portion—although his was double the amount he poured for her.

Myra set down the piece of meat she nibbled on and lifted the cup to her lips, slick with oil. Daniel wrenched his eyes away, unable to stop the flood of thoughts that her shiny lips brought on.

He downed the cup he'd poured for himself in two healthy swallows, then refilled. The whisky tasted like arse. 'Twas going to be a long night.

The piece of meat—Myra wasn't sure what kind—tasted like warmed over excrement. But that didn't stop her from shoveling it bite after bite into her mouth.

Nerves did that. She chewed fast, choked it down her gullet and heaped in some more. Opposite her, Daniel threw down one whisky after another. Mayhap she should switch to simply drinking whisky and avoiding the fare. He definitely appeared a lot more relaxed than when he'd first come in. The crease on his brow had receded and instead of staring at her like she had horns growing out of her head, he seemed to have found a particular interest in the brazier.

Myra reached for the jug of whisky. Too late, Daniel reached for it too. His hand circled over hers as she grasped the thin neck of the jug. Large, warm hands.

He yanked back as though she'd burned him, his stunned eyes meeting hers.

"Apologies, I didna realize ye were thirsty," he said, his voice low.

Myra smiled, trying to deflect the awkward situation she found herself in. There was something familiar about Daniel, the fact that she felt she could be herself around him was odd. She supposed it was simply having him trust she wouldn't kill him, his easy assessment and acceptance of her. But she

The Highlander's Lady

couldn't place where she would have ever met him, and determined that she must not have.

He was unforgettable.

Where had that thought come from?

She poured herself a little whisky, realizing at the last second that there appeared to already be some in her cup. Oh well. A whole cup of whisky wouldn't hurt her, would it?

Myra shrugged and took a long sip.

"Christ!" she shouted out.

Daniel's eyes popped open.

"Oh, my… I'm sorry, Daniel. 'Tis the whisky. It burns!" She slammed the cup down, her fingers coming to press against her lips, the reason twofold. The burning did not recede, and 'twas probably God's way of punishing her for taking his name in vain.

"No need to apologize, lass. Ye were startled."

Myra only nodded, grateful for him letting her little slip go, but also confused. When he'd let her sip whisky before it hadn't burned this bad, and the few sips she'd taken at Foulis hadn't either.

"This whisky is not as good quality as mine," he said. "Not aged long enough, I suspect. Or maybe the distiller is simply no good at his trade." Daniel shrugged and took another sip, giving the impression of not caring too much either way at the flavor.

His words clarified things somewhat. Myra felt her body warming. A tingling warmth that started in her belly and spread outward. She kind of liked it.

"Me too," Daniel said.

Had she truly voiced her words aloud?

"Aye, ye did, lass."

Clamping her lips shut, Myra reached for the cup again. She took another long sip. It still burned, but this time, she was prepared for it, reveled in it.

Confidence came with the warmth. She felt… Myra didn't know. She couldn't describe it. Strong? That was part of it, but she felt something else. Gazing at the man she'd handfasted to earlier in the day, she felt something entirely different.

Brazen. Her entire body tingled now, and her arms and legs had minds of their own and wished desperately to wrap themselves around the hunk of brawn sitting across from her.

"Oh," she gasped as her nipples hardened. Sensations she'd never before experienced whipped through her, making her feel heady, hungry for the taste of Daniel's lips.

This would not do.

She shoved the cup of whisky away. No more.

The drink was turning her into a wanton. A woman with little morals.

But was it truly wrong to want to touch Daniel? She had promised to be his wife after all. They would be together for the rest of their lives. They'd sworn to it in the woods and in the spring they'd swear to it before God.

She shoved the cup even further away.

Nay.

The plan was *not* to be with him forever.

Myra needed to get to Eilean Donan alive. Unscathed. And still a maid.

She would relay her news to the Bruce and then return to Foulis where she'd take up her position as laird until Rose birthed Byron's heir. Then her future would be decided.

Daniel was only a means to get to the Bruce. He would keep her safe. Be her guide.

That was all.

Clenching her thighs together, she was not at all pleased with the heat and tingling that grew between them. She squeezed tighter hoping to quell it but that only made the hunger emanating from the apex of her thighs grow.

The Highlander's Lady

What hold did he have on her? Was the whisky poisoned? Meant to seduce her? A magical love potion?

She glanced at Daniel out of the corner of her eye. He sipped casually on the whisky and again stared at the brazier. What was he thinking?

"Daniel," she started, but stopped when he jerked his gaze back to hers.

His eyes were dark, intense. She felt as though he could see right into her soul.

"Do ye dance?" he asked.

She nodded slowly. "Aye."

"Would ye care to dance with me?"

"But there is no music."

"There is. Listen."

Myra closed her eyes and could hear the faint sound of someone playing the pipes.

"May I?" he asked, suddenly closer.

She opened her eyes and found him standing right in front of her. She could smell him — earthy, leather, all man.

Myra placed her hand in his before she could think not to, again struck with the sheer size of him. Daniel had to be a giant. Highlanders were typically tall, but Daniel stood easily six inches above the tallest man she'd seen.

He gently pulled her to standing, tucked her close to him so that the heat of his body wrapped around her like a warm, sensual blanket. She had to keep herself from shivering. It didn't work. Her skin prickled, and Myra bit her lip to keep from sighing as her body molded perfectly to his. Daniel's hand wound around her waist in the back, the other holding her hand in his.

He started the steps of a dance she'd only danced once before. At Foulis. A sensual, wicked dance.

With —

Zounds!

Myra knew exactly why Daniel was so familiar now.

Eliza Knight

Chapter Nine

Myra stiffened in Daniel's arms.

She could tell he noticed the change when he started to take a step back, but Myra sank back into him. She didn't want him to ask why she'd moved away. Then she'd have to confess.

Confessing was on her list of things she *never* wanted to do, along with jumping off a cliff. Myra wasn't spoiled by any means, but when she didn't want to do something, she always attempted to get out of it. Besides, wasn't she allowed to have some secrets?

Somehow over the past couple of years she'd been able to completely thrust this man from her thoughts. How was it possible she hadn't recognized him right away? He was bigger now. Broader, his corded muscles thicker. Even happened to be more handsome — mayhap because he'd shaved the beard he once wore. His dark hair was now longer and most of the time it was in his face, covering his features in shadows and making her mad with the urge to swipe it all away. Age had done the man well, his features were more chiseled, more manly. No doubt he still had women falling at his feet, begging to be ruined.

Myra frowned against his shoulder.

A person did not change all that much, even if she'd had a hard time recognizing him until he'd taken her into his arms and she'd spiraled back in time. Swayed with him in that same perfect rhythm that had kept her up at night for months on end. His eyes were the same. Crisp, passionate, deep green eyes. Not shallow or cold. His eyes were windows to his soul, even if he tried to shadow them. Myra had been able to see the man beneath the warrior exterior.

She'd seen it years before too.

Myra supposed she'd just not wanted to remember. He'd broken her heart. Dashed her dreams with those eyes.

He'd not recognized her either it appeared. That notion had relief flooding her. She'd not made much of an impression on him on their first meeting at Foulis. She was sure of that. She'd found that out shortly after meeting him. They'd danced, just like this, their bodies swaying, the heat of him filling her. They'd laughed.

But when she'd gone to the garderobe to relieve herself, she'd stopped by her chamber, pulling out a linen square that she'd embroidered with a thistle and her initials. She intended to give it to him as a token, hoping that he would come to call on her in the future, perhaps even speak to her brother about a future together. Myra had been stupid.

When she'd returned to the great hall, Daniel was surrounded by women. He made eyes with them, laughed, touched, just as he'd done to her. She was nothing special to him. He'd treated all of them the same way. If that wasn't a blow to her soul she didn't know what was. Up until the moment she'd met him, Myra had never wanted to marry. Never wanted to be with a man. Not after what happened to

The Highlander's Lady

her mother. Byron and her father had made sure she knew how awful men were. But she'd thought Daniel was different.

He wasn't. Even if he made her heart stir still.

He'd not gone by Daniel then, he'd been called Murray, and she'd never found out his first name until meeting him in the woods. Byron had found her crying in the stairwell and sent her back to her room. Murray was deemed a womanizer just like any other man she'd found interest in. What had hurt the most though was with Daniel, she'd felt so much more than a physical attraction. He'd made her smile with his witty banter. He'd shown a genuine interest in her.

Then again, it appeared he showed genuine interest in every female.

Myra frowned, her brow furrowing so tight she started to get a headache. Or was that from the whisky?

Did it matter?

Now that she remembered who he was, she could not continue this farce. As soon as they reached Eilean Donan, she would be rid of him. End the handfast, dash the promises of a future together.

It didn't matter how sweet Daniel was. Or that he'd readily taken up the task of seeing to her protection. It didn't matter that she still felt the same way only stronger. Or that his hand at her waist felt like heaven.

Except it did. All of it.

Tears stung her eyes.

Dinna cry. Dinna cry. Ballocks!

A tear slipped from the corner of her eye and Myra turned her gaze toward the ground so Daniel wouldn't catch sight of it. She continued to sway in his arms, pretending as though there was nothing amiss. He didn't need to know she'd realized they'd met before.

Or that he'd broken her heart.

How foolish and naïve she'd been.

Well, she was no longer! Nay, now Myra was a woman full grown. A laird in fact. And she'd best start acting the part. Starting now.

She disentangled herself from Daniel and took a step back. Shoulders squared she forced a smile at him.

"Laird Murray, I do believe 'tis time for bed."

Daniel narrowed his eyes at her, but did not say anything. Most likely he'd been thinking they'd end this night with a bedding. Oh how she enjoyed disappointing him. He took her hand in his and she suppressed a shudder, although her knees felt very weak.

Daniel raised her hand to his lips and Myra bit her tongue. She wanted to shout for him to let go, not to—

Oh, sweet, lord in Heaven.

His lips brushed her knuckles. Heat. Sensuality embodied and all her thoughts of restraint, of irritation dissipated. Myra could feel her muscles relaxing, only to have her belly coil tightly. Her thighs quivered as his breath lingered on her flesh, and that one simple touch of his lips on her skin sent a hot current to race through her arm to her breasts.

She held her breath but couldn't yank away.

Daniel picked up her other hand.

Oh, nay! She couldn't have him repeating that move with her other hand, but she was helpless to stop him. Some part of her wanted him to kiss her hand. To feel the brush of his lips against her, even if it was such a simple, innocent move.

Ha! Innocence had nothing to do with it.

He kissed her other hand, his lips brushing tenderly against the knuckles until Myra was sure she'd swoon. She yanked her hand back so forcefully she lost her balance. Quick as lightning, Daniel reached out and wrapped his arms around her waist to steady her.

The Highlander's Lady

Myra held in a groan as he pulled her tight, his hard belly flattening to hers and something else hard, long and... Oh, my...

He pressed *it* against her hip. 'Twas impressive. Frightening.

She knew exactly what that was. Listening in behind the walls of Foulis she'd learned a lot.

Why now was she so curious though? She blinked rapidly trying to get visions of what his male parts would look like out of her mind.

Heat filled her face and she was sure she looked as red as a berry.

"Are ye all right, lass?"

"Pe—" She cleared her throat as her voice caught. "Perfectly." Myra shoved against him, standing tall. "Now, if ye will please leave me, I'd like to get some rest."

"I'm not going anywhere."

"What?" she faltered. "Ye must."

"We've handfasted, lass. Everyone here believes we're truly wed. I'll not leave this room until the morn."

She was going to be stuck with him in this room all night? Dizziness consumed her. Myra teetered back to her chair and sat down heavily. She was in over her head. Too much had happened. There had barely been a chance for her to grieve for her brother, for those in her clan who'd perished. She'd not even let the idea of becoming laird and being wholly responsible for all Munros sink in yet. And Rose. She'd just left her with the Sutherlands, not even sure that she was safe within those walls, even if Byron said she would be.

Byron had once thought Ross was trustworthy. Now he was dead.

Her heart fluttered painfully, and she felt all the blood in her head rush to her toes. Myra leaned back against the wooden chair, hot then cold, then hot again. Her fingers trembled and her lips went numb. Her vision grew blurry. Was she about to faint? She'd never fainted before.

"Lass? Ye look a bit pale." Daniel's voice sounded so far away.

Myra glanced up at him, trying to gauge just where he stood. He walked toward her, looking wobbly. Or was that her eyes?

He knelt before her. Touching her knee, her hands.

"Daniel," she managed to say. "I'm tired."

She was suddenly desperately tired. So tired she thought she might be able to sleep for an entire week. Through the haze of her blurred vision she saw him nod. But then her eyes closed. She could still hear. Heard him murmur something but she couldn't make out what it was. Her body moved into the air, pressed against a solid form. A comforting form. She snuggled closer.

'Twas nice, this body that held her.

He lowered her to the bed, which was not as comforting. Smelled of sweat and grease. Myra yawned, her mouth stretching wide and a murmuring sound coming from her throat.

"Sleep, sweetling. I'll be here."

"All right," she answered, liking the sound of his voice. Liking him calling her sweetling. Sounded almost like she was well and truly his.

What in holy hell?

Daniel stood back from the bed gazing down at Myra. She'd gone from blazing, to embarrassed maid, to fainting, vulnerable lass. She was an enigma. But he couldn't stop staring. Or stop wanting her.

The Highlander's Lady

She danced just as well as she did a few years ago, her body fitting to his. Her scent filling his nose, taking over his senses. Her breasts had been pert, soft globes pressed to his chest, and when his cock had pressed against her hip...

He blew out a long breath.

He was fucked.

There was no other term for it. He was well and truly being whisked through a torrential current and any moment he'd be falling over the edge.

Myra was dangerous. When she was close he could think of nothing but her. Of being with her. Of kissing her, touching her, dancing with her.

She was a distraction. How was he supposed to be of use to Wallace and the Bruce if he was busy chasing after her? 'Haps after they arrived and she relayed her message—with him by her side—he could send her back to Blair Castle while he continued with training the men for the impending battle.

She'd balk. He knew that. Myra balked about everything though. All he had to do was convince her that the safest, best place for her was at his castle. She could get to know his mother, the clan, her new home and he'd return to her in the spring for their nuptials.

Only problem was, how could he be sure she'd be there when he returned? He couldn't truly... Unless he bedded her now. And every chance he got until she left. Hopefully then he'd have planted his seed and she couldn't leave him if she was with child.

A sour taste filled his mouth. Daniel wasn't like that. He didn't resort to trickery. Shaking his head he walked around to the other side of the bed and laid down heavily. The bed creaked and groaned with his weight. Obviously the bed was not made for a warrior. He didn't bother to remove his clothing or boots. He and Myra were both safer this way. He crossed his legs at the ankles and put his hands behind his head as he studied the wooden planked ceiling. How reliable was the roof? The room smelled musty and moldy. He gathered when it rained the room was damp and a few buckets were placed around to collect water.

Myra made a sound in her sleep and he turned to stare at her. She was so peaceful, quiet in her sleep. Different than how she was when awake. Almost made him forget what a high-spirited woman she was. Almost.

Her skin was smooth and creamy looking, a touch of pink in her cheeks. Dark lashes fanned over her cheeks and beneath her lids her eyes moved back and forth. She was deep in sleep. His chest tightened for a moment. Myra trusted him. Even if she didn't say so when she was awake, and railed on everything he said, she trusted him all the same. Else she wouldn't be able to sleep so peacefully beside him.

Daniel wasn't a desperate man.

He blew out a breath and turned back to study the ceiling. He was damned well not going to force her. His wife would stay because she wanted to. And he was pretty sure he could make her want to stay.

If Myra decided to run away, he would simply track her down and convince her once more the right of things. The two of them were good for each other. He wasn't going to resort to trickery to keep her attached to him. And truth be told, if she wanted so badly to get away from him, then perhaps she wasn't the right one for him. He could be wrong. Daniel wasn't arrogant enough to believe he was always right—even if he was most of the time.

Myra snuggled close to him, her head somehow managing to fall on his shoulder as she curled up in the crook of his arm. Her warmth spread through him like sunshine and her breath softly fanned over his neck.

Daniel smiled crookedly. At least when she was sleeping she wanted to be with him. That was a start.

The Highlander's Lady

"Nay... Byron..." she murmured in her sleep then shivered. Desperation sounded in her voice, bringing to light all that had happened to her.

Myra was strong, no doubt about that. She'd been through one horrendous event after another. He was surprised she'd not collapsed earlier. Daniel shifted his arm around her back.

"Nay! Dinna die..."

Her words tugged at his heart and he wanted nothing more than to comfort her. Her breath quickened and she trembled in his arms. A glance at her eyes which still fluttered beneath her lids showed she was still in deep sleep. He frowned, wishing he could take away her pain but knowing there was no way to do that.

The lass was probably having a nightmare. Remembering the death of her brother. Daniel pulled her closer, stroking lightly through her hair, twirling a tendril around his finger. So soft. He didn't want to wake her. She needed to work it out in her mind. Mayhap her dreams were trying to tell her something. Or maybe it was part of the healing process.

Daniel's eyes widened as a thought occurred to him. The lass was muttering things. Reliving what had happened. He'd heard before that if a person talked in their sleep, it was possible to ask them questions and receive answers. Dare he? Was it worth the risk of waking her and being on the receiving end of her wrath?

Aye. Completely worth it.

Daniel pulled her gently closer, hearing her sigh a little in her sleep. She flopped a leg over his thighs and mumbled something. He gritted his teeth. The weight of her thigh a burning reminder of how much he wanted her. His cock was immediately at attention, just waiting for the go ahead from him. Nay. He'd not force himself on her. He had a task to complete. He needed information and God knew she wasn't willing to share when she was awake.

"Who did this lass?" he asked softly, praying he was right about her nightmare and what he'd heard of sleep talkers.

She garbled something unintelligible, snaked her arm around his waist, then whispered, "Ross."

Daniel gritted his teeth. Ross. The man had been the bane of his cousin Sutherland's existence. Magnus Sutherland had been nagged into agreeing to a marriage to Ross' daughter. The wench would have driven Magnus over the edge. Thank goodness his cousin stole away his English bride Arbella, else he may have flung himself before the first English army he saw and awaited his death. As if turned out, the Englishman he'd stolen Arbella from married Ina Ross—which made the entire clan a force to be reckoned with. Even though the English bastard swore he'd defected and believed in the Scottish cause, Daniel had always had his doubts, as had Magnus. What they'd not counted on was Laird Ross being behind the treachery.

Damn.

"Laird Ross killed Byron?" he asked softly, needing to hear her say it one more time.

"Aye... All of them."

All of them. Sounded so ominous. What was the state of Foulis right now? Anger sliced through him. When someone needlessly and violently attacked one of his allies... He would see to it the culprit was punished severely and then sent straight to hell.

Mo creach... Myra's journey to the Bruce just grew exponentially in importance. She was going to tell the Bruce of an enemy within his own group of trusted advisors. Ross was probably on his way to Eilean Donan now, if he wasn't there already. Ross was a major player in the Bruce's military. He was a bastard, a drunk and crude, but he knew how to plan an attack, how to train men. Wallace and the Bruce both trusted him.

The Highlander's Lady
    And he was the enemy.

Chapter Ten

Warmth filled Myra. 'Twas indeed a most wondrous way to wake. She snuggled deeper into the cocoon of covers she'd burrowed out for herself.

Wait... Keeping her eyes closed, she slowly extended her fingers and touched the hard, hot barrier beside her. Oh, my... Solid, muscled male met her fingertips.

That had her eyes popping open.

Daniel slept soundly beside her and the cocoon she'd thought was made of blankets and pillows was in fact the crook of his shoulder. Light streamed in from a break in the flap that covered the window. Morning. Had she slept beside him all night?

She tossed away the plaid that covered them both to see she and he were both fully clothed. They couldn't have consummated their handfast with clothes on, could they? And she would have felt it, right?

The Highlander's Lady

Myra chewed her lip, trying to recall all the various bodies she'd seen behind walls. There were indeed a few hurried instances where the lovers kept most of their clothes on.

But she had heard that it hurt for a woman the first time. Myra squeezed her thighs together. No pain. Only a dull throb which grew worse the more she thought of lovers and lovemaking.

Daniel let out a soft murmur that had Myra snatching the plaid back up. She glanced up at him to see if he was waking, but it didn't look like he was. In fact, he rolled toward her, slinging a heavy arm over her middle causing the air in her lungs to whoosh out.

Part of her liked the contact, liked to feel the weight of his arm on her, the other part panicked. She was trapped. Escape was impossible. She glanced down at his thick arm, the size of a tree limb. His leine shirt was well-made and creamy in color. It fit him well, but the way it rested against her it tugged tight in places outlining the shape of his upper and lower arms.

Myra had the urge to touch his arm. To trace the curves and lines. From the corner of her eye she again looked to his face to see if he was awake. His eyes were half hidden by a mass of dark hair that fell over his face but she could still see they were closed. Well, if he was asleep he wouldn't know that she explored his arm, would he?

Nay. And if he woke she would just tell him she was trying to remove his gigantic appendage from her person. Haughtiness would take attention away from what she was really doing. Myra had never been this close to a man. She couldn't give up the opportunity.

For shame. If anyone were to see her she'd be labeled a wanton, even if she was handfasted. A woman should never be curious about a man's body. Well, poo to that, she was going to touch him.

Since her right arm was pinned tight against his warm chest, she gently took her left arm from beneath the covers, feeling the chill of the room instantly. Gooseflesh rose over her limbs and her teeth almost started to chatter—she clamped her jaw tight to keep them still. Myra was certain the winter air seeping into the room had nothing to do with her sudden chill. What she was about to do had everything to do with it.

Using her index finger, she touched the top of his bare wrist, taking in the tiny dark hairs that dusted his arm. She slid her finger up until the leine shirt stretched to its capacity stopping her from going further. Daniel's arm hair tickled her sensitive fingertip. Corded muscle and sinew met her touch. He was thick. Where she could feel the bone on her arm if she followed it up to the elbow with her fingers, she could barely feel his. Daniel's flesh was hot. If he were a fire, he could heat a room with his body. Where she touched him sizzled and beneath the blanket the shared, warm air surrounded her.

Daniel sighed, his breath shifting her hair until it tickled her cheek. She stopped moving. Waited. One, two, three… He didn't say anything, didn't move. Still asleep.

She nodded, convinced, and turned slightly to see his still closed eyes. At his elbow, she flattened her palm over the thickest part of his upper arm. Massive. She couldn't even reach her fingertips around halfway. His arm was all muscle, thick, hard. Myra wanted to squeeze it, to see just how strong he was, but that would surely wake him. She settled for stroking up and down and over the bunches of muscle.

A sigh escaped her. She liked his arm. Hadn't realized how much touching a man's arm would make her feel…hot. Lightheaded. The sensations whipping through her body, playing with her mind, they brought to mind yearning. Wanting, desire. She'd never felt it before. Not until now. And it was intense. Myra suddenly wanted him to kiss her again.

The Highlander's Lady

She didn't so much mind the weight of his arm over her belly. In fact, she kind of wanted to remain like this for a while longer.

A loud grumbling sound from her stomach broke the spell. Thank God. She could not lay here all day stroking the man.

She flung his arm aside and hurried from the bed, screeching when her bare toes hit the frozen wooden planked floor.

"Good morning," Daniel said from behind her.

Myra hopped from one foot to the other as she turned to face him. His hair was rumpled, still half in his face as he gazed at her. The expression on his face looked…amused. Was it in reaction to her freezing or the molestation she'd done to his arm?

"Morning," she said, pleased with her clipped tone. If he did happen to wake to part of her exploration there was no need for his pride to inflate over it.

Myra turned away from him and poured water from the pitcher on the side table into the basin, then bent to splash some on her face. Felt like she was splashing frozen loch water onto her face. A violent shiver took over for a minute.

Placing her hands on either side of the table, she stood there, half bent, staring into the bowl of water. What was it about this man that made her half mad? She was not at all herself. Was that the way it was supposed to be? She couldn't afford to let herself become enraptured by him. To let her mind go. She had a promise to fulfill. A nation to save. The Bruce's life and every warrior who fought for him had their lives on the line.

The Ross was a traitor. Sided with the English, it was only a matter of time before he led troops to their camp. An ambush for sure. 'Twas the preferred method of the Sassenachs, and exactly how Ross himself fought. The bastard. Anger surged through her. Fury, regret, soul-wrenching pain. That man had taken everything from her.

No matter how much Daniel appealed to her, or how much her curiosity longed to quench its thirst, she could not allow him to become a distraction to her. There was too much at stake.

Myra had to think like a laird. Hell, she didn't even know how many of her people survived. If they even knew she'd survived. She'd taken Rose and fled. The only thing she could pray was that when they didn't find her or Rose's bodies, they knew she'd taken Byron's wife and child to safety.

"Are ye all right, lass?" Daniel touched the small of her back and Myra jumped.

She'd not even heard him climb from the bed. Squeezing her eyes shut for the span of a heartbeat she turned around to face him.

"Perfectly. Just trying to become accustomed to the cold. The bed was a mite warmer." She beamed a smile at him, hoping he'd not question her further.

"Aye. 'Twas warmer." His eyes which had been clear when she turned around were now shuttered.

He was hiding something from her. Or else he was trying to hide the fact that he realized she'd lied. Myra frowned for a second then walked toward the one small window. Pulling back the covering, she peered outside. The sky was grey and cloudy and the sharp breeze that whipped inside smelled of snow.

"'Twill snow soon," Daniel said, as if reading her thoughts. "We'd best gather the men and head out. I'll not spend another night here."

Here or in her arms?

Myra swallowed back her questions. She didn't care—or at least that was what she was telling herself. No more games. No more trying to figure out why this man wanted her one

The Highlander's Lady

minute and not the next. Once she relayed her message safely to the Bruce, she'd ask for an escort and return to Foulis. Where she belonged.

"Nor I," she replied softly.

She heard the splash of water as Daniel washed his face, but she refused to turn around. Having that vision of him, even for something so mundane, was intimate, she didn't want it in her mind. Didn't want to remember such an inane thing about him. No need for thoughts of domesticity clouding her mind.

There was a rustling of noise which she assumed was Daniel donning his weapons and packing up his satchel.

"I'm for the stables. When ye finish in here, meet me there."

Myra nodded and waited for the sound of the door closing before she turned away from the window. She located her hose and boots and pulled them on. Then found her cloak, which thankfully hadn't retained as much damage as her gown.

She'd brought nothing else with her. A bitter reminder of all she'd lost. Leaving the room behind, Myra descended the stairs into the rather quiet inn. Upon a table was a plate of stale-looking rolls. Grabbing one, she bit into it. Stale. Slightly moldy. But who was she to complain? There was nothing else to eat for now. And she dared not ask Daniel for something.

The Murray men were gathered in the courtyard, their horses readied and they appeared only to be waiting for her. Daniel eyed her wearily and she couldn't help but wonder what was going through his mind. 'Twas obvious he kept more inside than he wanted to and she suspected that was hard for him. He was not a shy man, and contradictorily not one prone to sharing his mind. Why did he act thusly with her?

"My lady," he muttered, offering her a hand.

Myra stuffed the last bit of bread in her mouth and placed her hand into his. He hoisted her up onto the horse and then came up behind her.

Oh, joy... She'd forgotten about how uncomfortable riding was with him. Myra stiffened her back so that she sat ramrod straight.

"How long shall we travel today?" she asked.

"As long as the weather will allow us," he said, gruffly and shifted.

Myra sighed deeply with resignation. Daniel was likely to shift and grunt the whole of it. She prayed however that they were able to travel until dark and until they found shelter and without any snow falling. Traveling in winter was treacherous. Especially at this time of year. The winter solstice was upon them. Snow was inevitable.

As it was, the grass was covered in frost and her breath came out in white puffs before her face. Myra wiggled her toes. At least they weren't likely to be frozen for a little while.

Daniel kicked his horse into a trot and Myra was unable to control her sudden fall backward. Her back hit the wall of his muscled chest, taking her breath away. She was quick to pull back upright, but it didn't matter. That sudden contact, however unromantic and unintentional still sparked something inside her. Zounds! No matter how hard she tried... Her body would always betray her when Daniel was near. Thank the saints he wasn't the enemy, at least in a literal sense.

Soon Daniel and his men were galloping over the deserted, packed dirt road. Myra was lost in her thoughts. Trying to think back to the day the castle was attacked. Was there any sort of warning?

Other than the visit from Laird Sutherland? What made her brother not take heed? He'd said in his last words from her that an attack from Ross had been warned of. Was it

The Highlander's Lady

because Myra was supposed to marry the old earl that Byron hoped it wasn't true?

There were too many unanswered questions that Myra would never see put to rest. Byron was gone and with him a piece of herself and the answers to her questions. Her heart ached for her lost brother. She prayed that those who survived thought to look in the darkened corridors behind the walls for her brother. But if there were no survivors he may still be there, his soul doomed to walk in Purgatory until a priest could be found to give him a blessing and his remains laid to rest.

Tears stung her eyes and she gasped for breath as her throat closed.

"Lass?" Daniel said from behind, his hold on her tightening. He leaned close, his breath tickling her ear. "What is amiss?"

Myra cleared her throat, not certain she could speak. The pain cut too deep and she had the sudden wish to drop from the horse and weep, but she couldn't. She had to be strong. She was a laird now. Swallowing through the knot in her throat she said, "A midge. I seem to have swallowed the annoying insect."

She felt Daniel nod, his chin bumping her head. He accepted her lie, even though there were no bugs flying about. 'Twas the middle of winter. How kind of him. It only made her think more highly of him. No good.

Myra stiffened her back, leaning forward a little, she made a pretense of patting the horse on the neck. What she didn't count on was the awkward position that put her in as they rode at a gallop. The momentum of the horse and her bending forward jostled her. She gripped the horse's mane tight to keep from falling.

"Zounds!" she shouted.

Daniel hauled her back toward him, the shock of his body planted fully against her once more taking her breath away.

"What the hell are ye doing?" he growled.

Myra didn't know whether to be outraged at his shout or relieved he'd kept her from falling and being trampled to death. She went for outraged.

"Petting your blasted horse!"

Daniel let out a growl. "Dinna speak of my horse like that."

"Or what?"

He tightened his grip around her, his lips skimming the shell of her ear. A shiver passed through her.

"Or I'll truss ye up like a stuck pig and have ye ride the rest of the way to Eilean Donan over my lap."

Myra swallowed. She had no doubt he'd do it. Not because Daniel was a violent sort of man, but there was something in his tone that made her believe him.

"Ye wouldn't," she said, as a pretense so he wouldn't realize she fully expected he would.

"Aye, I would."

She swallowed. "Then ye'd best hide my dirk at night." Myra made sure her tone was hard, sharp. She threatened his life, aye, and he didn't need to know she'd never be able to go through with it. She'd taken a life already this week.

That he knew of. The man who attacked her in the forest had in fact been the only person she'd ever killed. Just thinking about it turned her stomach. Too much violence had occurred in the past fortnight.

Life was hard. And she didn't expect it to be easy, even if she was born to privilege. She'd never been one to sit around while others served her. But wasn't she ever allowed at least a little reprieve?

What had Father Holden told her? *Life is challenging for all, 'tis only those who embrace those challenges, take the boar by its tusks, that make it.* He'd told her that after she'd spent an entire morning on her hands and knees scrubbing the chapel floors

The Highlander's Lady

as penance. Funny enough, she couldn't remember what she was being reprimanded for, but she remembered his words. They resonated within her. Mother had not been able to take those challenges. Granted, she'd been taken hostage and brutally assaulted by the MacDonald when Father refused to an agreement which Myra had never been made privy to. Shortly after she was returned to Foulis, a shell of her former self, Mother took her own life. 'Twas then Myra's own life had become harder.

Father and Byron were both harder on her. And she'd been hidden away. 'Twas a miracle she'd been allowed to spend that one glorious hour at the feast where she'd first met Daniel.

Then again, she'd cursed ever being allowed out after witnessing him with the other ladies. Jealousy was certainly an ugly monster.

Apparently, challenge was inevitable for Myra. She'd thus far been able to survive, to come out on top. However cowardly she felt on the inside, she definitely took the boar by its tusks each and every time it ran toward her, death in its eyes.

Defeat was not in her vocabulary and she wasn't about to let it in now. Myra squared her shoulders, making sure the blades nearly touched in the back. If she had to sit like a stone the rest of the day, she would.

Daniel chuckled. 'Twas then she realized he'd not replied to her threat.

Well, he did so now, and she could practically hear the sneer in his voice.

"Keeping your back straight and the stinging burrs in your words won't sway me, lass. I've held ye warm and pliant in my arms. Tasted your lips. Felt your passion ignite. I find—" He paused a moment. "I find your ire invigorating."

Bastard!

Chapter Eleven

Oh, how he loved to rile her up!

Daniel could practically feel fire blasting from Myra's ears as he threatened to truss her up. Not that he actually would, but he couldn't help teasing her about it. Her body was so stiff she could have been made from wood. One false move and she'd crack right down the center. He had to keep his jaw locked, teeth clenched to keep from laughing. He wished he could see her face. Her eyes were probably the size of trenchers, her lips pressed so tight they were white.

He'd get them pliant and pink again. Kissing angry. Now that was something that really interested him. He'd kiss her slowly, brushing his lips over hers and then slipping his tongue between her lips when she opened her mouth to protest. But she'd not be able to say anything because he'd make quick work of taking over her senses, making her quiver in his arms. Turn all the anger into passion.

The Highlander's Lady

Myra… Her enthusiastic nature was so powerful Daniel was sure to have his hands full. And he reveled at the thought.

Och! What the hell?

Here he went again. Completely distracted by the wench. She would be the death of him.

Daniel looked up at the sky, begging for a reprieve. Looked like he was going to get it too. The clouds had turned dark grey. Ominous.

A swift wind blew, sending sharp pangs of cold through his fingers even though he wore gloves. His plaid billowed around his legs and whipped at the back of his neck. A storm was coming.

"We need to find shelter," he called to Leo.

The man nodded. There were no inns along this road that Daniel knew of. They'd have to find an abandoned cottage or at the very least a cave. He'd even settle for one that was falling apart. As long as they had a wall and a partial roof they could make do until the storm passed.

Just a glance at the peripheral area showed there wasn't much hope for finding shelter. No dilapidated houses. No occupied huts either. They were on a stretch of land that consisted of moors and valleys. They needed to find water. Following a burn or loch would certainly put them in place to find someone willing to house them through the storm, or a place they could hunker down.

Only problem was, Daniel wasn't sure they had enough time to find one before the storm picked up and they could no longer ride. As it was, the wind was blowing sharply in first one direction and then another. Not a kind wind either. Great gusts that had Demon's head facing down as he forged ahead. They had to slow their pace or get carried away.

A cold drop landed on his nose. Damn. Too late now.

More cold drops of snow landed on his cheeks, nose and forehead, melting at the touch of his skin and then freezing with the gust of wind.

To the left a high rise cut into the sky. Maybe they could find a cave or even an overhang to huddle beneath. He pulled the reins to the left, and nodded to Leo toward the rise. Leo gave a short nod and hollered something to the men. Within moments they were all headed in the same direction off the main road, over fields thick with tall, dead grass and grains. Untouched land. Snow began to fall harder, white clusters of icy stars.

Myra reached up, a snowflake landing on her fingertip, lingering a moment before melting.

"So beautiful," he heard her murmur even through the din of the wind.

"Aye," he agreed.

She tucked her hands back within her cloak and to his surprise, huddled closer to him. He supposed in the face of freezing she was more willing to take some of his heat and put her stubbornness aside.

"Laird," Leo called.

Daniel glanced to his second who pointed ahead. Looked like the mountain split, a crevice wide enough that they could fit inside with the horses. Not really a cave, but the best they could find. Huddling in there would keep them safe from the wind, and keep most of the snow from falling on them. Would have to do. There didn't appear to be anything better now, and the snow was beginning to fall so thick he could hardly see in front of him. The world was slowly becoming a white, grey mass.

When they arrived at the split, Daniel was pleased to see that after the initially thin opening—which would still fit the horses—the space appeared to widen. He dismounted, helping Myra to come down beside him. She shivered in his

The Highlander's Lady

arms and gazed up at the sky. No doubt she was wondering if she'd live to see the morning or die in an icy grave. His men dismounted as well.

"I'm going to find wood for a fire," Leo shouted over the gusts of wind.

Daniel nodded. A fire was essential for them to live through the night. The temperature had suddenly turned frigid. Without warmth, they would all freeze overnight.

Leading the way, he paused at the opening, blinking his eyes to adjust to the darkened space. Wouldn't it be just his luck that they'd walked into a den of bears or wildcats? Luck was on his side for one—it was deserted. Grabbing the horse's reins with one hand and Myra's with the other, he led her inside, and then guided Demon in as well. They went all the way to the back.

"Will all the horses fit, Laird?" Seamus called.

Daniel glanced around. *Damn.* "Only three more. Go and see if ye can find another spot for the mounts." The animals had enough fur and fat to keep them warm, but he'd just as well not lose any to exposure. They were war horses, not wild cows.

Overhead the mountain jutted out creating a kind of roof so the thick snow fall came only in a few flakes within the crevice.

A few men arrived with armfuls of wood, dry enough that they could start a small fire to keep warm. Daniel settled his horse then turned to find Myra leaning against the stone wall, her eyes watching his every move.

"Are ye all right?" he asked, noting the bluish tinge to her lips. "Come, sit by the fire." He beckoned her close, spread an extra plaid on the ground and when she sat upon it, he wrapped her up in it. "Whisky?"

She nodded, but still didn't speak. Handing her the skin, he watched her take a gulp.

"I do like whisky," she said with a shy smile.

"Aye, me too." Daniel took a long swig.

Leo returned. "Found a spot for the horses not too far from here. They are all settled and hopefully come morning they won't have run off."

Daniel nodded. The men rustled in their packs, pulling out extra plaids and food. They passed around hunks of bannock bread, jerky and Leo gave Myra an apple.

She bit into the crisp fruit, sighing. Daniel wrenched his eyes away from the way her lips grew slick with apple juice and instead stared up through the tall mountains toward the sky. He could see only a sliver of sky, but it was dark grey and ominous. He prayed the snow fall stopped sometime in the night and that it didn't leave them trapped in the hollow of the mountain. His men and he were hearty enough to hold out until they could travel once more, but was Myra?

Sure enough, she was a brave woman, had the strength of mind that most women wished they had, but was she hearty enough in body to survive a snowstorm without the comforts of castle walls, a hearth and cooks to make her meals?

"'Tis cold, but I'll be fine," she murmured as if hearing his thoughts.

Daniel was sure this time he'd not said anything. He studied her as she finished the apple. "Aye, ye will."

"I can see the question in your eyes every time ye look at me."

"'Tis only natural."

"What? That ye'd think a woman weak?"

"Nay, that I'd be concerned for the woman I've pledged my life to."

She jerked her gaze toward his, surprise written into her features, almost like she hadn't thought he was actually invested in her.

"I gave ye my word, Myra. This may not be a love match, but that doesna mean ye are expendable to me. I mean to keep

The Highlander's Lady

ye safe. To see ye deliver your message and that ye make it safely home with me."

She swallowed, her throat bobbing as she studied him. He could tell she wanted to say something, but didn't. Instead she burrowed deeper into the extra plaid he'd given her and munched on her bannock.

Daniel turned his attention to his own meal, contemplating the future. There was so much at stake. Myra's message, the Bruce's life, the Ross' treachery, the damned English…his marriage.

"I've need of privacy," Myra said quietly and moving to stand. She clutched the plaid blanket tightly around her and even though it was slight, he could see she was trembling from cold.

Daniel jumped up beside her. "I'll escort ye."

"'Tis not necessary." She shook her head, and he could tell from the set in her jaw that she would argue.

Well, he wasn't going to let her out into the storm on her own.

"Aye, it is."

Myra glanced at him again, that questioning look in her eyes, and he realized she too felt the stakes. She too was leery of what would happen. How could he comfort her?

With a quick nod, she turned away from him, walking toward the opening of the mountain crevice. Daniel followed close behind.

Once they'd slipped through the opening, the atmosphere was instantly changed. Snow swirled around on the ground with the wind and fell in droves atop their heads. The grey clouds grew darker with the setting sun. It would only be a few more minutes until they were blanketed in blackness. Daniel pulled his plaid up over his head, and watched as Myra did the same with the cowl of her cloak.

"'Tis magical," she said, doing as she had on the horse and sticking her hand out to catch a few flakes.

"Aye, 'tis that. But can be deadly."

She nodded, then did something completely surprising. Leaning her head back she caught a clump of flakes on her tongue, instantly melting them. Myra laughed and did it again. Daniel stood mesmerized. The pure joy in her laugh, the innocent playfulness, it showed there was so much to her than the tortured soul he knew she was. He could see that woman he'd danced with at Foulis.

Without thinking, Daniel reached out, his fingers stroking her cool, reddened cheek. Myra leaned into his touch, her eyes closing. For a moment time stood still and he couldn't believe how fate had once more put them together. She pulled away, her face in shadows.

"I'll be right over there." She nodded toward an oversized fir tree, thick with needles.

"Call if…"

"I'll be fine."

He nodded and watched, still slightly dazed as she hurried toward the tree. 'Twas obvious things were changing between them. Was just a matter of them both embracing it.

Daniel kept his senses alert for danger. The last thing he needed was for his bride to be taken while she relieved herself. The wind howled, making it hard to hear if any person or animal approached. He walked a path back and forth from the left to the right of the fir, ready to rush behind it when she finally emerged.

She beamed a smile at him. "Ye look ready to mess yourself, Daniel. Is aught amiss?"

Oh, she had a way with words. If he didn't know she was a lady, he might have questioned her upbringing.

He grinned at her and resisted the urge to pull her into his arms so he could show her just how he was feeling. "All is well. Let us go and get warm by the fire."

The Highlander's Lady

Myra nodded and rushed toward the opening. The men all huddled together around a separate fire, leaving the other to Myra and Daniel. They sat close, Myra rubbing her hands together over the flames.

"Lass…"

She glanced up at him, a question in her eyes. How could he phrase this without giving her the wrong idea?

"For the purposes of warmth, ye might consider sharing our plaids."

Her delicate brow rose and he had the urge to kiss the arc of it.

"Share your plaid?"

"Aye." He nodded toward his men. "Nothing else. I'd never compromise ye in front of my men."

"But ye would if they were not here?"

Daniel chuckled. "Ye play my words back at me. Nay, if ye recall our night in the inn. Ye slept in my arms the whole night through and not once did I touch ye inappropriately." He paused, watching her lick her lips nervously. "Ye however, did take a moment to quell your curiosity."

Even in the shadows of the fire he could see the blush on her cheeks. Her mouth opened in shock and outrage and she let out a snort.

"Ye know not what ye speak," she said with a shake of her head.

Daniel grinned wider. "Dinna I? Did ye not trace your pretty little fingers all over my arm? I tell ye, there are other parts of my body jealous of this appendage." He raised the arm he spoke of, feeling the strokes of her fingers as though she were doing so now. He'd been shocked when he'd awoken to her touching him, exploring his muscles, the point of his elbow, but he'd not stopped her. In truth, he was just as fascinated as she was, but he suspected for different reasons.

Myra's blush grew deeper. "Ye're a boor."

"Mayhap I am, but it was ye who touched *me*."

"Would ye rather it was the other way around?"

Daniel couldn't believe his ears. He scooted closer to her. "Aye."

Myra's face paled; clearly she'd not thought he'd answer in the affirmative.

"But I willna — unless ye want me too."

She shook her head vehemently. "Nay. But I will share your warmth."

"Good, then we shall be sure to wake in the morning, instead of freezing to death" he teased.

Scooting even closer, Daniel opened the plaid he'd wrapped around himself and invited her inside. Myra nestled beside him, her shoulder against his ribs. He felt the curve of her shoulder keenly, liking the pressure of her body beside his, and not only in a sexual way. It was comforting to have her with him, to feel her warmth.

"Will ye not tell me what happened?" he asked.

"Happened?"

"Aye. What happened that ye ended up in the woods alone?"

"Oh, that."

She stayed quiet for so long, Daniel wondered if she'd fallen asleep. But then she sighed deeply and glanced up at him. Her eyes sparkled, flickers of the fire dancing in their depths. The world around them tunneled away, leaving just the two of them. He flicked his gaze over her mouth, wanting to kiss her, but also not wanting to break the spell. She looked on the verge of telling him something.

"I told ye I have a message to deliver."

"Aye."

"'Tis a matter of life or death."

Daniel put his arm around her, offering his warmth but a measure of comfort too."

"Death? Whose death?"

Myra pressed her lips together, her eyes still searching his. "Can I trust ye?"

"Aye. I am your husband; ye shall never have to fear that I'd betray ye. I am your protector."

"That is not the same thing."

"What do ye mean?"

"Ye can still be my protector and betray my trust."

"How?"

"If what I tell ye displeases ye, ye could make sure I not deliver it, all while making sure I am still protected. This message is not about myself. 'Tis about all of Scotland and Scotland's king. If ye betray me, the entire country and everyone who lives here will feel the weight of your duplicity."

Daniel nodded. Whatever it was she held within her beautiful head, it was heavy.

"I'll not betray ye, lass. Never."

"Even if ye dinna agree with it?"

"Even then."

"Truly?" She gave him a look like he was mad.

"My word is my honor, without it, I have none. I give ye my word, ye can trust me and I'd never betray ye."

"Thank ye."

But she said no more, instead she laid her head against his shoulder and snuggled deeper within her plaid.

Daniel leaned back against the stone, resigned to fall asleep with no further information tonight. But strangely, he wasn't upset about that. Nay, in fact he felt that they'd grown closer. He understood that trust was the foundation of a good relationship. Oddly enough, he didn't expect her to just tell him all. While she still hadn't told him everything, he'd gained a lot. He was growing closer to her, gaining her trust and soon, when she was ready, she would tell him what she knew, and he'd be able to better protect her—and Scotland.

Daniel closed his eyes, leaning his head back. The cold of the mountain was dulled by the warmth of his wool plaid.

"Did ye remember Byron Munro?" she asked quietly.

"Aye, lass. He was a good man."

"Was?" she stiffened.

Damn. In his near sleep he'd said the wrong word—*was* when he should have said *is.*

Quick to reply, he said, "I was at my cousins' when his widow arrived."

"Oh," she said.

He waited for her to say more, to admit she was Byron's sister, but she didn't. He was glad she didn't pull away, that her stiffened muscles relaxed, and he remained on alert until her breaths grew even.

"I remember ye too," he whispered, knowing she wouldn't hear him.

Chapter Twelve

Myra woke with a start, but was soothed by the warmth of Daniel's strong body, where she nestled in the crook of his arm. The weight of his hand on her hip, the steady sound of his breaths were soothing. She blinked her eyes open, finding herself once more studying him as he slept, and feeling completely at ease.

She didn't dare explore him this time—not only because his men were within view, but because he'd woken last time and had not stopped her.

Oh, the humiliation at realizing he'd been completely aware of every touch, stroke, squeeze. Her face flamed once more with the memory of it and how much she wished to do so again.

Slowly she picked up his hand and removed it, then with just as much stealth she climbed from the beneath the plaid they'd shared. Myra stretched her arms up over her head and studied what bit of the sky above she could see through the thin mountain gap. Clouds still covered up the blue of the sky, but instead of grey, they were now white. Snow no longer fell, but the air was frigid.

Not wanting to wake Daniel to escort her to the giant fir for the privacy she required, Myra picked her steps carefully to the edge of the gap. The grounds outside of their shelter were covered completely in a blanket of thick white snow. Thank goodness they'd found a place to rest. As it was, the snow dusted onto the floor of their refuge rising in a slow arch, she guessed at least six inches deep.

Myra contemplated returning to the warmth of Daniel's sleeping embrace instead of having to stick her feet into the deep snow. Granted, she wore thick leather boots, but they weren't very high, rising just a couple inches above her ankles. Her bladder however was not willing to contemplate returning to bed. With a heavy sigh and a muttered oath, Myra plunged her foot into the snow, instantly feeling the cold through her boot.

She shivered and rubbed her arms beneath her cloak but trudged ahead. Half walking, half running she made it to the fir tree. After finishing her business, she stood to return, but a sound stopped her.

Sounded like a snort or growl.

"Oh..." she said under her breath, praying it wasn't a wolf or wildcat.

There was nothing in sight, but the snorting sound was ominous and echoed off of every surface.

Eyes on the cave she walked slowly back toward it, praying that she made it before whatever animal warned her of its intent to attack actually did so. Then came the distinct roaring squeal that tore her heart from her chest and had panic setting in deep.

A boar.

Boars were fast as devils and mad as demons. If one caught up to her there would be no escape, she'd be speared

The Highlander's Lady

through and through by one of its deadly tusks. Fear like she'd never known set in. Myra lifted her skirts, let out a scream and ran. From behind, pounding, angry snorts followed her. Blood rushed in her ears and her breaths came so fast she nearly choked on them.

As she ran, her feet sinking deep into the snow, her toe caught on something sending her flying forward. Myra landed hard on her hands and knees, sinking into the snow, but that didn't stop her from moving. To stop meant certain death. She scrambled on all fours, her hands stinging with the cold until she was able to gain her footing. Men spilled from the mountain gap, weapons drawn. The roar that split the air from Daniel's lips was more chilling than the sounds of the wild boar that chased her.

"Daniel, help me," she squeaked, throat tight.

Sword drawn, Daniel searched the area. His eyes immediately met hers, then looked behind her.

"Myra!" Daniel ran toward her, his long legs stretching over more ground than hers could ever manage. He lifted her into the air, his arm around her waist, and ran back to the cave, thrusting her inside. He didn't say anything, didn't look at her again, but whirled back around to fight off the enraged wild beast that was charging at first one of his men and then another.

Myra leaned against the cold stone, pressing her cheek against the hardness and allowing the cool to calm her somewhat. But it didn't work. Her heart still pounded, her breaths were hitched and fear raced through her veins. She was no longer afraid for her own life, but for Daniel's and his men. But mostly Daniel.

Not allowing herself to blink, she stared wide-eyed as the men all shouted trying to distract and confuse the boar. They waved their arms, and when the boar charged, they swung their swords, some slicing, some missing.

Myra pressed her hand to her heart, fearing she might faint. Daniel too arched his sword and swung, his feet leaving the ground as he leapt with the force of his assault. Time stood still as he swung downward just as the boar leapt into the air, its sharp, long tusks aimed right at Daniel's chest.

"Daniel!" she screamed, the sound cracking the air. Nay! She couldn't lose him.

Daniel's sword struck home, slicing through the boar's neck, just as the animal's own daggers skimmed his chest. Daniel and the beast both fell to the ground in a heap of heaving breaths. Myra ran toward him.

She couldn't lose him now. Not when she'd just found him... Not when she was starting to feel... Even if he'd broken her heart before, she still—

"Daniel," she sobbed, dropping beside him in the snow.

Myra grabbed onto his thick arms, rolling him onto his back. Two streaks of red stained the front of his leine shirt.

"Oh, God... Ye're hurt."

He gazed up at her, his eyes filled with some unexplained emotion, and he shook his head. "Nay, not too bad."

"Ye're bleeding."

"I've bled many times."

Leo and a few other men grabbed the boar by its legs and dragged it away.

"Seems we'll have a savory meal to break our fast," Daniel said.

Why was he being so casual? Myra wanted to strike him. He'd scared the life from her. She'd been so afraid of losing him, even come face to face with a feeling she didn't want to confront. An intense feeling for him that gripped her heart and squeezed.

Myra shook her head. Nay. She wouldn't even consider it. She was confused. All the stress of the attack at Foulis, killing the man in the woods and nearly being skewered by a boar

The Highlander's Lady

had made her emotional. Such stresses often put odd thoughts in one's head, and even drew people closer because of them. Myra refused to believe she had anything more than friendly feelings for the man lying on the ground in front of her. Anything else she was feeling was purely a condition of the events leading up to this moment. Nothing more.

"Lass, 'tis all right." Daniel brushed his fingers over her cheek and she leaned into his touch.

"I thought…" Myra's voice broke and she took a moment to try and compose herself. "I was scared."

Myra watched Daniel clench his teeth, his jaw muscles flexing. She met his gaze and watched as his eyes changed from nonchalant to intense. They darkened, his whole face appearing to do so.

"Me too."

Her eyes widened at his confession. "Ye were?"

"Aye. Watching ye run for your life… Time seemed to stand still."

"That was how it was for me," she whispered.

Silence filled the space between them as the things they said, and the things that were left unsaid, sank in. Those feelings returned, unwanted as they were. Chills snaked up and down her arms.

Without thinking, Myra leaned down, her breasts pressing to his chest as she touched her lips to his. His skin was cold, his breath hot.

She shivered, gripped his shoulders, never wanting to let go. Daniel slipped one arm around her waist, holding her tight, the other threading into her hair, pulling her mouth ever closer. As one, their tongues touched, an instant spark of heat that had them both losing control. They kissed with desperate abandon, knowing that moments before either one of them could have been killed.

In that kiss, they told each other how much they needed each other, and yet, Myra knew they were not meant to be, just as Daniel must know it. Abruptly, he broke the kiss. Myra felt the loss keenly, and more so, what that meant. Kneeling back, she pushed to stand. She offered him a hand, but he didn't take it. Instead he easily stood, not even using a hand in the snow to brace himself. Another testament to his strength and dexterity.

Myra's cheeks flamed with untamed emotion and frustration. She was glad for the cold that had turned everyone's skin a tinge of red.

"We are both safe now. Dinna go out alone, again." Daniel's tone was a mix of fear and anger. He took her by the elbow and led her back inside the mountain crevice.

Guilt flooded Myra. She'd thought to wake him, but didn't. If she had, perhaps he would have sensed the boar to begin with. He wouldn't be hurt as he was now. She glanced around the men, witnessing a few others with scratches from the boar's tusks. No one appeared to be overly harmed. At least that was on her side, she wouldn't be blamed for someone's death or ghastly injury.

Those who'd taken the boar to prepare it for cooking made a makeshift spit to roast the animal. Myra prayed the scent of cooking meat didn't bring any hungry animals—or men for that matter. Daniel must have had the same fear as he issued orders for the men to take turns on watch.

Myra settled back against the wall within the plaid once more, trying to regain some feeling in her fingers. They were frozen through and an irritated red from being in the cold and from landing in the snow. She closed her eyes for a moment, sending prayers of thanks to the Heavens for having kept her safe and for keeping Daniel safe. Her heart finally settled, no longer paining her with its rapid beats. Tears threatened to spill but she willed them away. Now was not the time for tears.

Now was the time for contemplation.

The Highlander's Lady

Why had she kissed Daniel? What compelled her? But more than a simple kiss, she'd hungered for his touch. Thrust her tongue against his, gripped his shoulders like she feared being wrenched away.

She just needed to get to Eilean Donan. Once there, she could unburden herself with the news for the Bruce and then she could return home. Distance herself from Daniel. Return to where she felt safe...only, she felt safe with him. He made her not want to return to the walls of Foulis. Made her want to explore the world, to enjoy this newfound freedom, even if it meant a lifetime of not knowing what to expect.

"How long do ye intend for us to stay here?" she asked him.

Daniel turned from tending the fire to glance at her. Some unexplained emotion flashed in his eyes before he turned back to spin the boar.

"We shall stay and eat. I'm hopeful the afternoon sun will melt a bit of the snow and we can be on our way. If it doesna, we will leave in the morn."

"I must reach Eilean Donan. 'Tis urgent. How far away are we?" She'd lost track of time, days and felt rather hopeless at having no idea where she was.

"We are only a few days away, lass. I will get ye there." He stood from his spot beside the fire and sauntered toward her, his strong legs bared at the knee. Flashes of masculine flesh, a sprinkling of darkened hair. Myra wrenched her eyes away to gaze at his face. There was a spark of humor in his eyes and she cursed him all the more.

Daniel sat beside her, his masculine scent filling the space between them, intoxicating her in a way she didn't like because she liked it *too* much.

"Have ye any more whisky?" she asked.

Daniel grinned, using that wicked curl of his lips that sent her body to tingling.

"Aye." He leaned over and pulled the wineskin from somewhere to his left. "Here ye are, my lady."

Myra took a long gulp, savoring the burn as it made its way down her throat. The stuff was dangerous to be sure. She passed him back the skin and watched from the corner of her eye as he too took a long gulp.

"Do ye want to dance?" Daniel asked, completely surprising her.

She squinted her eyes a little as she studied him. How inappropriate it would be to dance with his men all about. The way Daniel danced was not…proper. Made her melt and tingle.

"Nay," she answered, just to spite him.

Daniel's smile slackened and Myra found that pleasing. If he thought they'd pass the time…dancing…he was sorely mistaken. Lucky for her she was covered by the thick plaid, else he could see what the thought of dancing did to her. Gooseflesh covered her arms and her nipples hardened, surely visible even with her gown and cloak covering her.

"Nay?" he mocked.

"Not even a little bit. Why do ye ask? Were ye hoping for a *dance* here in the cave? I dinna enjoy dancing with ye."

Daniel leaned forward, his elbows resting on his knees and he turned back to study her. His expression was penetrating, as though he could see within her, knew she was untruthful. "I thought to pass the time. And ye're lying."

Myra's lip twitched, but she held back the smile that wanted to come out. "Why would ye say such a thing? I never lie." She pressed her hand to her heart, pretending to be offended.

"I can tell."

The man was far too confident. "How?"

The Highlander's Lady

"When ye lie your left eye twitches just the tiniest wee bit." He pinched his forefinger and thumb together, a slight smile creasing his lips.

His words shocked her. Myra was speechless. He'd studied her so well?

Daniel shrugged and took another swig of whisky. When he passed her the skin she shook her head, but he wasn't looking.

"Nay, thank ye."

"I like to dance," he said, leaning back against the rock once more. "With ye."

His shoulder bumped into hers, but neither of them moved. She tried to ignore his words and how they made her feel. Having his solid form beside her was comforting, despite her best efforts not to find it so. The men who were not on watch ignored them both, chatting amongst themselves. A few played a game with pebbles, some slept and another had taken over the spit. The scents of the roasting meat made Myra's mouth water. She couldn't remember the last time she'd had a decent meal. It had to be before the attack on Foulis—actually, a couple days prior, since she'd been ordered to fast as punishment.

Her belly rumbled loudly and Daniel chuckled. "Ye're hungry."

"Aye, that obvious?"

Daniel nodded. "Your rumbling belly could wake an army."

"Gratitude," she said sarcastically.

Daniel placed his hand on her knee and squeezed as he laughed. The gesture wasn't meant to be sensual, she knew that. But her body took his touch and made it into so much more. The heat of his fingers seared a path through the layers, up her thigh to her belly where it settled in an aching pulse. The squeeze was firm, and only brought to mind the way he'd gripped her behind as he'd kissed her at the tavern.

Myra wanted to yank away, to push his hand off her leg, if only to settle her mind. Why then couldn't she move?

Her breath caught as her mind warred with what to do, and in that time, Daniel removed his hand and raked it through his unruly hair.

"Do ye ever wear your hair back?" Myra asked, knowing he had when he visited her at Foulis.

Daniel glanced at her, studying her several moments before he answered. "Sometimes."

Myra nodded. "Such as?"

"Formal occasions mostly."

She smiled. "Ye put the beast away and show the world ye can be tamed?"

Daniel winked. "I canna be tamed."

Oh, why did he have to wink at her? Her insides went all to mush and all she wanted to do was crawl into his lap and beg for another kiss. Myra glanced down at her hands. The skin had turned back to normal color, but now it was extremely dry, cracked in spots. Her knuckles stung.

Daniel took hold of her hand and stroked his fingers gently over the cracks in her knuckles, traced her fingers, a frown on his face. His fingertips were coarse, yet tender, sending shivers through her, and she tried with all her might not to let on.

"Ye need gloves," he said quietly.

"There wasn't time."

His eyes locked on hers. "Ye've yet to tell me what happened. I swear I'll not tell another soul."

The seriousness of his expression told her he spoke the truth. And she trusted him. After all, he'd risked his life for her. Nearly been impaled. Myra nodded.

"I know. 'Tis the telling that is hard." She swallowed, knowing that if she did share the tragedy of Ross' treachery she'd have to live through every moment. Not thinking about

The Highlander's Lady

it was the only thing that had kept her from completely breaking down.

Daniel took her hand between two of his, applied gentle, reassuring pressure. "I can help."

There was no way he realized the depth of his offer, or how much help she needed. Knowing someone was on her side, there to share the burden, support her, was an extraordinary feeling she'd never thought to have. Daniel had somehow cracked the wall she'd built around herself. If they were to remain married—which she was sure they would not—he would have another clan to deal with. Daniel had made it clear he'd blown off the duties of his own clan in exchange for battle.

What's to say that he wouldn't do so again? He'd made a promise to his clan, for certain, but if another battle came, would he once again put off his duties to his own people? If he had two clans that counted on him, what then?

Myra believed he had the best of intentions, that Daniel believed in the things he said. There was nothing sinister or false involved. Myra trusted him with her life, but she didn't trust him with her father and brother's legacy.

The Munro clan was her responsibility. Daniel would have to prove himself to her. But how?

Daniel let go of her hands to lean back toward his satchel. He pulled out two large leather gloves.

"Here. Take mine. I canna have ye losing your fingers on the way to seeing your duty done."

"But ye need them." She tried to keep the shock from her voice.

He sent another stunning grin her way. "I'm a Highlander, lass. All I need is my horse, my whisky and my woman."

His woman.

Chapter Thirteen

Daniel's head felt as though someone had hit him hard with a mace. In fact, his chest felt a little like that too.

He'd handfasted. Claimed her for his own for life. And yet, saying the words, *his woman*, aloud… It did something to him. Sparked fear in his heart. Fear his promises would not be returned. Fear for her life and the added responsibility. He wasn't a coward. He wouldn't back down and he wouldn't take those words back. Daniel was ready for the responsibilities that were his. Ready to own them, to be the man he was meant to be.

All the same, he'd never wanted to wed before now. Never wanted to be with a woman for eternity until he met Myra. The first time.

But her subsequent rebuff of him had thwarted his ideas altogether and he'd never wanted to experience that again. He couldn't understand why she would have done so. It all came back to his father's own scrutiny. There was something they

The Highlander's Lady

saw in him that left a bad taste in their mouths. What it was Daniel couldn't point out.

Even now, he didn't sense that she disliked him. The exact opposite was revealed to be the case. She'd even kissed him, unbidden, in the snow. Fear had flashed in her eyes and she'd pressed her lips to his. His own emotions had been flying, battle rush flowing through his blood. He'd wanted to toss her onto her back and make mad passionate love to her. Of course, then she would have probably snubbed him and he'd be right back to feeling like he did at Foulis.

As it was, either she recognized him and teased him for it when she blatantly lied about not liking to dance with him, or… He didn't know. She'd practically admitted to lying. So what was her purpose?

Daniel chanced a glance her way. She'd put on his gloves, and he smiled at how huge they were on her petite hands. Like a monster swallowing a wee bairn.

Myra too stared at her hands. Her cheeks were creamy with hints of rose in the center. Her lips, thank goodness no longer blue, but lush and ripe, meant for kissing. Lashes, long, thick and dark accentuated the rich brown of her eyes. Daniel could stare at her all day, memorize every curve, every detail. He enjoyed the arch of her brow and how when she looked at him it would curve upward nearly half her forehead. She was so expressive. Never had he met a more enchanting creature.

"My thanks, Daniel." Her voice was smooth, a sensual caress to his starved self.

"Ye're most welcome. I pray they keep ye warm."

"I can already feel the difference." She smiled at him and rubbed her hands together, the loose fingers flopping over one another.

"Anything to make ye more comfortable."

She cocked her head to the side. "Daniel…"

"Aye?"

"Why are ye so nice to me?" She pursed her lips, looking very contemplative.

"Is it not the way a man should be to his woman?" How many men had she had encounters with? He glared at the boar on the spit, wanting to punch anyone who'd treated her wrong.

"Well… I suppose."

"Ye suppose?" His eyes widened, meeting hers.

Myra bit her lip and he regretted his somewhat loud tone.

She shrugged. "I've never been handfasted before…only betrothed. And, well, he was an arse."

"Who was he?"

"It doesna matter."

"Aye, it does. Are ye still betrothed now?"

Myra faltered then shook her head. And her eye twitched. Damn. Things just became exponentially complicated.

"Who were ye betrothed to? And be clear 'tis past tense because ye'll not marry another."

Myra's eyes narrowed on him, but she did not say a word. Daniel didn't know whether that was good or bad, but he was leaning toward bad.

"Answer me, woman. I'll know who's to come after me."

"He has not right to me."

"Aye, that's a fact—ye're mine. I dinna let anyone take what's mine."

Myra clearly clenched her teeth, her parted lips showing how they ground together. He was making her angry, probably had her thinking he was a brute again, but he cared not. A spurned man was one to be reckoned with. Daniel wasn't worried about not being able to protect her or himself from whoever the man was, he only prayed it wasn't one of his own allies, as he would have just created a new enemy.

If he was honest, he also wanted to see who it was she would have accepted for marriage after rejecting his own

The Highlander's Lady

presence. The rational part of him said that she wouldn't have had a choice. She was a lady. The sister of a powerful laird. Her betrothal would have been made with an ally to gain lands, money, to solidify borders or to create a bond between two clans that were in the past at war. And he'd never asked. Even still, he wanted to know who had taken the spot he longed for. Who she might think about when he sank between her thighs.

"The Bruce will not allow our marriage."

That was a strike to his ego and his heart. She was spurning him once more. "Well, madam, we shall see," he said through gritted teeth, then stood to check on the boar.

Daniel could not look at her. Her prickly side had been charming before, but to hear her blatantly say the Bruce wouldn't allow their wedding was harsh. Well fu—

"Daniel." She tentatively touched his arm with her fingertips as she came to stand beside him. "I didna mean ye and I."

Now he felt like a fool. And he still couldn't look at her. He'd reacted like a spoiled child and she'd come all calmness and sweetness to show him she'd not said what he'd thought. Daniel blew out a breath and raked his hands through his hair. He didn't like at all how she'd changed him. He was a hardened warrior, yet around her he was overly conscious of how she felt about him and his own feelings. 'Twas making him mad.

"I know it," he said.

Myra removed her hand from his arm and from the corner of his eye, he watched as she studied him for several moments before turning her gaze to the boar. "Looks like 'tis nearly done."

"Aye."

But small talk was not what he wanted. Daniel needed more. If he was going to get it, he probably needed to share a part of himself. Taking in a deep breath, he turned to face her.

Placing his hands gently on her shoulders, he locked his gaze with hers, moved her back to their place against the wall where they might have more privacy away from the ears of his men.

"Myra..." Where should he begin? "My father passed a year ago, leaving the clan in my hands."

She nodded, her eyes never leaving his. He was glad to see she gave the impression of being interested in what he had to say.

"I was foolish. Irresponsible. Didna want to take my place as laird. My father—" Now came the hard part. He glanced down at his feet, then sucked in his pride. "My father often lamented of my abilities to run a clan. Found me lacking."

Myra's mouth parted a little, her eyes crinkling with what looked like disbelief.

"I've never known why, save for my joy of life, my interest in more...entertaining activities than attending a clan meeting."

"Daniel..."

"Nay, let me finish afore I lose my nerve. I'm a damn good warrior. I can quell a dispute easily. I've never lost respect in that area. But I couldna make my father believe in me. When he passed... I had a lot of doubts about myself. Had a lot of doubts about my place in the world. Then I met ye."

"Me?"

"Aye, Myra Munro."

She gasped, tried to take a step back, but he held onto her shoulders.

"Dinna be afeared. I've known ye from the beginning."

Her expression shuttered and he wished more than anything to have her regard back.

"I know ye didna want me back then, that ye dinna want me now, but know this, I will protect ye with every breath I

The Highlander's Lady

have. I am a different man. I've grown up. I'm Laird Murray, and I know my place now."

Myra swallowed several times, glancing around her as though trying to find the words to respond.

"Ye dinna need to say anything, I know ye were trying to hide your identity from me. That ye didna wish to wed with me and that now I've forced a promise from ye in exchange for your protection."

Myra shook her head. "Nay, nay, I knew who ye were too, even if ye do look more wild than before. But I dinna understand…"

"Aye? Tell me, I wish to make it clear to ye." Daniel was relieved she hadn't bolted.

"I dinna understand what ye meant about me not wanting ye."

Daniel's hands slid from Myra's shoulders down to her elbows.

"What dinna ye understand? I danced with ye at Foulis, I waited for ye for days, and ye disappeared."

"Days?" She shook her head again, her face filled with confusion. "Nay, ye didna even wait a few moments."

"Myra, I did," he said, his voice impassioned.

"Nay. When I came back to the great hall, ye were surrounded by other lasses… Ye laughed, winked, touched them…"

Mo creach… What he'd once considered to be a blessing—his seeming ability to attract women like bees on nectar—was now his curse.

"Lass, I didna return any of their regard for me. I merely flirted."

"But that was what ye did with me."

Daniel shook his head. "Nay, with ye it was much deeper. I flirted, I wanted, I dreamed."

"Dreamed?"

Daniel was starting to feel like a sappy lad. But he'd caught her attention once more, and that was what he really wanted. Hoped that by confessing some of his inner demons, she'd feel comfortable to do the same. Daniel had never shared his inner most self with anyone before. Not even his rebellious friends from before his father's passing. This was something new to him, and while he'd been scared to death to admit his feelings to her, now that he was getting them off his chest, he felt oddly lighter, freer. Scared the hell out of him at the same time it was exhilarating.

"Aye." He gazed deep into her eyes. "And I was sorry to hear of your brother's passing. He was a good friend of mine."

"And ye have so little of them," Myra teased.

"Ye know me well."

Myra glanced down at their feet, then she too placed her hands on his elbows as she gazed at him. A change took place in her eyes. She too was opening up. Would she tell him what he wanted to know? Even if she didn't, this was still progress.

"I confess to recognizing ye too." She shook her head. "'Twasn't at first. But when we danced at the tavern—I could feel it. The memory of your arms came rushing back. The way ye made me feel…and with it the vision of ye surrounded by women. When I saw that, I didna think ye thought more of me than ye did of those women. I felt naïve, expendable."

Och! How could he have been so stupid? She was an innocent, and he should have pushed all those women away. Shouldn't have let her leave him in the first place. "Ye are anything but," he said quietly.

"Ye say that, and I believe ye mean it, but…"

"But what?"

Myra bit her lip and Daniel had to resist the urge to run his thumb over her plump, inviting mouth. Instead, he took

The Highlander's Lady

her gloved hands in his, brought them to his lips and kissed them.

"I've shared with ye something I've never told another soul. I trust ye with my secret — my father's dislike of me. Will ye share a part of yourself with me?"

Myra nodded, squeezed his hands in return.

"When I was little, I have this vision of my mother. She was walking on the moors, away from the castle. Her gown was white, flowing wildly with the wind, her hair, dark like mine whipped all around her. I remember thinking that the sky looked purple and pretty like a thistle, but then there were flashes of lightning. No rain yet. But a wicked storm brewing." Myra gazed off into the distance as if recalling that vision.

Daniel could picture it too, sensed the eeriness of it. Sensed how it would have permanently imprinted in the mind of a young child.

"'Twas dawn and I'd woken early. My nursemaid was asleep on a pallet before the hearth and I was looking out the window to see if I could spot a deer on the grounds below. They always liked to come close to the castle in the early morn and I wanted to catch one as a pet." She paused a moment, licking her lips. "There were no deer, just my mother."

She flicked her gaze toward his and smiled shyly. "Might I have a sip of whiskey?"

Daniel nodded and handed her the skin. He didn't want to say anything. Didn't want to break the spell of her willingness to share part of her past. Wanted to know where this story went. He'd heard her mother passed away when she was young, at least that was what Byron had told him, but Daniel had never learned how. He'd been too young when her death occurred to recall it and he'd never been close to their father although his own had.

Myra took a long gulp of whisky, her eyes closing as she swallowed. She swiped away a drop that dribbled down her chin with the too big gloves, wiping the excess on her gown.

"I watched her walk until I could see her no longer. She just disappeared. When my nursemaid woke, I told her what I'd seen and she told me it was probably a dream. But when I went down to break my fast as I was allowed to do each morning in the great hall, my mother wasn't there. Father was frantic and shouting orders to his men. He was afraid she'd been taken again."

"Again?" Daniel couldn't help asking, although he kept his voice quiet.

"Aye." Myra nodded, fiddled with the wineskin but did not take a sip. "She was kidnapped by an enemy of our clan. I never learned what happened exactly, but the horrors of it were hinted at to me. She was abused. Men were to be seen as evil. My father no longer let me be seen, he was so afraid I'd be taken. We no longer hunted. I wasn't allowed to leave the castle walls again and the only way I could participate when any guests visited was through the walls."

"Through the walls?"

Myra nodded, and a moment of panic flashed in her eyes.

"Ye can trust me, lass."

"The hidden corridors."

"Ye mean ye watched the festivities hidden away and ye didna participate?"

She nodded, her eyes filled with sadness. "Aye. I found comfort in it. There is a hidden corridor behind nearly every wall almost like the castle is within a castle. My father taught me every hidden doorway and corridor within Foulis."

"Fascinating." And it was, but he couldn't help but wonder at the quality of life for someone always hidden, always scared. Although it happened with an attack, he was glad she was no longer buried within a stone tomb.

She smiled. "Aye, 'tis."

She took his hand in hers again and he wondered if it was intentional or if she did it without thinking. He couldn't tell.

"I never saw her again, Daniel. She left us."

"Did they ever find her?"

"Aye. Weeks later." Myra squeezed her eyes shut and Daniel did react this time. He pulled her close, resting her head on his shoulder as he stroked her back.

"What happened?"

"She drowned herself." Myra's voice had turned monotone.

"I'm sorry, lass."

She nodded. "'Twas tragic. But even though 'tis a sin to take one's own life, I think she was happier doing it. She was in hell. Mother was never the same when she came back. I dinna know what unimaginable things they did to her, but it changed her. Her eyes were shadowed. She didna sing or play with me anymore. She was quiet. Haunted looking. Nothing father did could bring her back. Nothing anyone did worked."

"How did your father deal with the loss?" Daniel's heart went out to her.

"He was angry. Brooded for days. Went to war with those who'd harmed her. But nothing could bring her back and I think he realized that. Eventually he stopped. Didna talk about her anymore. Only worked with Byron to be the best laird he could be. Made sure I was safely hidden. Made sure I was punished when I did wrong. Father Holden and I became quite close as I was often in confession."

Daniel chuckled lightly. "With your nature I can hardly believe it."

"Why do I think ye are lying now?" she said with a little giggle.

Daniel pulled her closer, liking the feel of her cuddled against him. The warmth of her body, the softness of her. He was glad too that she was more light-hearted after having revealed such a heavy truth of her past.

With two fingers on her chin he turned her face up toward his. "I would never lie to ye, Myra."

Then he lowered his lips.

Chapter Fourteen

A million years seemed to pass before Daniel's lips reached hers. Myra's eyes fluttered shut as his breath caressed her face and his warm mouth brushed hers. She sighed into his kiss, unable to resist his touch. There was something so intoxicating about Daniel's kisses—more so than whisky. The intensity he put behind each intimacy made her feel boneless in his arms.

As much as she wanted to push him away, to force herself to become indifferent to him, she simply could not. Myra turned more fully against him, her breasts pressing slightly to his chest sending tendrils of desire floating through her entire being. She snaked her arms around his middle, feeling the solidity of his physique beneath her fingertips.

Each time they kissed it was different—always wonderful—and this time it was once again completely unique. This kiss wasn't timid as their first had been. Nor was it carnal as their kiss in the tavern was. It wasn't filled with panic and the rush of nearly losing each other. This kiss was sweet. Slow. Heady.

Myra trembled in his arms. Wished they were in a different place so she could more freely explore his body. As it was, she kept her hands strictly in place on his back even though she itched to stroke up and down his spine, over his chest. Her nipples were taut peaks and rubbed against his chest sending an ache to pulse in a line from her breasts to her center.

Daniel touched her lightly on her waist, not as shy as she. He caressed her ribs, her spine. Every little touch tickled and sent frissons of need to throb through her.

And it was over too quickly. This time Myra pulled away. Acutely aware of where they were and who could watch and how continually kissing Daniel would change both of them irrevocably.

She was already in too deep. Already wanting more than she should. There was too much between them—beyond a simple handfast. More than she'd ever considered. At one time years ago she'd had a brief fantasy of it. Believed there could be something such as true love. Why did he have to make her feel that way again? Daniel showed her that he could be trusted, that he was invested in her and her clan. He was a changed man and she believed she could count on him.

Myra wanted desperately to pull him in just as she frantically tried to push him away.

"Myra," he whispered, his voice a hush. He brushed her cheek with his fingers, forcing her to look deep into his eyes.

Myra bit her lip, her mind a jumble of confused thoughts.

He'd witnessed her at her worst and still accepted her. He'd poured his heart out to her unknowing how she would react. And she could have stomped on him, remained indifferent or done exactly as she had. Let him in. She'd never talked with anyone about her mother before, sensing that it

The Highlander's Lady

was a topic best left alone with her father. When she'd tried with Byron he'd always changed the subject or yelled at her, and even her nursemaid was unwilling to offer her a word. The woman only burst into tears and called her a poor, poor lass, while patting her on the head.

Even Father Holden, for as close as they'd become over the years, was not willing to speak with her about it. Orders she supposed from her father. When her mother left them all, committing the gravest of sins, she'd become a ghost to them all, just a figment of Foulis' imagination.

A near figment of her own. She could barely remember what her mother looked like. All Myra remembered clearly was her long hair. The softness of it. The scent of rosemary and lavender that clung to her. And a song. She remembered the lyrics clearly, could hear them in her mind.

The wee birdies sing, and the wild flowers spring…
And in sunshine the waters sleeping…
But the broken heart it knows, nay second spring again…
Though the woeful may cease from their greeting…

"Daniel, I—" Myra placed a hand on his chest, feeling the thumping of his heart though his shirt. "Have ye ever felt like ye've fallen down a well and it will take an eternity for ye to climb out?"

He nodded slowly. "I feel like I've been climbing for a long time."

"Me too. When I look toward the light it just gets farther away."

He placed a gentle hand on either side of her face. "We have each other now. Though it may not be as ye wished, but together we can forge a way to climb to the top."

Myra pressed her lips together, trying to believe in what Daniel said.

"Meat is ready, my laird," one of the men said who turned the spit.

The spell was broken, and Myra's stomach grumbled loudly, her mouth watering from the succulent scents of roasted meat. Daniel stood and went toward the roast. The men who were not on duty all gathered around, cutting hunks of meat and blowing away the heat, creating puffs of steam around their faces.

Daniel cut off a hunk, blew on it and handed it to Myra. "Ladies first."

"Such a gentleman."

"Never. Highlanders are not gentle," he said with a wink.

Myra took off her gloves and grasped the meat with her fingers, pulling it off his dirk. Juices slipped down her fingers, forging a warm, greasy path. She sank her teeth into the meat and tried not to moan from both the taste and texture. There was truly nothing as delicious as roasted game. Oh, how hungry she was. Myra tried to eat delicately, but there was nothing for it. She shoved the hunk of meat into her mouth and took out her dirk, ready to cut off another hunk.

"This is amazing," she said between bites.

Daniel chuckled. "'Tis good indeed. I'm glad ye're eating. From the sounds of your rumbling belly ye've not had a good meal in a while."

"I canna remember when."

"Did ye not eat at Foulis?" Daniel asked, cutting off another hunk for himself.

Myra watched as his men cut off another portion then left the cavern, switching posts with the men who'd been on watch.

"Whenever I wasn't fasting."

"Fasting?"

"Aye. I…tended to do a lot of penance."

Daniel winged a brow. "Why's that?"

Myra shook her head and smiled. "I told ye I spent a lot of time with Father Holden—confessing."

The Highlander's Lady

"Tell me of your latest indiscretion."

Myra's smile faltered. "Listening in on a meeting my brother had with another laird."

"How did they catch ye?"

Myra shrugged, biting into her meat and taking her time chewing.

"Byron had a six sense when it came to me spying on him. But what could I do? I was mostly confined so as not to become a victim like my mother had. 'Tis boring to sew and study all day."

"I take it ye spied a lot."

"Aye."

"How often do ye serve penance?"

"More often than not."

Daniel chuckled. "I like your spirit, Myra."

Myra felt her cheeks heating at his compliment. "Thank ye. Ye'd be the only one."

"Fitting since I'm the only one that matters."

His words were flattering in one respect—that a husband should enjoy his wife for who she is, but they were also a bitter reminder that she'd lost everyone.

"I'm full." Myra put her dirk back into the small leather loop at her hip. "And a little sleepy. I think I'll take a nap afore we leave. 'Twill be soon, aye?"

Daniel studied her a moment before answering. "Aye, soon. What did I say?"

"What?" His question caught her by surprise.

"Ye've shut down, Myra. We've not known each other over long, but in that time I've gotten to know ye a little."

That unnerved her. Before today she'd still felt like she was safely hidden behind a façade. Now he knew exactly who she was and they'd shared intimate parts of themselves.

"Your words... They were just a reminder of what I've lost."

Daniel frowned. "I didna mean it like that."

"I know ye didna, but it was said all the same. 'Tis the way of things. We say one thing and taken out of context it means something different."

"Are ye truly full? I wouldna want ye to starve yourself because of something stupid I said."

Myra was heartened by his concern. She touched his elbow briefly, before realizing what she was doing. It was becoming so much easier to touch without thinking. She had to stop…else she would not be prepared to leave him once she relayed her message to the Bruce.

"I am truly full. My thanks for your concern."

Daniel nodded. "Mind if I continue to eat, or did ye need me to lean against?"

"I think I can manage on my own." She flashed him a grin.

Daniel smiled, so charming, she felt her insides melt and her sadness ebbed a little. "Good, more for me. I'm starving."

Myra laughed a little then turned to sink back within the nest of warmth the plaid and her cloak created. She was truly exhausted and a bit of rest would be good before they had to brave the weather once more.

Closing her eyes, Myra was struck with a fierce anxiety. It'd been over a week since Foulis was attacked by Ross. There was no telling if he'd already been to Eilean Donan and wreaked havoc there as well. On the road they'd not have found out. The tavern they'd stayed at was not likely to have heard the news yet should such a thing have happened. Myra's heart beat harder and her fingers felt tingly. She tried to calm her breathing, telling herself that if that were the case, there was nothing she could have done about it.

Rose came first. Byron's heir came first. She'd taken them both to safety and then set about her way. The weather couldn't be controlled. 'Twas winter. Snow was inevitable,

The Highlander's Lady

and even if they'd not been stuck in the snow, they'd only be a few hours further along.

Even still, knowing all this, she couldn't calm down. There was so much riding on her relaying her message. The entire War for Independence. Scottish Freedom. So many lives. All of their future. If she failed in her mission, or she arrived too late, there would be nothing left for anyone born of Scottish descent.

Myra shifted, no longer comfortable. Her mind raced so she couldn't fall asleep. When they arrived at Eilean Donan—if the Ross had not yet been there—she would insist on an immediate meeting with the Bruce. She would not allow them to make her wait, even if she had to barge in on him while he was in the privy. 'Twas life or death. He would understand. He had to. She would force him to see.

The Bruce was a reasonable man, or so she believed. If all of Scotland wanted him as their king, then he had to be good. If Wallace fought for him—Daniel fought for him—he must have made a good impression on them. Myra admitted to herself that when it came to politics and safety, she trusted Daniel wholly. Her father and Byron had also fully supported the Bruce. Byron had even fought alongside him at Stirling.

Aye, Robert the Bruce must be reasonable. And there was no reason he wouldn't agree to see her. No reason that he would be willing to risk his neck. He would gladly hear her news and bless her a thousand times for saving his life. He'd offer her escort and an army to Foulis so she could reclaim her castle. Then he would allow her to watch as Ross was executed—slowly.

Sometime later, Daniel shook her shoulder. "Lass? 'Tis time to move out."

Myra blinked her eyes open, not remembering having fallen asleep. Her head felt heavy, her body achy. She stretched as much as she could then took Daniel's offered had to stand.

He pulled her a little too hard and she bumped into him, instant heat filling her. Moving away from him was hard. She busied herself with gathering the extra plaid he'd given her.

"Keep that. 'Twill likely be cold upon the road."

Myra nodded, and put on the gloves he'd given her. The men tamped down the fire and wrapped the remaining meat in a cloth. Thank goodness there was plenty left over for the evening meal.

Leo and several others brought the horses, already saddled up. Within moments she was seated upon the horse in front of Daniel, the extra plaid wrapped tightly around her, thankfully creating another barrier between them.

This time she wasn't so stiff-backed when they rode. She allowed herself to relax, even bumped into him a few times without completely panicking. The last thing she needed was more aches and pains. This journey had proven hard enough already. Besides, Daniel was warm and Myra was freezing.

Snow no longer fell, and the sky had changed from white clouds to mostly blue. The sun shone high, melting some of the snow. The trees sparkled as the ice that had frozen to their limbs melted and dripped to the ground. The horses could go no faster than a trot as the ground was still covered in several inches of wet snow.

A brisk wind blew every so often, whipping Myra's cowl from her head and causing her hair to pull free of its braid, hitting her and Daniel's face with stinging slaps. She noted that he had tied his hair back, likely for the same reason.

"I'm not sure if I'll die from exposure or being whipped by your hair," Daniel teased.

Myra laughed. "I fear 'tis the same for me. Mayhap you'll be so kind as to cut it with your dirk."

"Oh, nay, I'd never. Your hair is far too beautiful to suffer such a butchering."

"Suit yourself." Myra twisted into her seat to gaze up at him. "Your face is already covered in welts, what's a few more?"

"Truly?" He frowned and reached up to touch his cheeks.

Myra laughed aloud. "I but jest!"

Daniel shook his head. "Sadly, I thought it might be true. Your hair could be its own weapon."

"If only I could control it so well."

Daniel chuckled. "Women would most definitely be a formidable force if they could all use their hair to render us helpless."

"What's to say we don't already?" Myra winked.

She'd never winked at a man before, but found it to be such a natural reaction. To her surprise, Daniel started, his eyes locking on hers.

"And your eyes... Are they too a weapon?" he asked.

"I shall never reveal the secrets of feminine weapons," Myra teased.

What was happening? She'd suddenly become this bold woman. Winking and teasing a man about feminine wiles. Daniel brought out this side of her and it was not unwelcome. She enjoyed teasing him, playing with words. She liked the way he looked at her, a mixture of wonder and desire. It made her feel special—and this expression was not one she'd ever seen him use on another. Not that she'd been with him all the time, but he'd certainly not looked at the women at Foulis that way, nor the wench at the tavern who offered to service him. It almost seemed liked that expression was just for her.

Oh, zounds! What was she doing getting carried away? They were simply flirting. They'd shared a few kisses; it meant nothing. 'Twas simply what one did when pledged to marry. They had to get along somehow and it appeared they did have a few things in common besides enjoying each other's company. Daniel couldn't possibly think of her as someone special. She was simply a means to an end. His clan would no longer pester him about marrying and he could be comfortable knowing that he'd once been close to her family. That was all.

Then why did thinking about it like that hurt so much? Why did she want it to be real, to have his regard? To be special?

A male's weapon, she supposed. Causing women to fall at their feet and beg for love and affection. She couldn't remember so many interactions between her mother and father. She'd simply been too young to recall. Myra thought back on Rose and Byron. They appeared affectionate. Byron would place his hand on Rose's shoulder and she to him if one was sitting and the other not. Their hands would brush every once in a while at meals, but come to think of it, Myra could not truly recall any affection.

That didn't mean there wasn't any behind closed doors. Rose seemed to be very happy and likewise had Byron. Oh, horse poo. Relationships between men and women were too complicated.

"Now what has ye frowning?" Daniel asked.

Myra's eyes came back into focus and she realized she was staring up at him. She bit the tip of tongue and tried to come up with a quick reason.

"Just curious about how much time we have left upon the road."

Daniel raised a brow.

Myra rolled her eyes. "My eye was not twitching."

"So ye say. Won't be long now. A few days mayhap. In fact—" He turned to his man Leo. "Send three men ahead to Eilean Donan to advise of our arrival. Let them know a lady— my wife—shall be accompanying me and that I'll need an immediate audience with the Bruce."

The Highlander's Lady

Myra's stomach fluttered. In just a few short days she would be presented to the future King of Scotland as Lady Murray—wife of Laird Daniel Murray.

Chapter Fifteen

Daniel stared into the distance. The air was frigid where it hit his bare knees. He'd wrapped his plaid around the both of them which left his legs partially exposed. The sun shone like a bright golden orb, larger than usual due to its glowing affect with the whiteness of the snow. Winter was always Daniel's favorite season. He loved Yule festivities, the beauty of snow and ice. Sitting before a roaring fire with a maid or three. Now he could envision sitting before the hearth with Myra on his lap. He'd hold a cup of warm, spiced wine to her lips, then kiss the droplets that spilled. They'd make love on the bearskin rug in his chamber.

His body immediately reacted to that thought. Blood fired with an intense hunger, need for Myra. All that passion surged to his cock, making him rigid. If she moved just an inch backward, she'd know it—and he'd be groaning with the pain of un-fulfillment. 'Twas going to be wicked hard to wait until they returned to Blair, made things official and he could

The Highlander's Lady

finally make love to Myra with all he had and more. He wanted to hear her sighs of pleasure, cries of passion. Knowing he was the only man to have ever kissed her was certainly a powerful feeling, but to teach her how to make love, to pleasure him… That was something altogether potent.

However, the journey to Blair was not imminent. Daniel wasn't even sure of how long it would be until they traveled to his home. He'd planned on staying at Eilean Donan until the spring. That was three months away at least.

Until that time, how could Daniel be satisfied with tame kisses and touching? He wanted it all. 'Haps the Bruce would insist they wed for certain with him rather than wait until spring. Daniel's mother would be angry she missed it, but considering the alternative—not marrying at all—he thought she wouldn't balk too much.

What if the Bruce did not suggest such? Daniel's lips curled when a clever, thoroughly debouched idea came to mind. 'Haps the lass would be open to practicing other exploits without actually completing the final act. There were so many other things lovers could do for pleasure…

And just like that, his cock pulsed even more, grew hard as stone and was not likely to calm for some time. Daniel tried to think of something else, anything to get his mind off ravaging Myra atop his horse, upon the grassy meadow, against a tree…

He groaned under his breath and shifted in the saddle.

"Is aught amiss?" Myra said, her teeth chattering.

Daniel gritted his teeth as he wrapped her tighter in his plaid. She was cold, and he'd not let his lusty thoughts interfere with keeping her warm.

"Aye. 'Tis frigid."

She nodded and allowed herself to snuggle a little closer. This ride was so much different than past rides together. No more stiffness—other than his cock—they'd crossed a bridge of sorts.

Daniel continued to study the landscape, intent on getting his mind off the lush behind that kept nudging against his thighs and sporran.

The road was clear of other riders. Occasionally when they passed someone traveling the road, and Myra would stiffen until it was clear the passerby was no threat. Most of those they passed minded their own business, and Daniel was grateful for it. 'Twas too damn cold.

They'd left their mountain shelter after the nooning and though they wouldn't be able to travel for more than a few hours before the sun set, it had been imperative that they set about their way.

Not only did Daniel not want to get caught in another snow storm which would only delay them further, he wanted Myra to relay her message. In just a couple of days they would reach Eilean Donan and he still did not know everything behind the attack from Ross and what the message was that Myra needed to communicate. But he was aware that whatever she needed to relay was crucial.

Life and death.

Those were Rose's words. Myra believed so too. He only wished she'd open up to him about it. They'd established a trust of sorts—her supple body against his, their kisses, the truths they shared were evidence of that. Even still, Daniel had his doubts about whether Myra would bring up the topic. She was a stubborn lass, and he could say with near certainty she wouldn't broach it without being asked. That fact was a great testament to her loyal nature. She would indeed make him a good wife.

Leaning forward so that his mouth was close to her ear—he convinced himself he did this because of the wind when in fact the breeze was quite tame—he said, "Myra, I want to ask ye something."

She turned sharply, nearly knocking into his face. "Aye?" Her brows were narrowed and she looked at him uncertainly.

Her abrupt movements could have been bad. He could have ended up with a broken nose as well as a hair-whipped face. He jolted back with a sharp laugh. "I think ye do have it in for me."

Myra smiled, the gesture brightening her countenance. "Mayhap. What did ye want to ask me?"

"'Tis about Foulis."

Immediately she shuttered her eyes, her face expressionless and she turned back to face the road beyond. "What do ye want to know?"

"I want ye to trust me," Daniel said softly against her ear.

"I do." She nodded, almost like she was telling herself as well as him.

"Then, please, Myra, tell me what happened. I want to help ye. To protect ye. Your people are my people too now — albeit we have not officially wed, I do consider ye my wife all the same."

"Daniel…" Myra sighed deeply and he could sense her hesitation.

Would she shut him out again? Daniel wasn't sure he could accept that. They had to move forward, not backward.

"Dinna deny me again." His voice came out harsher than intended and Myra stiffened, sitting taller which moved her a few inches away from him.

The wind whistled down through the space between them, reminding Daniel just how cold it was outside.

"Myra—"

She shook her head, cutting him off. "Ye've been very patient with me, Daniel. I know that to offer me protection, marriage and not to know the extent of what ye're getting into, must be…difficult."

He nodded, then realized she couldn't see him. "Aye. But it didna sway me not to. I only seek to know so I may better protect ye."

"Ye're a good man." Her voice was soft, full of some unspoken emotion.

No one had ever told him that before. He was stunned by how much it meant to hear those words. Hadn't realized how much he needed to hear that he was a good person.

"Thank ye, lass."

She didn't say anything for several moments prompting Daniel to speak again. "Does that mean ye'll not tell me more?"

She chuckled. "Nay, 'tis that I was trying to think of a way to say it. But there is no way to phrase it that makes it any less painful for me."

Hearing the scared tone in her voice made Daniel's heart clench, made him want to hurt whoever hurt her. If he could, Daniel would take away all of her pain. He'd absorb it so she didn't have to. "Take your time. We've a long ride."

Myra nodded. Daniel settled in, thinking it would be awhile before she spoke, and he didn't mind in the least. There were plans to be made for the training of the men, for how he'd approach the Bruce, for the different ways he'd seduce Myra…

But he didn't have to wait as long as he thought.

"I was in the chapel—'tis attached to the gallery above the great hall—when I heard a loud crash and shouts."

Myra's gloved hands slipped around his as he held her at her waist. Daniel tried to picture Foulis and recalled the great gallery above where Byron had several musicians playing during the feast. The chapel must have been well hidden for he didn't recall seeing a doorway. Good thing since it probably saved her life.

The Highlander's Lady

"I called for my maid but she wasn't there. When I opened the door I heard the most horrendous noise. A battle cry."

A chill slipped up Daniel's spine. He could only imagine her fear. Myra shivered in front of him and he pulled her closer until her back rested upon his chest once more. He'd offer his strength to her now, and prayed it would help calm her, give her the courage to continue with her story. Then again, Myra was so filled with courage, he wasn't sure he could ever give her more. She was the strongest woman he'd ever met. Been through more than most and come out on top. He was proud of her.

"I took to the hidden corridors—the ones I told you about. I searched the castle until I came upon Rose, Byron's wife. She told me that Foulis had been attacked, that Byron was dead. That everyone was dead." She choked on the word dead, her voice strained.

Daniel placed a comforting kiss on top of her head, took a moment to breathe in her heady scent.

"She was wrong. I found Byron hidden within the walls. He wasn't dead yet. He told me of his ally's treachery, that I had to save Rose and that I had to give the Bruce a message." She sighed heavily. "I've done most of what he asked so far. Rose and her bairn are safe within the walls of Dunrobin. And now I just have to deliver the message. Pray that Eilean Donan is still standing."

"Why would it not be, lass?" Daniel kept his voice low, unthreatening. He waited, chest tight, for her answer. Her words were ominous and sent a surge of urgency through him.

"Because the Earl of Ross attacked Foulis. Ross is the Bruce's most trusted ally, yet he is not loyal to Scotland. He is in league with the English."

Damn... Daniel gritted his teeth, the base of his skull starting to throb. He'd gathered from her dream that Ross played a part in the massacre, but he'd never dreamed the man was in league with the Sassenachs. Demons all of them, minions to Longshanks, the devil himself. A demon within the midst could prove fatal. Myra's journey to Scotland's future king was even more vital than he'd originally thought. The Ross could have already made it to the war camp and attacked—brought in an army of Sassenachs. After having destroyed Foulis the man would be feeling all powerful. An ally that was actually your enemy was a man's worst nightmare.

There was one thing, however, that did not make any sense. "Why would he attack Foulis?" Daniel asked, suddenly confused.

Myra let out another deep sigh, as if she'd been expecting him to ask this but hoped he wouldn't. "Because my brother knew of his change of allegiance. He'd been warned. 'Twas the conversation I'd overheard. Byron wouldna have allowed us to marry. Ross is a prideful man, and starving for power and coin. The more the better. Knowing Byron was going to call off the marriage prompted him to take Foulis by force. Thank God I escaped, or else I'd be..."

Daniel shuddered to think. "Are ye telling me ye were betrothed to Ross?"

"Aye. And I would rather walk in my mother's footsteps than to marry the man."

Fear pulled at Daniel's gut. If he were in her shoes he'd consider the alternative of an eternity in Purgatory over marriage to a monster too. He too thanked God she'd been able to escape. That he'd found her upon the road. He pulled her even closer. "I willna allow ye to do either."

Myra hugged his arms. "I believe ye. Thank ye, Daniel."

"Ye dinna need to thank me, lass."

The heaviness of what lay ahead sank in deep. Daniel had not expected it. He'd known it couldn't be good, but he'd not realized that they may find Eilean Donan occupied by the English and the entire rebellion put to rest, the future of Scotland destroyed.

He urged Demon into a faster trot. The sooner they got there the better. Damn the snow. If the road was clear he'd have been able to make it to the castle that much sooner.

Daniel was often of the mind that all things happened for a reason. Something positive had to come from it, even if only a lesson learned.

Myra felt a shift in the weight upon her shoulders. The burden she'd been carrying had been substantial and now that Daniel knew what was at stake, what had happened to her, she felt as though she wasn't completely alone in the world.

There was something about him that drew her in. Beyond being physically attracted to him—damn her wanton body!—she was inspired by him. Wanted to share with him her innermost thoughts, dreams, fears. Myra had never felt that way about anyone. It was both unnerving and liberating. She didn't know how it happened.

Maybe it was by the burn when he'd seen the blood upon her hands and simply offered to watch her back while she washed up. Perhaps it had been when he'd offered to marry her without knowing who she was or what her intentions were. Or even still maybe it was at Foulis all those years ago when he'd seen her lurking in the shadows, spying, and he'd pulled her into his arms and danced with her, made her feel magical.

When her feelings had changed was a question she'd never be able to answer, the fact of the matter was, she had. 'Twould only make it that much harder for her to leave him once they'd reached Eilean Donan.

Oh, he'd told her that the Munro clan was his responsibility that he'd not take that duty lightly, and Myra believed him. The problem was, he had his own clan to worry about, his own duties to perform and she didn't feel right about saddling him with her responsibilities and burdens. He may not have known to extent of what he was getting into when he offered marriage. If she were to just dump the major issue of Foulis' disaster in his hands she would not feel right about it. Doing so wouldn't be fair to Daniel.

A brisk wind blew, causing her to suck in a sharp breath. What she wouldn't give for a blazing hearth, soft goose down blanket and a cup of spiced wine.

Daniel's hand on her waist was a warm, welcome weight. She pressed her own gloved hand over his, eternally grateful for the large gloves he'd given her. Her fingers wouldn't fall off—she'd met an old man missing his pinkie who told her it'd frozen off— and that was an immeasurable comfort.

Over the next two days, the snow melted quicker than any Highland winter that Myra had witnessed, perhaps a gift from the Heavens so they might reach their destination sooner. With the leftover boar, oatcakes and jerky, they were all fed well each day. When night fell, Daniel and Myra slept as they had in the cave, leaning against one another for warmth. There were no more shared kisses, but from the intensity of their gazes it was certain that they both suffered from a powerful yearning that was soon to have them both caving into their desires.

After stopping for a brief rest in the late afternoon, the smaller group finally came within view of Eilean Donan atop a rise. A mist curled around the base of the castle, making it look as though it floated upon the water. The setting sun streaked orange and pink across the sky reflected on the water. They arrived just in time, it appeared, as in the distance

The Highlander's Lady

the sky churned with eerie grey clouds. Another storm would be upon them.

"Eilean Donan," Daniel said. "Has been a long time since last I saw her."

They stopped far enough away not to be spotted by the guards atop the battlements.

"'Tis magical," Myra said.

"Aye."

"Can ye tell who…"

Daniel grunted. "Nay. Without getting closer I'll not be able to see what the men on guard are wearing. Either they'll be dressed as they should be in plaids or they'll be wearing the devil's clothing." His voice held such a strong vehemence for the English that Myra shuddered. Anyone who stood in Daniel's way would suffer for it.

She was acutely glad to be on his good side.

"Come, the trees below will hide us and give us a better view."

The horses trotted quietly down the mountain ridge. Daniel was careful to stop at any sounds that she sometimes didn't even hear.

"There are scouts in these woods to be sure. Sassenach or not, but I pray not."

Myra nodded, trying to keep her own eyes peeled for anything out of the ordinary. They made it to the base of the ridge, staying hidden within the shadows of the trees. The sun had set further and Myra could see that the guards on top of the walls had begun to light torches. Winter sun fell quicker than any other time of the year. They'd not make it to the gate before darkness fell.

"I canna see well enough," Daniel muttered.

"My laird, if ye'd allow me, I'll sneak closer and have a look," Leo offered.

Daniel nodded. "Aye, take another with ye."

"Aye, my laird."

Two men disappeared moments later. Myra was shaken by how easily they slipped away as though they had magical fae powers of invisibility.

"I've often prided myself on my ability to disappear, but I had walls to hide behind. Your men dinna."

Daniel chuckled. "Aye, my men are good. The Murrays are known for it. They'll be back soon enough with news."

Myra prayed it was good news.

Chapter Sixteen

"Scots upon the battlements, my laird."

"'Tis good news," Daniel said.

Myra let out the breath she'd been holding since the hour before when the men left to scout the area.

"There is some bad news though, my laird."

"Dinna hold it in, Leo. I'll know all now."

"Aye, laird. We spotted a band of warriors camped just to the east of here. Armed to the teeth they were. Donald is fairly certain they are Ross men."

"Donald?" Daniel addressed a warrior who nodded. "What made ye think they are Ross men?"

"My mother was raised a Ross. We visited the clan often. I recognized at least two warriors who I trained with."

Whatever sense of relief Myra had felt moments before quickly receded. They were here. Her mission would soon be completed and she'd have to make the decision of whether or not to leave. Chills snaked up and down her arms and she shivered. Daniel tightened his hold around her waist.

"What were they doing?" Daniel asked.

Leo answered this time, "Looked like they'd set up camp either for the night or they've been there a day or two. Wouldn't be surprised if they'd been there longer, keeping watch. Is there any reason the Ross clan would be armed outside of Eilean Donan? I thought they were allies with the Bruce."

Daniel shook his head. "I dinna know. But it isn't a good sign. We canna wait. We must go to the castle now," Daniel said.

Myra was surprised and pleased that Daniel kept the information she'd told him a secret. In the face of danger, a band of armed warriors not far away, she'd thought for certain he would tell his men so they could be prepared.

His men nodded their agreement with Daniel.

"We must split up," Daniel instructed. "If we were to travel as one large group, we'd be noticed."

He gave orders for which men were to go where and with whom. Myra and Daniel were to be alone. He pulled the plaid further over them. To the outside eye, they were indistinguishable.

"I dinna want the Ross warriors to see ye, lass."

"I know, me either."

"I'm hoping they may just think we are a couple seeking shelter if they should spot us, but I pray that we pass without their notice."

Myra nodded, sinking more firmly against him.

"Dinna be afraid," Daniel said softly, his voice soothing her nerves.

"I'm not."

"Good, lass."

Myra smiled. Daniel truly was a caring soul even if he came off as a brute sometimes. His strength gave her strength, courage.

The Highlander's Lady

They crept forward at a snail's pace. Painfully slow going it was, so much so, Myra was sure they'd be noticed. Demon kept silent, not a snort or misplaced step. They could have walked right through a camp of men without being heard.

Blood roared in her ears and her nose tickled just to spite her. But she didn't sneeze, thank the saints. She was strung so tight, Myra was sure she'd snap. The only thing keeping her from jumping off the horse and bolting was Daniel. He was a solid force in a hundred moments of unrest. Looking back, she was fairly certain she would not have made it this far without him.

"Thank ye," she whispered.

"Hmm?" he whispered back.

"Thank ye, Daniel," she whispered.

Daniel didn't say anything, but instead found her fingers, entwined them with his and squeezed. She wished to take off her gloves to feel his fingers threaded through hers. When they finally made it to the castle—because they would, she prayed—and they had a moment to be alone, would she touch his bare hand to hers? Ask him for another kiss? Perhaps even a little more? Myra would not consummate their union, that would only solidify it, but she was curious to see just how far their passion could reach without crossing that boundary.

Having the Ross warriors so close put a damper on her plans to leave unnoticed. She'd not want the Bruce to spare any of his men if there was going to be an attack either in order to take her home. Myra would have to wait out the certain battle.

They grew ever closer to the castle, the stone bridge just a short gallop from the line of trees where they stood.

"Lass, I'm going to break through the trees. I canna make Demon run at full speed, else we'll draw attention to ourselves. Keep tucked against me."

"I understand."

Then they were out of the trees. The sky was purple, the sun nearly set all the way. Few stars shone in the sky as clouds had begun to fill the heavens. Luckily the clouds were not quite as grey as before when the storm had overtaken them.

The men upon the battlements turned their attention onto Myra and Daniel. She watched a couple notch their bows and prayed they were not quick to loose their arrows. Daniel must have felt the same way. He positioned his arms more fully around her, tucked her head under his chin as if to shield her.

The horse's hooves clomped loudly over the bridge, and all around them everything else was a hushed whisper. Daniel stopped before the gate and peered up.

"Laird Murray to see The Bruce."

"Aye, we've been expecting ye. Where are the rest of your men?" the guard shouted down.

"They are coming… Let me in, I've news."

The guard called to those on gate duty and within moments the gates were opened. Daniel walked Demon into the courtyard, where they were met by a large, imposing man. He looked rough, with a long unkempt beard. But his eyes were soulful, and he was even a bit handsome.

"Murray, good to see ye."

"Wallace, 'tis good to be among friends."

This was William Wallace. He looked every bit the part. She'd heard such tales of the fierce warrior. He was as tall as Daniel, and just as broad.

Daniel swung his leg off the horse and then turned to help Myra down. He slipped his hands around her waist and lifted her effortlessly. Setting her down a little too close, Myra was instantly aware of their proximity. Her body reacted immediately, nipples tightening and belly flipping.

She stared at his chest, not wanting to look up, sure if she did he would see the desire in her eyes. Positive that everyone

The Highlander's Lady

else would see it too. When she'd watched behind the walls, she could read passion in the lovers' faces. If she, an innocent, could see it, then the seasoned, debouched warriors surrounding her would know it in an instant. But more, she was worried Daniel would see it.

"Is this your wife?" Wallace asked, breaking the spell that had held Myra in place.

She swiveled around and met the warrior's gaze, lifting her chin.

"Aye, this is Lady Myra," Daniel said, pride in his voice. He placed his hand on the small of her back, sending a shiver of desire up her spine.

"A pleasure, my lady." Wallace gripped her hand, and stopped halfway to his mouth when he took note of the overlarge gloves. He glanced up at Daniel. "Your wife doesna have gloves of her own?"

"'Tis a long story—and an urgent matter. We would speak with ye and the Bruce."

Wallace dropped her hand and Myra took that moment to remove the gloves not wanting further attention.

"Aye, your men did say ye'd beg an audience. I thought it would be about a plan for training the men. Ronan is eager to see ye about that as well." Wallace motioned them to follow him inside the castle.

"Aye, good. I'm eager to see him."

"Who is Ronan?" Myra asked.

"He is my cousin. Brother to Laird Magnus Sutherland."

Myra's eyes widened. She recalled him saying he'd been at his cousins' when Rose arrived; she'd just completely forgotten that fact.

"Ye are a fearsome family," she commented.

William Wallace laughed so loud it boomed all around. "Aye, they are that! No one's been able to best me afore I met the Sutherlands and this Murray arse. Pardon my language, my lady."

Myra tried to hide her smile.

"'Tis nothing she hasn't heard *or* said afore," Daniel said with a snicker.

Wallace laughed all the more while Myra's face heated to a fiery flame. She nearly drew blood, biting her tongue so hard from retorting. When she got Daniel alone she'd give him the rougher side of her tongue—maybe even throw in a few choice words he'd not heard before.

Myra had learned quite a bit of foul language while traipsing the darkened, secret passageways, and she used them often when alone. Shouting a curse or muttering one behind someone's back always made her feel better. Gave her a sense of power in a world where she had few choices.

Daniel took her hand in his and squeezed. She tried to pull away but he only held on tighter. It was then she realized their flesh was touching. Their palms were flattened together, fingers entwined. His hand was large, warm, and sent rippling sensation up her arm to warm her chest. Her ire dissipated and instead an odd heat seeped into her.

Daniel leaned in close as they followed behind Wallace. "I must warn ye, lass, this is a war camp, not a castle such as ye might be used to."

"What do ye mean?"

"This place is overrun with boors."

Myra gasped, imagining the raging wild animals running around and goring anything in sight. "Truly? Is that how ye train? Is that not dangerous?"

That had Daniel laughing just as uproariously as Wallace had. Myra frowned.

"What has ye laughing like a loon?" she asked.

"Ye, lass. I didna mean actual boars."

They entered the great hall and Myra instantly knew exactly what Daniel had meant. The room was packed with men who shouted crude jokes, men wrestling, eating greasy

The Highlander's Lady

meat and tossing the bones to their dogs, burping, farting and all manners of disgusting behavior. The blood drained from her face and she had to remind herself she was not here for a social visit but to save the future King of Scotland's life. To save Scotland from tyranny.

Myra squared her shoulders and looked several of the men in the eye, a frown on her face, hopefully as fearsome as her nurse's had been when she was growing up. Those who met her gaze stopped whatever they were doing, standing stock still as they gaped at her.

"Men! We've a lady present. Contain yourselves," Wallace bellowed.

The room suddenly became silent as a grave. Daniel pulled her hand, moving her further into the room. She would have been perfectly fine where she was. The place smelled like rotten food, foul bodies and...*shite*. Myra crinkled up her nose and forced her belly not to roll.

Slowly the men came to form a disorganized crowd in the middle of the great hall.

"That is better. Now clear out," Wallace ordered.

The men grumbled but did as they were commanded, nodding at her as they passed. Myra tried her best to be pleasant, but some of the men were so gruesome looking she was sure to have night terrors recalling their visages.

"Would ye care to have a seat, my lady?" Wallace asked, pointing toward an overlarge chair in front of the hearth covered in a fluffy, warm-looking blanket.

"Aye, thank ye," she said.

She tried to let go of Daniel's hand, but he wasn't willing to part with her. He walked with her toward the chair. It was only when they were within a few feet that the blanket she'd seen got up and jumped from the chair.

Myra shuddered. She could see the fleas jumping all over the furry monster from where she stood. Her skin automatically itched, and she felt as though a thousand bugs crawled all over her. Knowing it was a figment of her imagination she refused to scratch. But Lord, the urge was overwhelming.

"I think I'll stand."

Chapter Seventeen

Wallace shrugged then moved to sit at the long trestle table in the middle of the room. Daniel followed and Myra felt she had to do the same. She swiped off some crumbs from the bench and sat down, relieved she didn't slide off from all the grease. The place could use a thorough scrubbing.

A bump on the top of her foot made her jump and she swore a critter just run over her foot. Trying not to cringe, she concentrated on Wallace and what he was saying to Daniel. Doing so helped to ease her nerves a bit. Awkwardness didn't even begin to describe how she felt sitting out in the open with so many strange people surrounding her. Found herself looking for cracks in the walls, oddly placed furniture and anything else that might indicate a hidden doorway. Not hiding was something she needed to learn well. Daniel would keep her safe.

"The Bruce is not here at present. But he should be back soon. Anything I can help with? That eager to begin training?"

The large warrior's smile was contagious and Myra found herself smiling in turn. But her smile faltered as she realized that the Bruce was not within Eilean Donan's walls. All the struggles she'd been through had been for naught.

"Where has he gone?" Daniel sat forward, his brow creased. Myra followed suit.

Wallace too sat forward, sensing something was off no doubt. "What's amiss, Murray?"

"We've come with urgent news. My wife must speak with the Bruce immediately."

Wallace shook his head. "Impossible. He is not here."

"When will he return?" Daniel's tone turned impatient and Myra felt her own nerves reaching the breaking point. She had to stop herself from interjecting.

"A couple days I suspect."

Daniel's hand clenched into a fist on top of the table but he didn't say anything. Myra watched his knuckles growing white.

"What's this about?" Wallace glanced at Myra, catching her eyes. "Ye can trust me."

Myra touched Daniel's arm. He jerked, then seeming to remember her presence, he glanced at her. Unspoken words passed between them. She nodded and Daniel returned the gesture before giving his attention back to Wallace.

"My wife's home was attacked over a week ago. Her brother Laird Munro was slain."

Wallace's face filled with compassion. "My prayers are with ye, lass. Munro was a good man."

Myra swallowed back her tears, gave an imperceptible nod. At the moment she wanted to bolt. To leave this castle with its beautiful shell but inner stink. Her skin felt like it was crawling and Myra curled her hands into fists to keep from fidgeting or scratching.

"Who attacked Foulis?" Wallace asked.

Again Daniel turned to Myra for her permission, and she gave it.

"The Earl of Ross was behind the attack. Munro found out some information about the bastard and Ross sought to silence him and take what he believed belonged to him—my wife."

Wallace's face paled where he wasn't covered in hair, and his eyes flashed with anger and fear. "The Bruce has left to meet with Ross. The man has been...a great ally to our cause."

Nay! Myra shook her head, disbelieving what she was hearing.

Daniel let out a deep breath. "Aye. But the news gets worse."

"I think I may know what ye're going to say." Wallace's tone was hollow and Myra could practically read the plans he was etching.

"Ross is in league with the English. If the Bruce has gone to meet him, it's a trap. Where were they to meet? My men saw a band of Ross warriors camped within the woods."

"They were to meet at a nearby inn. Ross sent a message that he had news of a possible ambush..." Wallace's words trailed off.

Myra's stomach plummeted. The future of Scotland was walking into a trap.

"Did he take any men with him?" Daniel asked.

"Aye, but only a half-dozen. He feels safe around here. Every Scot wants him to succeed. Well, at least that's what he thought."

"I fear the warriors outside the walls await but a signal from Ross before they attack. I'd fortify the walls." Daniel stood. "I need to speak with Ronan."

"Wait!" Myra said louder than she'd planned. "What about the Bruce? Shouldn't someone go and get him?"

"Aye, I will see about it." Wallace stood and stomped away, anger in his every step.

Daniel's grip engulfed Myra's hands as he pulled her to stand. "'Twill be all right, lass. Ye've given your message and now we can all work to see Ross brought down."

Then why did she feel such dread? Why did it seem like everything was falling apart?

Myra nodded. "I think I need to rest. I'm so tired." And that was partially true. She was completely exhausted. Her mind numb from having to be constantly on alert for nearly two weeks, all the suffering and loss she'd been through. Her body ached from travel, fighting off attackers and the physical rush of being in danger. The emotional turmoil started to take its toll. But in truth, she felt the need to be alone. To sink into the comfort of obscurity.

Daniel's face showed lines of strain. He was tired too, that much was obvious.

"Let us find ye a maid…" He glanced around, an eyebrow raised. "Not sure that will be possible."

As if on cue, an older female servant melted from the shadows. "I can show ye both to your chamber. I am Marta, Housekeeper to Eilean Donan these past twenty years."

Myra smiled at the older woman who stood proudly before them.

"I would be grateful for a chamber."

Marta nodded and motioned for them to follow her up a winding staircase. "These chambers are meant for honored guests and I'm sure that would include ye and your husband, my lady."

Myra's tiredness ebbed a little. They would have to share a chamber? Ugh. She hadn't the strength to argue it. Besides a chill had settled in her bones that only ebbed when she was in Daniel's arms. They'd make do. After all they'd been sleeping beside each other for the last couple nights. She would just make sure that they slept fully clothed—boots and all. Although, the alternative was enticing…

They came to a chamber, decent in size, but smaller than her chamber at Foulis. There was a double bed pushed up against the left corner, a small hearth on the right wall, a wooden chest at the end of the bed and a table beside the bed with a washbasin. Two narrow slitted windows were fitted inside tiny alcoves that someone had set small vases of dried flowers in an attempt to make the fortified arrow slits homier.

"Will ye be needing anything else, my lady? My laird? I can rummage a bath for ye."

"That would be wonderful," Myra said, hearing the tiredness in her own voice.

Marta nodded and retreated from the room.

Myra went to the slitted windows and glanced outside. The darkening clouds had moved closer and she was that much happier that they'd arrived. But there was something so ominous about that threatening storm, as if it culminated everything she'd been running from and toward.

"Are ye all right, lass?" Daniel came up behind her, placed his palm on the small of her back. "I know this wasn't the news ye were hoping for."

Myra shook her head, glanced back at him for a moment before turning back toward the storm. "Nay. 'Tis not good, especially knowing warriors are waiting just behind those trees. Feels like I missed the mark by a few moments. Story of my life." She laughed bitterly.

"Myra, none of this is your fault. Ye could not have predicted that Ross would turn against his own people, his own country. Ye could not predict that he'd gain the trust of our revered king and draw him out alone. These are things that no one could have predicted. Not even Byron."

Myra glanced down at her boots, dirty around the tips. The hem of her gown was dirty too and could use a good washing. In fact, she'd be glad for a new one that fit.

"I know it, but it doesna mean I feel better about it."

Daniel softly took hold of her elbow and pulled her into his embrace and she let him, wanting to feel his strong arms around her, wanting him to take away some of the burden she carried. He ran his hands up and down her back, massaging the tightened muscles.

"What can I do to make ye feel better?" he asked softly.

"Kiss me? Make me forget." Myra was just as shocked by her own words as Daniel appeared to be. He, however, recovered from it much quicker than she did.

His lips descended on hers in yet another kiss that was completely different and magical in every way. Sparks shot from their connected lips to raise flames on every inch of her body. She melted into him, sinking against the muscled length of his chest, stomach, thighs. Myra shuddered, unprepared for the onslaught of sensation brought on by all that hard flesh touching her softer curves.

Daniel deepened the kiss, his tongue sweeping inside her mouth to tease hers. Myra leaned even further into him, wanting, needing so much more. Everything that had happened before, led up to this one, intense, desire-filled moment, and she didn't ever want it to end. She gripped his shoulders, kneaded the muscles, ground her hips against his, frustrated when his sporran got in the way.

Instinctively, she reached down and undid the buckle that held it in place, hearing the piece thud as it hit the floor. Daniel pulled back a moment, his eyes wide, matching her own, but Myra couldn't think on what she was doing. Thinking would only make her stop, and she didn't want to do that. Right now she needed to feel loved, cherished and whenever Daniel kissed her, touched her, she felt those things. She wanted to forget the past two weeks and to just *feel*.

She tipped up on her toes and pressed her lips once more to his, crushing her breasts against his chest.

The Highlander's Lady

"Myra," he growled, low and sensual, the sound sending ripples of rampant desire up and down her arms. "What are ye doing, lass?" He may have asked the question, but he didn't stop her. His lips claimed hers once more, fierce and demanding.

He reached down and gripped her rear, lifting her slightly as he tugged her pelvis once more close to his. She gasped when a new hardness pressed against that sensitive spot. His sporran was no longer there. Nay, the rigid length that now touched her, probed against her delicate parts was his...

Myra shuddered, loving the new sensations that his arousal brought about. Tentatively, she explored his arms, his back, her fingers gliding over the ridges and sinew. He was so muscular, built like a rock. What would it feel like for all that firmness on top of her, inside of her? Her legs trembled and she felt suddenly boneless.

Daniel lifted her into the air, his mouth skimming to her chin, her ear, where he bit the lobe lightly, then toward her neck where he teased the flesh with the tip of his tongue, kissed then suckled.

"Oh," she moaned, completely out of sorts, only living for the delicious and wicked movements of his tongue.

"I want ye, lass..." His voice was husky, vibrated against her neck, made her nipples ache for the same attention he'd paid to her flesh. "But I won't take ye all the way."

What was he talking about, taking her all the way? She nodded, not fully understanding, until her body hit the bed. She sank into the softness of the mattress, the plushness of the pillows.

"Wait," she said, a bit frantic. "What do ye mean?"

Daniel came down on top of her, that weight that she'd been wondering about feeling even better now that it was covering her, pressing her firmly to the mattress. She wanted to spread her thighs and wrap her legs around him, just as she'd seen the lovers do behind the walls. There were so many questions she'd had when watching that were now being answered.

Daniel leaned up on his elbows, sucked her lower lip into his mouth as he watched her. She shivered, arched her back and didn't want him to answer, just act.

"I willna take your virtue."

She was glad for it, but had to know... "Why?"

Daniel's eyes widened, perhaps not having expected her question. "Do ye want me to?"

She shook her head. "Nay, not yet. Not until we reach your home."

He nodded. "That is what I thought as well. Why did ye ask why?"

Myra shrugged, the movement making her breasts rub tantalizingly against his chest. "I was but curious about your reasoning. I know my own reasons."

He nuzzled against her neck. "I want ye bad. Can ye feel it?"

Daniel pressed his hips forward, that hard length touching her in such a way she couldn't help but cry out. "Aye!"

"I want ye, lass, there is no doubt, but I also want ye in my own bed."

She didn't know why, but the way he said it, the possessiveness of it, imagining what his bed would look like made her want the same thing.

Then came the logical side... She shouldn't want it. Especially since she was still planning on returning to her own castle. Her people. She had responsibilities, that didn't include Daniel or making love. Instantly she was contrite. Here she was behaving like a selfish wanton while her people suffered, while the Bruce could be suffering from a butchering.

The Highlander's Lady

"What?" Daniel asked. Seeming to notice the change in her, he stopped kissing her and pulled back.

She wished to take back the moment. For once she could have something for herself, couldn't she? She'd just have to pray in the morning. Fast for a day or seven. Hide in the garderobe with nothing to comfort her save a hair shirt. Until then she was seizing this moment as her own. Before she could act, a knock came at the door. Daniel was quick to get off of her, the bed shifting with the loss of his weight. Myra sat up, legs hanging over the side of the bed and straightened herself out.

When he answered the door, the look that Marta gave them showed she knew what had been happening. Myra's face heated. Was she that obvious? Was Daniel? She looked toward him, besides his missing sporran he looked completely normal, his usual fearsome self.

So what had the housekeeper seen? Myra groaned inside. She was never very good at hiding her feelings. From the swollen feel of her lips, the tingling on her neck where Daniel's stubble had scraped her skin, it was possible that she hadn't needed to give anything away. One look at her probably told the woman what had happened.

"Your bath, my lady," the housekeeper said, keeping her eyes on the wall ahead.

A few servants filed in with a wooden tub, linens, soaps and buckets of water. Myra waited patiently as they finished preparing her bath and then left just as quietly as they'd served her.

"Your bath, my lady," Daniel said with a wicked glint in his eyes.

"Shouldn't ye be leaving?" Myra raised her brow in challenge.

Daniel slowly shook his head. Just that simple gesture and what it implied had gooseflesh rising along her limbs.

"I dinna intend to go anywhere. In fact, I intend to join ye."

"What?" She gaped at him.

"Aye." He stalked toward her, prowess in his every move. His knees touched hers and he reached out, his finger sliding over her bared collarbone until he hooked inside her gown at her shoulder. "I intend to...take care of ye."

Oh how his words had so many different meanings. And Myra didn't blink an eye. She wanted him to.

She stood, suddenly feeling every bit as bold as she had before. "Then I'd best get out of this gown."

Daniel's mouth fell open a little, his pupils dilated—again she'd taken him by surprise. Had he thought she wasn't serious? This is what she so desperately wanted. To escape. To feel what it was like to be with a man who wanted her.

Who knew what the future held? She didn't. And as Daniel said before, she couldn't predict it either.

Chapter Eighteen

What in all holy hell was going on here?

Daniel's hands trembled as though he'd never been with a woman before. Truth be told, he'd never been with a woman like Myra. She was skittish one moment and a fiery wildcat the next. Her prickly nature drew him close at the same time it pushed him away.

But he wasn't going to let anything get in the way of pleasuring her. Stilling his hands through sheer willpower, he stepped toward her, let his heated gaze rove up and down her body until her cheeks matched the flames in the hearth. He noted how her own hands trembled.

Not as bold as she wanted to let on. Good.

Daniel reached for her, stroking his hand over her hip and then settling on the small of her back. The room was silent save for her catch of breath and the occasional pop from the hearth. Blood pounded in his ears as it made its way down to his cock. He tugged her close until she was flush against him. Her eyelids fluttered at the impact, her mouth parted in a silent moan. He felt the same way. The heat of her body against his, the feel of the apex of her thighs cradling his arousal. Even through the blush on her face, she kept her gaze locked on his. Bold temptress.

"Ye want me?" he asked.

She nodded.

"I want to hear ye say it."

"Aye," she whispered, then louder, "Aye."

She licked her lip, making him want to take her tongue into his mouth.

"But first, I want a bath…and to reach your castle."

Daniel grinned and winked at her. "Aye. Ye'll get a bath, and I'll teach ye something of lovemaking, but I'll leave your maidenhood intact—although not unblemished."

"Oh," she said on a breath.

Desire coiled inside Daniel, ready to spring, ready to toss her onto the bed and ravish her.

"Get undressed," he said, his voice low, husky.

Myra nodded, took a step back and slowly took off the gilded belt at her hips. He watched her fingers as they skimmed over her gown until she lifted it over her head. She tossed it to the side, the sound of her fluttering fabric mixing with their heavier breaths. The chemise she wore was still too tight, her nipples hard little buds pressed tightly against the fabric which hugged the mounds of her ample breasts. Before he could think better on it, Daniel reached out, traced the outside of her right breast, watching as her chest rose and fell in a more erratic pattern. Good God, he'd never been with a more perfect woman.

"Daniel," she breathed.

His eyes snapped back to hers. They were cloudy with desire, her lids partially lowered. She stepped closer so that her breast filled his hand, the hard bud of her nipple pressing against his palm.

"I've never…felt anything like this," she said.

"Me either," he confessed. There'd been plenty of women, many breasts, but none as flawless as Myra's. None so honest in their reaction to his touch.

He slipped his fingers into the edges of her chemise on her shoulder, the softness of her skin branding his fingertips. Sliding his fingers down toward the ribbons between her breasts, he tugged lightly. The fabric fell open, exposing the delicate creamy swells. Daniel slid the fabric off, letting it fall to the floor in ripples of fabric. Myra let out a gasp, gooseflesh pebbling her skin, and attempted to shield her nakedness.

"Ye're cold. Best get in the tub afore the water completely cools," Daniel said, trying with every ounce of his willpower not to let his eyes dip below hers.

Myra nodded, turned and hurried toward the tub. His eyes did drift then over the round, fullness of her arse. Perfect for grabbing, stroking… He had to stop himself from touching. She lifted one perfect, long, sculpted leg into the tub, then the other, sinking low into the water, covering her breasts from his view.

Daniel let out a long breath he didn't realize he was holding. This was going to be the longest, most excruciating bath of his life.

He cleared his throat. "Mind if I wash your hair?"

She shook her head and dunked under the water, coming up and using both hands to wipe the water from her face. "'Tis not completely cold yet," she said.

Daniel pulled up a chair behind her, stroked his fingers over her wet hair and massaged her scalp. He could have spent the rest of winter sitting here, touching her, exploring her body.

Myra sniffed one of the balls of soap before handing it too him. "'Tis lemon."

"Smells good," he replied. "Are ye surprised?"

She laughed nervously. "A little. I admit when we first arrived, I did not think they'd even have clean water let alone sweet smelling soaps."

"I believe it must be the housekeeper's doing. The Bruce has not been the same since his wife died."

Myra nodded. "'Twas the same for my father. I suspect losing the one ye love is devastating to the soul."

Daniel suspected she was right. Even when he'd only watched the wild boar bear down on her he'd seen red fury. If she'd been killed he wasn't sure what he would have felt—and he didn't love her. Did he?

Just thinking on the word made his hands tremble once more. His chest tightened acutely. Must have been something he ate. He made quick work of washing her hair, hoping doing something so mundane it would help him to get over whatever ailed him. Love was not an emotion he had the luxury of. Not now, not ever. He was a warrior. He would bring his wife home to Blair then return to war with the hopes that she was with child should he not ever come home.

But those thoughts only turned his mind dark. He shoved them aside and instead concentrated on the lushness of her hair, the tangy scent of lemons and the small sighs she made as he massaged her hair into a thick lather.

"Ye wash hair much better than my maid," Myra commented.

Daniel chuckled. "I think 'tis because I enjoy it a lot more."

"Ye're probably right about that," Myra said, a smile in her voice. Her eyes were closed, head tilted back. Soap bubbles skimmed the top of the water and the only bit of flesh he could see were the two points of her knees poking out.

"I need to rinse your hair," Daniel said with reluctance. He'd enjoyed touching her... Then again, he'd not yet begun to bathe her body and that was certain to be more tempting than washing her hair.

Myra sank under the water and Daniel made quick work of rinsing the suds from her hair, then gently brought her back to the surface. He leaned in close, pressing his nose nearly to her scalp and inhaled her scent.

"Smells good," he murmured.

Myra sighed. "Aye, I've not had a proper bath in quite a while."

Daniel tilted her head so she could see him, and he smiled wickedly. "Ye consider this proper? I wonder what ye'd think is wicked?" As he said the latter, he stroked his hands deliberately over her shoulders to the warm, wet globes of her breasts. His breath came out in a shudder. Her skin was perfect silk in his grasp. Daniel lowered his lips to hers, brushing tenderly as he continued to play with her sensitive flesh. He massaged her breasts, brushed his thumbs over her nipples, felt her harsh exhale against his face.

"Nay, 'tis not proper at all." Myra moaned, arching her back.

Daniel had to slow down or else he'd end up in the tub with her...which actually was exactly what he wanted, but would only end in taking her virginity which he'd promised not to do yet. Regrettably he pulled his hands away and scooted his chair to the side of the tub.

"I need to wash your body." The words and their meaning were practical, but uttered in the face of a woman who was flushed with desire, lips parted in the most sensual way, they could only be considered risqué. Not to mention they brought to mind all manner of things he wished to do with her.

Myra nodded and handed him the linen square the servants had left. Daniel picked up the ball of lemon soap he'd used to wash her hair, dunked the cloth into the water and then rubbed soap vigorously onto it. Doing so did not make his task any less meaningful as he'd hoped.

Daniel held out his hand, grateful when she simply laid hers in his. Stroking the cloth up and down her arm, he watched the suds bubble on her flesh. He rubbed over her shoulders, down her other arm and back again. For the longest time, he avoided her breasts while he washed her neck, chest and arms.

"I think my arms are thoroughly clean, do ye not?" A small, teasing smile curved Myra's lips.

Daniel laughed. "I suppose they are."

"How about my legs?" She lifted one foot onto the edge of the tub, her skin slick with water. Her eyes were wide as though she surprised even herself with her bold move. Oh, how she tempted him... And she must know it too. He resisted the urge to stroke over her thigh with his bare fingers and instead soaped up the cloth even more.

"I'm happy to oblige ye," he murmured. Daniel took the soapy cloth and slowly swiped it over the tips of her toes, the sole of her foot, chuckling as she jerked and then laughed.

"That tickles."

"What this?" He did it again.

Once more she jerked and laughed. "Stop!" The joyous sound of her tinkling laughter made Daniel smile and realize how much more there was to live for in life.

He did stop tickling her foot. However, he massaged the cloth up over her calf, kneading the muscles, admiring her lithe limb, and then swiped beneath her knee, making her jolt.

"Does that tickle too?" Daniel grinned mischievously.

Myra bit her lip. "Nay..."

He grinned wider, and instead of using the cloth, tantalized the sensitive flesh at the back of her knee with his fingertips. Myra gasped and pulled her leg up higher,

The Highlander's Lady

bending her knee closer toward her chest. The move, meant to cease his tickling did something else entirely.

The soap bubbles parted to clear water...completely exposing her mons.

The dark raven curls of her sex parted to reveal the pink petals of flesh beneath. Daniel gritted his teeth, his eyes riveted to the spot. How he wished to dive beneath the water and kiss her sex. Breathe in the essence of her womanhood, taste her heat, feel her thighs quiver on either side of his face. Seeing where his gaze was drawn, Myra quickly covered herself with her hands, long fingers delving between her thighs. He knew she meant to hide herself, but it only increased his desire.

"Och, lass..." he started. Daniel swiped wet hands through his hair, turned his gaze toward her face. He could take it no longer. Daniel reached forward, threading his hands through her damp hair and bent his mouth to hers.

He captured her lips in a deep, demanding kiss, swiping his tongue inside. He took control of her mouth, claiming her once more as his own. Myra did not back down, in fact she met his tongue full force. Gripped his shoulders, tugging him closer. Where her wet hands touched his shirt left cool, damp spots clinging to his flesh.

Daniel slid his mouth away from hers, down her tender neck, nipping at the spot where her pulse vibrated. He slid lower, not stopping until he'd captured a taut nipple between his lips. Myra moaned aloud, the sound thrilling him, making his cock harder than stone. There was no going back now. They'd crossed a bridge—not *run* over it.

He sucked a little harder, gripping her breast, massaging it as he feasted on one nipple and then the other. But it was not all he wanted. After seeing the pink of her sex, he wanted that too. Wanted to taste her with the fierceness of a starving man. He slid his hands around her waist and lifted her into the air.

"Daniel, what are ye doing?" she asked, her voice shocked, swollen mouth open.

Daniel answered with another kiss. He grappled for the linen towel he'd seen beside the tub, and glided it over her wet skin. His entire body was afire, for even the act of rubbing the cloth over her lush limbs, flat belly, round breasts and buttocks was completely erotic. She was everything he wanted and more. Fear of losing her again lingered on the edges of his consciousness. If only she felt the same way about him.

She shivered, bit her lip and stared at him, waiting for an answer.

"Drying ye off."

"But I've not yet finished my bath."

"I'll put ye back in soon."

"What are ye doing now?"

"Ravishing ye."

Her mouth fell open, silent question still on her lips. Resistance to kissing her was futile. He did so with abandon, sucking on her plump lips and running his tongue over her smooth teeth. Tossing the damp towel somewhere behind him, he picked her up again, one hand behind her back and the other beneath her knees. She clung to him, shivering—he hoped mostly from desire and not only the chill of the room.

Daniel laid her gently on the bed, coming down on top of her, wishing to keep her warm. She watched his every move, curiosity and hunger in her gaze.

"How will ye ravish me?" she asked.

"Ye're not as shy as I'd have expected," he murmured. "Then again, ye've surprised me at every turn."

Myra smiled wickedly, even though she blushed like mad. "I've seen many things behind the walls of Foulis. Things that have made me...curious. I'd never thought to be in a position to experience them."

He raised a brow. "Oh, aye? Like what?"

Myra's eyes widened, her lips forming a shocked little O.

"Did ye think I wouldna ask?" he teased, nipping at her chin.

"Well…nay."

Daniel chuckled deeply as he slid his lips over her neck, and then up to her ear to whisper. "I want to know everything ye saw. Did ye see lovers kiss as we have?"

"Aye…"

"And do this?" He slid his tongue along her chest until he reached her breasts where he once more teased her nipples to taut peaks.

"Mmm…" she moaned, gripped his shoulders.

"What about this?" He moved lower, taking his time to kiss her belly, her hip, lick and nip her sensitive flesh. Her stomach quivered, her fingers dug deeper into his shoulders, slid up to rake through his hair. He liked the way she touched him, the way it sent shivers of pleasure rushing through him.

He glanced up, saw that her gaze was firmly placed on his, watching his every move. Daniel slid even lower, nudging her thighs apart. He breathed hotly on her mound. Myra's lips parted in a carnal moan, but still she watched him.

"And this, lass? Did ye see lovers do this?"

She swallowed hard, her breaths coming in pants. And then she nodded. Her eyes were afire, her cheeks flaming red, and she pulled on his head, as though begging him to do just what he wanted.

He'd not wait any longer to taste the slick, pink folds she offered him. Daniel nuzzled her dark curls, widened her legs. Used his thumbs to part her slick folds and then delved inside. He tasted her slowly, lazily, reveling in every one of her hitched breaths and moans. Their eyes remained locked on one another. Scorching. Exhilarating. Blood rushed with intense force through his veins. Daniel quickened the pace, flicking his tongue rapidly over her little nub of pleasure. Watched her watching him.

Myra cried out, her eyes finally closing as her head fell backward. Her thighs shook as they clenched his face and her hands fisted in his hair. Daniel was relentless in his pursuit of her pleasure. He slid a finger inside her tight sheath, in and out, mimicking what he wished to do with his cock. His own desire raged and pulsed, but he wouldn't stop. Not until—

Back arching, legs stiffening, Myra let out a shriek as a climax rippled through her. Her sex quivered, slick and hot. He continued to lave at her until the fluttering of her peak subsided.

Myra fell back against the pillows, her body trembling, expression sated. She smiled, blinked open hazy eyes and gazed at him.

"That was..." She licked her lips, fingers clenching in the bedclothes.

"Aye?" he goaded.

"Amazing."

"Everything ye thought?" He kissed her inner thigh, sliding up her body.

"And more." She slid her hand up his arm, touched his neck and tugged him close for a kiss.

Daniel let himself sink against her, his cock fitted against the heat of her. He delved his tongue inside her mouth, kissing her with all the passion he possessed. But he had to pull back, or else he would flip up his plaid and drive home.

"Is it always like this?" she asked.

"That and better."

"With...everything?" Her cheeks flamed redder than they already were.

"Are ye referring to the bedding?"

She nodded.

The Highlander's Lady

"Aye. At first there might be a pinch, since ye're a maiden, but after 'twill only be pleasure, I can promise ye that."

She smiled. "Thank ye, Daniel."

"For what?"

"For caring about my pleasure."

"Aye, lass. I'd not be married to a woman I didna wish to see fulfilled."

"There are men who dinna," she said thoughtfully, glancing away.

"What do ye mean?"

She shrugged. "'Tis only I doubt that the Ross would have sought to please me."

Daniel shook his head. "I canna imagine that he would. The man is evil, selfish and only out for himself."

Myra nodded. "He's the incarnation of the devil himself." Her voice was filled with bitterness.

The moment of spellbinding perfection vanished. Daniel was once more filled with rage. Ross would pay for what he'd done to Myra, to their country. He prayed that the Bruce was safe and that Wallace and his men were able to get to him soon.

A loud, swift knock sounded at the door.

"Daniel, I need to speak with ye."

Daniel sighed deeply, his gaze meeting Myra's. "'Tis my cousin Ronan. I'd best see what he needs." Louder, he called to his cousin, "Be out in a minute."

Myra nodded. "Aye. Please…"

Daniel shifted off the bed and grabbed her chemise, tossing it to her before he picked up his sporran. He glanced toward her, taking in the sudden vulnerability that covered her expression as she shyly slipped back into her chemise.

"Will ye tell me what is happening?"

Daniel stepped forward, pressed his palm to her cheek. "Rest assured, as my wife, ye will always be informed."

Chapter Nineteen

As soon as the door closed, Myra sank onto the bed and let out the breath she'd been holding. What in the world had just happened? How had she allowed it to happen? Her body had taken over her mind, that was how. Desire had drugged her, intoxicated her and she'd been helpless to do anything but enjoy the pleasure Daniel gave her.

And enjoyed was an understatement. She wanted him to rush back to the room and do it again. She wanted to explore his body, kiss his— What had she heard the women say? Cock? Kiss his cock and see if he gained just as much pleasure from it as she had. Having watched a woman do so before, she had an idea that he would.

A sharp knock jolted her from her thoughts. Myra rushed to throw the simple gown over her head and then opened the door. Marta greeted her with a discreet nod.

"My lady, we would clean up the bath. And I've brought a new gown and underthings for ye. They were the late lady of the castle's, and I thought ye could use them."

Marta held out a soft wool gown, dark green in color with gold ancient swirls on the hem and sleeves.

"Thank ye."

"'Tis my pleasure, my lady. They ought to get some use and 'tis a shame for ye to be in that wretched gown, pardon my frankness."

Myra smiled. "'Tis horrid, I agree."

Myra swiftly removed her old garments and donned the new ones. She ran her hands over the soft new hose, rolled them up and proceeded to tug on her boots. She had no intention of staying in this room. If Daniel was going to allow his wife to always be informed, then he wouldn't mind if she came down to find him and Ronan while they spoke. And if he did mind, she would simply find a way to listen in. After all, she was very good at sneaking around.

"Your husband has requested that ye sup in here. He bade me tell ye that he would return as soon as he could, but not to wait for his return before ye eat."

Myra frowned. So he would tell her she could be informed but then make sure she didn't come down with him? Placing her hands on her hips, she tapped her fingers as she thought on the housekeeper's words. She nodded, instead of responding. There was no way she was going to stay put, but the housekeeper didn't need to know that.

"I've already asked the kitchen to send up a platter. Should be here—" Another knock interrupted her. "Now, I see."

Marta opened the door and in came three servants carrying trays of food and drink. They set it out on the small table that had previously held her soaps. The servants bowed their way out, and Myra waited patiently as Marta straightened the room and then left as well. Finally. She thought Marta would never leave.

The Highlander's Lady

The scents the food sent up smelled heavenly. Myra grabbed a hot pastry filled with meat, burning her tongue on the first bite. She blew out her breath, trying to cool her tongue and then took another hot bite. Delicious. She shoveled down the pastry, but the rest would have to wait. She needed to find out what it was Ronan needed to speak with Daniel about. Could be about the Bruce, could be about Ross, she didn't know, but she intended to be informed now, not when Daniel was ready for her.

Before trying the door that led to the corridor, Myra examined every wall, corner, nook and cranny within the room to decipher if there was a hidden entrance. Sadly, there wasn't. Well, she could easily find her way downstairs as everyone else did—the actual staircase.

She slipped out the main chamber door, glad there was no one outside or within view. The corridor was dark and shadows jumped every few feet. Myra took a moment to gain her bearings and let her eyes adjust then tried to remember which way she'd come from the stairs. The left she thought. Oh, why hadn't she paid more attention?

Moving toward the left, she walked silently down the hall until she came to the end. No stairs. Ugh. It had been the right then. She turned around and began walking the other way. Coming to a stop, she plastered herself to the wall when someone stepped up to the door she believed was hers and placed their ear to the wood. Who could be eavesdropping on *her*?

Biting her lip to keep from asking that very question, she watched as the figure retreated in the opposite direction. Well, this put her in a conundrum. Should she follow the disturbing eavesdropper or try to find Daniel? There was always the option of getting information from Daniel later. She wouldn't be able to figure out who was spying on her though.

Myra slid along the wall, keeping a safe distance from the person who slipped just as stealthily as she down the stairs and rounded a corner away from the great hall. They came into the light just long enough that she could see it was a female servant. Not one she immediately recognized. As Myra continued to follow the woman, she tried to think back on every face she'd seen since arriving. The somber, noble profile of the person she followed did not match any of the servants she'd come into contact with so far.

Suddenly, the woman stopped, stilled as if listening. Myra jerked within an alcove just as the servant turned. Had she made a noise and not realized it? Myra shook her head. No. She'd been sure to be silent. The woman was most likely on edge from having been spying. Myra's nerves prickled. The click of heels sounded just outside the alcove—almost indiscernible save for Myra had been waiting for it. She held her breath. Expected the servant to peek into the alcove, but appearing to have lost her nerve, the woman took off at a run.

Damn!

Myra slipped from the alcove and tried to follow, but lost the trail as the woman dashed down one corridor and then another. Myra stopped when she reached the kitchens, Cook and her many servants glancing up from their work.

"Can we help ye? Did ye not find the meal satisfying?" Cook asked, a frown marring her features.

"Nay, 'twas delicious. I was simply looking for someone."

One of the scullions turned to glance surreptitiously toward the back entrance to the kitchens. Her spy would be long gone now…

"There's no one here." Cook's lips pressed together as she glanced around the kitchen.

Myra was immediately on edge. They knew who'd been spying on her, who she'd been looking for, but they would keep quiet about it. That made her nervous. Were they in league with Ross? Were all the occupants in danger?

The Highlander's Lady

She suppressed a shiver and made her way back toward her room. Waiting for Daniel within the confines of her chamber may be safer considering they could have very well just landed inside a den of vipers. As soon as she closed the door behind her, Myra lifted the heavy slab of wood and barred the door. She looked under the bed and behind the chairs and tapestries to make sure no one hid within. All was empty.

Now she simply had to wait for Daniel's return.

Myra sat in one of the wooden chairs and stared at the mound of food before her. Her foot tapped nervously on the floor and she kept her arms crossed over her chest. She felt like an easy target, her only weapon, the dirk at her hip. She knew how to use it, that was for sure; she only prayed no one but Daniel tried to come through her door. Even Marta was suspect in her mind. The woman had after all taken an enormous amount of time in leaving when she'd left the food.

Myra leaned her head back against the chair. She'd thought for certain once she reached Eilean Donan she would be safe—well relatively safe, given that Ross was considered an ally to the future King of Scotland.

The handle of the chamber door jiggled violently causing Myra to jump. She gripped the dirk at her hip and tip-toed toward the door, prepared to strike.

"Myra, 'tis Daniel. Open the door."

Acute relief filled her. She sheathed her dirk and lifted the bar. When he came in, she was surprised how glad she was to see him. She was also surprised by the instant sweep of desire that filled her. Turning away from him, she walked toward one of the slitted windows and pretended to be occupied with gazing at the courtyard below—except, she suddenly was. There was the woman, racing across the bailey toward the stables.

"Daniel, who is that?" she asked, her voice frantic.

Daniel rushed toward the window and gazed out, but the woman had already disappeared inside the stables.

"Who?"

"A woman. Let us wait. She may yet come out."

"Why?"

Myra told Daniel of how she'd seen the person spying and followed her, only to lose her in the kitchens.

"Why were ye out in the corridor?"

She'd forgotten about that one part... "I was looking for the privy."

Daniel seemed to take her at her word. "Are ye sure she was spying and not simply coming to check on your meal?"

Myra shook her head. "Nay, she was most definitely spying."

Daniel nodded. "I've an idea this place is full of the enemy."

"What do you mean?"

"Ronan believes there is more than just Ross who has sided with England. We must be constantly on alert."

Myra's heartbeat shot up. When she spoke, her voice came out a croak. "Truly? Here?"

Daniel nodded, then pointed below. "Is that her?"

Myra glanced down, seeing the woman sneak from the stables back toward the kitchen. What could she have been doing? Delivering a message? Sending one? She could only nod, her throat suddenly swollen. They were in danger.

"I'll be back."

"Nay, wait! Dinna leave me here. Take me with ye."

Daniel frowned and shook his head. "Nay, I canna. 'Tis too dangerous. Ye must stay here. Bar the door."

"If ye leave me here, I will only follow ye," she threatened.

"Myra"—he gripped her shoulders, forcing her to glance at him—"dinna be foolish. I've just told ye there are enemies

The Highlander's Lady

everywhere and we're not even sure who is who. I need to go speak to the servant and find out what she's about. Ye'll only be a distraction."

Myra tried to be offended but she couldn't. He was right. Daniel would be quicker about getting the information if he didn't have to worry about her. Not that she would prove to be the distraction that he thought she might be, but that wouldn't change his mind. Even if she was silent as the grave, invisible, he'd still worry. Then he'd not get the information.

"Would ye feel better if ye'd more of a weapon than your dirk?"

She nodded solemnly.

"Then take my sword." He pulled the claymore from his back and held it out to her.

The handle was carved and studded with a large emerald. And was heavier than a tree. She'd not expected that. Myra used all of her strength to hold it.

"Hurry back."

"Aye, my lady." He bowed low to her in a show of mock chivalry, which only brought a smile to her face.

"Ye can try to jest, Laird Murray, but I know deep inside ye're a gentleman."

"Only for ye."

She wished to kiss him, to pretend that none of the dangerous problems were clouding above them. But that wasn't possible and it wasn't realistic. She shoved him playfully toward the door.

"Go, so ye can hurry back and tell me what the scamp was doing."

Daniel chuckled as he departed. She quickly put the board up on the door and sat down to wait, the weighted claymore carefully on her lap. One wrong move and she might cut herself. Whisky would be good about now. She glanced at the jug of wine and poured a healthy cup. Wine would do too.

Daniel snuck down the back servants' stairs until he reached the kitchen at their end. Muffled voices sounded through the door which was open a crack. He glanced inside and watched them work. Watched as the woman who'd spied on Myra took off her cloak and hung it on a hook, then proceeded to knead a mound of dough. Her strawberry blonde hair was pulled back tightly in a bun at the nape of her neck. She didn't have the look of a servant, but rather a lady. 'Twas odd. Very odd.

What appeared to be the head cook walked over toward her, nudged her shoulder and whispered in her ear. They exchanged a few words and nods, then the cook left the other woman to her task of making bread.

Daniel pushed the door open, and enjoyed the startled look on the faces of those who were guilty of some form of deception.

"What are ye about?" he asked the lady-look-alike point blank.

Her startled expression quickly turned serene, bored even. "Kneading dough."

"Ye know what I'm asking." Daniel crossed his arms over his chest.

"I'm sure she doesna, my laird," the cook started, but Daniel cut her off.

"Out. Clear out."

"We're trying to feed an army!" she blustered.

"Then advise your kneader to accompany me outside for a moment."

The lady looked terrified at that, shaking her head. But the cook straightened her spine and said, "Go, lass."

The Highlander's Lady

As if understanding there would be no getting out of it, the woman squared her shoulders, grabbed her cloak from a hook and slipped it over her tight form. She reminded him a bit of Myra in her resolve. He followed her out, conscious that she may turn a dagger on him.

She swiftly rounded on him once they were outside. "What do ye want?"

"What is your name?" he asked sternly.

"None of your business."

"Is that any way to talk to a laird?"

"Depends. Ye dinna know who *I* am."

She had him there. Was it possible she was of higher rank than he was? Daniel decided to change the subject.

"Why were ye spying on my wife?"

The woman huffed a breath and glanced from side to side as if routing out her escape.

"Ye canna run. I will only chase ye."

"I wasn't spying."

"Then what were ye doing?"

"I was…checking."

"Checking? What the hell does that mean?" Daniel could feel his temper beginning to flare.

"I canna tell ye." She folded her arms.

"Then I shall have to inform the Bruce and Wallace there is a traitor in their midst."

At that she practically snarled at him. "Ye'll do no such thing."

"Watch me," Daniel snarled right back. Who the hell did she think she was?

"The only thing I'll be watching is ye embarrassing yourself."

That was not the response he expected. Daniel frowned further, unable to form words in response.

"Mind yourself and your wife, and stay out of my way."

She tried to push past him, but Daniel shot out his hand to grasp her above the elbow, and none too kindly.

"My wife's safety, and the safety of Scotland is why I'm standing here with ye, lass." He kept his voice low, allowing the deadly threat of his anger to seep into his words.

"I worry for Scotland's safety as well."

"Then why do ye lie?"

She rolled her eyes and yanked her arm back. "I dinna lie, ye big oaf. I'm on your side. I was simply checking on your wife to make sure she was all right. There are a lot of traitors trolling the camps."

"How can I trust ye?"

She shrugged. "I canna force ye too. But I can promise if ye press the issue, ye will only suffer for it."

"At whose hands?" He waited for another lie to come from her mouth, but was wholly unexpecting what she said next.

"The Bruce. Your cousin Ronan."

"Tell me your name."

"Julianna." Ronan rounded the corner, a look of possession on his face. The woman he'd called Julianna, the spy, reddened in the cheeks and ducked her face.

"Ye two know each other?" Daniel asked his cousin.

"Aye, and ye?" Ronan scowled, his light hair falling over his eyes giving him a dangerous look. The man looked so much like his older brother, Magnus, it was uncanny.

"Only just met. She was…checking in on Myra."

Ronan nodded slowly. "A word, cousin?"

Forcing back a growl of frustration, Daniel followed his cousin.

"What is it?" Daniel asked, watching over Ronan's shoulder as Julianna slipped away.

"Dinna press her."

The Highlander's Lady

"Why?" He studied his cousin, seeing the frustration and admiration written on his face.

"I've yet to figure her out, but I do know the Bruce and Wallace both think very highly of her."

"Is she a lady in disguise?"

Ronan shrugged. "I dinna know."

"Are ye taken with her?" Daniel couldn't believe it. The great and mighty Ronan taken with a woman—and a hellion at that!

Ronan glowered at him, crossed his arms. "I ought to call ye out for that."

"Go ahead. I could use a good fight."

Ronan grinned. "Let's go then."

Chapter Twenty

The floor beneath Myra's boots was surely wearing thin from her pacing. Where the hell was Daniel? He'd said he'd be back quickly. Had the woman lured him into an alcove and killed him? Offered him a cup of poisoned wine?

Every scenario flashed before her eyes. All of them bad. All of them ending with Daniel's death.

This wasn't going to work. She had to get out of this chamber and find out what was happening. But just as she reached the door, shouts came from outside. Myra rushed back toward the window to see what was happening. From the fields beyond the walls, she saw men—warriors—rushing the castle walls. Oh, Lord! Pray be friends and not foe!

Friends would not rush a castle, battle cries ripping from their throats.

Had to be the Ross warriors. That meant they'd gotten a signal. Wallace had not been successful in his retrieval of the future king.

The Highlander's Lady

"Dammit!" Myra stomped her foot, envisioning all of Scotland crumbling around them.

Whirling in a circle, she took in the room, trying to figure out what she could use as a weapon. The claymore was just too damn big. Candle sticks, the basin… There was nothing in this forsaken chamber! She'd have to make do with what she had. She could certainly thump someone into unconsciousness if she had too. Myra gripped her dirk in one hand and shoved the candlestick under her arm as she opened the door to her room. Hand free of the door handle, she held the candlestick in a defensive measure. The corridor was once again empty. This time she welcomed the eerie silence.

Myra crept down the hallway toward the end—the opposite direction of the main stairs. There had to be a set for servants. She found it at the end of the hall, hidden within what appeared to be an alcove. Clever. She'd missed them before. The stairs were dark. Why didn't anyone light torches in this place? Well, she supposed she knew the answer to that. It would use resources they could save for a later day. Today was that day—they were being attacked!

Taking the stairs slowly, sliding one foot along until she reached the edge of each step, she descended. There were no noises from below. Not like when she'd been attacked at Foulis. At her own home the sounds of the enemy echoed all around her, the stuff of nightmares. Here, it was as though she were all alone in the world.

Myra paused in her steps to listen carefully. She no longer heard the shouts from outside. Was that even possible? Were the walls so thick that they would disguise the sounds of an attack? That didn't sound very good for the castle inhabitants. Was it possible she'd gotten it wrong and they were not being attacked? Only one way to find out. She finished descending the stairs and pushed open the door to the kitchen. Inside, she took note that the kitchen staff looked scared, gripping spoons and knives so hard their knuckles were white.

"What is happening?" she asked them, hoping they would not shun her as they had before.

A woman with reddish-blonde hair turned around. That same aquiline nose. 'Twas the woman who'd spied on her. Myra stiffened. "Ye…"

The woman nodded. "I'm no enemy, my lady. That I can promise ye."

"Are we under attack?"

She shook her head, hesitated, then nodded. "In a way, aye."

Myra's hands faltered, she dropped her arms to the sides, no longer in attack mode and frowned at the strange woman. "What in all of Purgatory does that mean?"

"I'm Julianna."

"And? Will ye not tell me what ye're talking about?" Myra said through gritted teeth.

Julianna glanced around at the other servants, then letting out a long, annoyed breath she said. "Aye. The Ross warriors have been camped outside of our walls for days on end. Every so often they make a run for our walls, trying to scare us out. They know the Bruce is not here and they hope that we will abandon the castle."

"How do ye know they are Ross men?" Myra was instantly on alert, recalling what Daniel had said about the castle being full of enemies. Julianna had been spying on her after all.

"I know."

Myra waited for her to explain further, but it soon became evident she would say no more.

"Then they will not breach the walls?"

"Nay. We will not allow it."

The Highlander's Lady

Myra cocked her head, studying Julianna. She was a strange one. It almost felt like she spoke in riddles.

"Where is Daniel?"

"Fighting with his cousin."

"Fighting?" They were under attack! Julianna had only been stalling!

"I can see from your expression what ye are thinking, my lady. I assure ye, we are not under attack and that they fight only with each other. 'Tis a warrior thing." Julianna waved her hand as if dismissing the topic. "Should ye like to try an apple tart?"

It was evident that Myra wasn't going to get any answers from Julianna, and she was definitely not hungry for a tart. She whirled on her heel and headed toward the arched door that led to the great hall.

"Where are ye going?" From behind came the click of Julianna's heels as she tried to catch up with Myra's quickened steps.

When she reached her side, she walked just as fast. Irritation boiled deep. Myra stopped walking altogether and faced a stunned Julianna.

"Ye make no sense, and I wish to be away from ye." She lifted her chin, trying to put the servant in her place.

"I'm afraid that is impossible." Julianna's jaw was set in an alarmingly tight edge.

"Why?"

"I was charged with...watching over ye."

"By who?" Myra crossed her arms over her chest.

"My brother."

"Who is he and why does he want ye to watch over me?"

"Never ye mind who he is, save know that he is powerful. He wants me to watch over ye, because he's heard a rumor about ye."

Myra's ire was piqued, and she glowered at the woman. "So your mysterious brother thinks that I'm a threat?"

Julianna shook her head vehemently. "Let us go to your room and I shall explain."

At that, Myra laughed heartily. "I dinna think so. Know that I can defend myself, but I'll not willingly invite ye in to kill me."

This time Julianna laughed. "I'd not harm ye at all. I'm to protect ye."

"Well, I dinna need your protection. I've Daniel's and my own." She shook the candlestick at the woman.

Julianna nodded, then leaned in close. "I swear to ye, I'd not harm ye. I canna tell ye all here. The walls have ears," she whispered.

Myra glanced around at the shadowed corners and darkened alcoves. "Does no one here like to light torches?"

Julianna laughed once more. "There is plenty of light from the windows."

There were three meager windows in this passageway, all at least ten feet apart. Hardly conducive to seeing.

"Fine. Ye can come to my room, but I warn ye, I have no problem stopping ye if ye try to harm me." Myra hoped she wasn't making the wrong choice.

Julianna nodded, and swept past her and headed toward the stairs leading up. Myra had no choice but to chase after her. Julianna stopped every few feet to listen, then would continue on. Myra did followed suit, not hearing anything, but feeling uneasy just the same. She craved the peace within the walls. Once they reached her room, Julianna went to bar the door and Myra shot out her hand to stop her.

"Nay, leave it unbarred."

"Suit yourself," Julianna replied, her brow furrowed. "But if the door crashes open, be prepared."

Myra stood, arms crossed and watched as Julianna inspected her chamber for anything out of the ordinary, similar to what she herself had done before. She allowed it to

The Highlander's Lady

go on, but as soon as the woman was finished, she wasted no time in asking what she needed to know.

"Who are ye? What is going on?"

Julianna smiled. It was a friendly smile. Not at all what she'd expected. It was unnerving and threw her off her guard.

"Ye've nothing to fear from me. We can be friends."

"Not if ye keep deferring all my questions."

"All right, I'm not one to beat around the bush. Now that we're inside your chamber and there is obviously no one here to listen in on us, I shall tell ye. We received word of Ross' defecting to the English, although he would seek to keep it a secret, and in turn, murder the Bruce. 'Twas his mission from Longshanks."

"And? Where is the Bruce?"

"He's away, safe."

"How do ye know this? Not even Wallace knew it."

"Robert had to keep a few things secret, even from his own men."

"But not from ye? Are ye his lover?"

Julianna laughed. "Dinna be silly. We are family, nothing more. Blood is thicker than water, and so Robert trusts me wholly with his counsel."

"I still dinna understand. If ye knew that Ross was bad, why did the Bruce do nothing to stop him from massacring my entire clan?" She seethed with anger, for the unjustness of what happened to her, her brother's death, the pain and loss of so many.

Julianna did look sad then, but it was only a flash before her features were smooth once more. She looked so regal, so well acquainted with her own feelings. Myra shivered. There was much more than what met the eye with this woman.

"There was not enough time," she said quietly. "Robert was very saddened when he heard the news, which was why he left immediately, pretending to agree to Ross' request for a meeting. He knew it would be an ambush. Knew that ye would be coming here. I too am sorry for all ye've been through, and for the loss of your brother. If I lost my brother, I would not know what to do with myself."

Myra's heart clenched and the pain of Byron's death, all she'd lost and the uncertainty of her future, was felt acutely all over again. She swallowed back her tears, and lifted her head, smoothed her features just as Julianna had, and found that it was not as difficult as she thought it would be.

"Why did Wallace not know of what happened at Foulis?"

"I suspect there was not enough time for Robert to tell him."

"Aye, indeed, Wallace ran out after the Bruce believing him to be in danger. Why would he not tell him? Makes no sense to me." Myra felt her pain turn to anger once more. Too many games. Too many people keeping things hidden when knowledge would have made everyone's lives that much easier.

"I dinna get in the way of Robert's thoughts or machinations. I simply listen and follow his orders."

Myra growled under her breath and turned in a circle, frustration rattling her bones. Where was Daniel? She needed to sort this out with him, not with Julianna.

"Myra..." Julianna came closer, reached out her arm as though she'd comfort Myra, but then dropped it back toward her side. "There are no words for what ye've been through. No words for all that is going on. I but thought ye should know ye're not alone. That ye did a good thing in coming here. The Bruce will surely see ye rewarded."

That was the last straw for Myra. "I care nothing for a reward! I only came here because it was my brother's dying wish. If not for that, I'd be at home, at Foulis, putting my castle back together. Helping my clan rebuild their homes. Taking care of my brother's widow and unborn bairn. Not

The Highlander's Lady

here! Dinna mistake me in my allegiance to the Bruce, he has it, but dinna also think I have no other responsibilities."

Julianna was visibly taken aback. "Then we'd best make sure ye return soon."

Myra huffed. The woman had no idea what was at stake within Myra's own life, or that going back wasn't that simple and she wasn't about to get into it with her.

At that moment, the door opened. Myra whirled around, ready to take off the head of whoever barged into her chamber only to see that it was Daniel. He leaned against the frame, filling the doorway with his body. He was magnificent and recently cleaned up. Even wore his hair back in a queue as she remembered him. His eyes were sharp and stared from her to Julianna, question in his gaze.

"Apologies for intruding. I didna know ye had company."

"Julianna was just leaving," Myra said sharply.

Julianna raised a brow. "I shall find ye…soon."

Myra wanted to shout for her not to bother, to go back to the kitchen and bake bread, but she knew that was not only rude, but unnecessary. Julianna did not mean to frustrate Myra. She was only trying to help as best she could. Juliana didn't have to confide in her, and yet she'd done it all the same.

"Thank ye!" Myra called after her.

Julianna turned and smiled, dipping her head in silent acceptance of Myra's unspoken apology. She closed the door quietly.

"What was that about?" Daniel's voice was brusque and he crossed his large arms.

Myra tried not to laugh at the stern look on his face—it was all too obvious he was working hard to keep it there, for his eyes kept glancing down at her breasts making her face and other parts fill with heat.

For a few moments she contemplated whether or not she would tell Daniel what had transpired. She would. The truth of it was, she trusted him. Completely. He was the only person she'd been able to trust since her brother's murder. Whenever she was with him, she felt safe. He would protect her, of that she had no doubt.

"The Bruce knew of Ross' change of heart before we arrived."

A black cloud filled Daniel's face and she was certainly glad she was not on the receiving end of his anger.

"What? How is that possible?"

Myra shrugged. "Julianna claims the Bruce knew of Ross' defection to the English. She didn't say how."

"And instead of warning anyone, they kept this information to themselves?" Daniel's eyes blazed with anger.

Myra rushed toward him, took his cold hands into her warm grip and squeezed. "Daniel, dinna be angry for my sake. There wasn't enough time for them to warn anyone. At least the Bruce knew and when he accepted the invitation from Ross to meet, he didna walk into a trap."

"How was it that Wallace didna know of it? He is supposed to be the Bruce's right hand."

That part, Myra didn't understand either. "The only reason I can come up with is he informed the left hand and didn't think the right needed to know."

"Who is his left?"

She shook her head, studying Daniel's large hands. He had scratches all along the knuckles and his skin was rough. "I dinna know. I suspect it is Julianna."

"Julianna?" Daniel looked bewildered. "The kitchen wench?"

"She is more than that. She is his family."

"Of what degree? Ten times removed? The Bruce would not have his family working his kitchens."

The Highlander's Lady

"Are we not all family in some way? Maybe she was adopted in. I dinna know. I could hardly ask her. She speaks in riddles."

"That I agree with."

"Can I get ye some wine?" Myra asked, hoping to calm Daniel's anger.

He nodded and slumped into a chair. "With Wallace chasing after the Bruce and the Bruce not truly in danger, what are we to do about the Ross warriors?"

He said *we*…

"Have ye spoken to Ronan about it?"

Daniel snickered. "Sort of."

"What do ye mean by that?"

"We had a wee fight."

She noticed then the redness beneath one eye. Must be where he scratched up his knuckles as well. Myra smiled. "Who won?"

"I did, of course."

"Of course." She poured him a cup of wine. Outside the sun was setting and the moon shone silver behind the clouds. "What did ye think of the bluster the Ross warriors put on?"

"I found it…childish. Annoying. Thought we were under attack but the bastards only threw filth over the walls and then ran away."

Myra crinkled her nose and sat across from Daniel, handing him the cup.

"Are ye not going to have any?" he asked.

"I forgot. This whole mess has me tied up in knots." She rubbed her eyes, trying to rub away the tension that had built behind them.

"I'll get it for ye." Daniel set down his cup and stood gracefully for a man of his size. He poured her the cup and set it before her, then held his cup to hers. "To us."

"To us."

Somehow, they would make it through this unscathed. And somehow she would find peace and happiness... She hoped.

Chapter Twenty-One

"I have a confession to make."

Myra jerked her gaze up from the cup of wine Daniel had given her. "Confession?"

He nodded, his expression grim. "Aye, lass."

He said nothing further. When the room filled heavily with the words he left unsaid, so full of doubt, question and fear, Myra broke the silence. "Well, tell me what it is, Daniel."

She sat forward, steadying her breaths, trying to ready herself for what he would confess.

"I know ye plan to escape. That ye never planned to stay married to me. I canna allow that."

That was not at all what she expected. Picking up her cup of wine, she took a long slow sip. Despite her efforts to remain calm, her heart kicked at her ribs painfully and her stomach swirled with the stress of it all. He knew. That meant she wouldn't be able to easily remove herself to Foulis. He would only follow her there. That meant there was no escape from this marriage.

Like it or not, she was going to be Lady Murray. Lady of his castles. And what of her own people? Myra slowly sat back in the chair, feeling the wood dig into her spine and shoulder blades as she pressed herself hard against it, almost as though she wished to become the chair. The wine left a sour taste in her mouth, made worse with his confession. How the hell had he figured it out, and why did he want so badly to see it through?

Not that a part of her didn't also want to...

'Twas naïve of her to have thought that he would never figure out her plan, that he wouldn't confront her on it. How many other things had she been naïve about? Her ability to rule Foulis until the bairn was born? Her ability to be a wife? Perhaps she should creep back to where she belonged, within the castle walls and tell Daniel he was better off with one of the women his mother found for him.

"Lass?"

Myra glanced up, her eyes connecting with his. Daniel gazed at her, concern written in his features, and regret. He'd not wanted to tell her he knew she'd leave, so why had he?

"Will ye not say anything?"

Myra swallowed hard, keeping her gaze steady on his.

"What makes ye think I'll run?"

Daniel's lip quirked into a smile. "Ye think I jest?"

"One can never be too certain about anything," she challenged.

"Truer words have never been uttered." He slapped his hands on his knees and leaned forward, his breath tickling her nose. "If ye must have me say it aloud, ye're eye twitches whenever talk of our marriage is uttered."

"Ye're lucky 'tis not my fist clutching a dagger twitching."

Daniel chuckled. "'Tis good to see ye've not lost your sense of humor. Ye know the one thing that drew me to ye

The Highlander's Lady

when I met ye all those years ago was your vibrant personality. Why did ye shut me out, Myra?"

Confusion struck deep. "Shut ye out?"

"Why did ye not come back?"

"What are ye talking about?"

"At Foulis. We danced, we laughed, I went to get ye more ale while ye said ye needed a moment and then ye did not return."

Myra did not recall that being the case at all. Vivid memories of returning to the great hall only to see that Daniel had filled the space where she'd been with several other ladies ran rampant in her mind. "That is not true. And we've already had this discussion."

Daniel shook his head. "Not all the way, we never really delved into it. Tell me the way of it, because I waited three days for ye to come out of hiding."

Hiding. That was what she'd done after seeing that. And aye, three days was how long he waited, but she'd not thought he'd waited for her. She thought he was just using all that time to get sow his oats with the other ladies present.

"Ye were not waiting for me, Daniel. Let us not pretend that I meant something to ye back then, just as I will not pretend that I mean something to ye now."

Daniel's nostrils flared and he jumped to his feet. His plaid swung angrily against his knees, hands fisted at his side. "Ye are even more naïve than I thought, or ye know just the right way to twist a man's kilt to make him angry."

Myra jumped to her feet too. How dare he start flinging insults at her? She stepped forward, her boot tips hitting against his. Tilting her head all the way back, she glared daggers up at the giant whose gaze was equally enraged. The power of her anger overcame her fears and her hands flew to her hips. She was not going to back down.

"If ye think so low of me, why would ye want to marry me? Is it pity? Ye feel bad that Byron's been killed so ye wanted to help out his lowly, unimpressive sister? Or is it even worse? Ye have a vendetta against the Ross and ye knew he and I were to wed so ye thought to steal me away instead?"

"Are ye mad or daft, or both?" Daniel growled, his face coming within inches of hers.

"How dare ye!"

"How dare I? Ye slur my manhood and my honor with your insults. I should take ye over my knee and paddle some sense into ye. Lucky ye are that I'm the one who found ye covered in blood in the woods. Another man would not be so kind to ye and your stubborn, ill-tempered mouth."

Myra gasped, rage flushing her cheeks. For once, she was speechless. But not for long.

"Well, I'm sorry that ye had to come across me then. Sorry for having agreed to be your wife. But I'm not sorry for who I am. That is something I'll never be sorry for."

Daniel took a step back, his expression changing for a moment before he whirled around and faced the hearth. He stomped toward it, leaving Myra feeling cold in his wake. Where had the fight in him gone? What had she said? Mayhap he was simply realizing the error he'd made in choosing her to be his wife.

Even though she'd thought the same thing, as much as said it…now she had doubts. Regrets in fact for having spilled the words.

"At Foulis," she started, then stopped. Myra huffed a breath and trudged toward the slim windows, pulled back the fur covering and felt every bit of the chill wind that swept into the room. Her breath came out in a puff of steam and gooseflesh covered her arms, the cold and the emotions storming inside her making her nipples hard. The sky was clear, for once since she'd trekked out of the secret passage of her castle. Hundreds, thousands of tiny golden stars dotted

The Highlander's Lady

the sky, and though there were no clouds she could still smell the snow.

"At Foulis?" Daniel said from behind her.

She'd not heard him approach. Myra didn't turn around. She took a few moments, several deep breaths and worked up the nerve to say what she had wanted to say a few moments before. 'Twould hurt her pride, embarrass her for certain, but if she did not say it now she was certain she would come up with every excuse she possibly could until she never told him. That would leave too much unsaid between them.

"At Foulis, I thought I'd found something special in ye," she managed to say, though her voice sounded strangled. "I rushed off thinking I'd come back to ye worshiping me, showering me with affection. Ye're right. I was naïve, and since that moment, I've changed. I've grown up."

Daniel's hands slipped onto her shoulders and he squeezed gently, reassuringly. "If ye'd come back to me I would have."

"Ye see, that's the thing ye dinna understand, Daniel. I did come back."

"When?"

"I told ye afore, moments later, not long. Ye were surrounded by women. Smiling, laughing, touching their arms, just as ye'd done to me, and I knew that I was not special."

Hot breath caressed along her ear as Daniel whispered, "Ye were special. If only ye'd watched a moment longer ye would have seen me shake them all off. I only had eyes for ye. Waited with baited breath day after day for ye to return to me. But 'twas as if ye vanished. Gone. When I asked of ye, your brother…"

"Dinna say it. I have an idea of what he said."

"Do ye?"

"Aye. I believe the negotiations were already being considered with Ross, although they were not finalized until recently. My father believed it would be best for our clan, and I think my brother would have pushed ye away. In any case, Byron was overprotective of me. Worried over me worse than my nursemaids."

"Why?"

"'Tis a long story."

"We've nowhere to go."

Myra let go of the fur flap, feeling the instant warmth as the cold air was not able to stream in so easily. She turned around, aware of how close to Daniel she stood. Every whisker on his face seemed to catch her attention, diverting her from the conversation. She knew that it would be rough and yet soft at the same time. Without thinking, she reached toward his face and stroked two fingers over his stubble. Daniel closed his eyes momentarily. When he opened them his pupils were dilated.

"Ye think to distract me," he murmured.

Myra gave a small smile. "Mayhap I was distracting myself."

"Do ye need a distraction? Is it so difficult to talk about what happened in the past?"

"Aye, 'tis."

Daniel grasped her hand in his, pulling it away from his cheek to his lips where he kissed her softly on the back of her hand. She resisted the shiver that raced up her arm. "Myra, I would never ask ye to do something ye dinna wish. Of that, ye must be aware. I didna make ye tell me your message to the Bruce, let ye share when ye were ready. If ye are not ready to share with me the pains of your past, then dinna."

How could he do that? Make her admire him...dare she think it—love him?

Damn... She wanted to pull her hand away as much as she wanted to sink against him, feel his lips on hers. Feel his arms wrapped around her. Myra bit her lower lip, turned her

The Highlander's Lady

gaze back toward his, terrified that her feelings would be showing on her face. Could he see them? See how he affected her?

"Thank ye for understanding." Myra swallowed, waiting for Daniel to say something. What, she wasn't sure. She could stand here and gaze into his eyes all day, fantasize about his kisses, his mouth on her flesh. When her thighs began to quiver and her nipples hardened, she blurted out, "Why did ye not tell me sooner about..."

"Ye wanting to leave?"

"Aye."

"Ye seemed to want to keep it from me. I didna want to force ye. I'm not a monster, lass. I figured in time ye'd change your mind. But time has passed and I didna think it was fair to let the farce go on. Didna want to wait until ye disappeared. I care...for ye. I dinna want ye to leave."

He *cared* for her. Hardly the vast depth of emotions she had started to feel for him. Myra was utterly disgusted with herself. How could she have allowed herself to fall so deeply for Daniel—without even realizing it? And he only *cared* for her. She cared for her maid. Cared for her horse, the several hunting dogs her father had owned. Myra cared for apple tarts and whisky. She didn't care about Daniel. Nay, 'twas all too obvious to her now that she didn't simply care for the brute. Love had somehow found its way into her heart. Damn him.

Glowering, she took a step around Daniel toward the hearth where he'd sought solace from her moments before. How had she gotten into this mess? When she'd left Foulis, she'd had three goals—take Rose to safety, relay the message to the Bruce and return to Foulis where she could ascertain the damage done and set about fixing it. All that had been blown away in the wind the moment Daniel placed his lips on hers.

This was his fault. Her feelings, both love and mortification, were all his doing. But what could she do about it? Heat leapt from the fire, warming her more than she wished. She was already overheated. Frustration ran deep and Myra had to keep herself from stomping her foot or running from Eilean Donan screaming.

The question was, what did *she* want? What did she want from Daniel, from life, from herself?

"Myra..." Daniel's voice sounded strained, as though there was so much he too wanted to say but didn't.

'Twas good to know she wasn't alone, even if she didn't know what it was he was thinking. Slowly, she turned, watching the way her skirt swished about her ankles, wishing to be back in time. Back in a place where she didn't feel so exposed.

"Myra, what did I say this time?"

How could she say it was more what he didn't say? She couldn't. Wouldn't.

"Listen, lass, 'twould seem we both got turned around somewhere. When we first met...'twas, I dinna know how to say it, but perfection comes to mind. Ye are the most amazing woman I've ever met. One I am proud to call my wife, if ye'd still have me."

"Daniel—"

He held up his hand stopping her. "Let me finish, please."

Myra nodded, intensely curious about what he would say.

"I admit to being hard on ye, to saying things that might have hurt your feelings, but I want ye to know, I would never change who ye are. Your spirit, your fire, they are some of the reasons why I knew the first moment I met ye that ye'd make me a good wife. But not just a wife, a companion. I want a woman that I can grow old with, that enjoys my company, not

The Highlander's Lady

the coin in my coffers. I thought ye could be that woman, and I still hope that ye can."

His words made her soar on the inside. Even if he didn't admit to feelings stronger than simply caring, Myra realized that he did in fact have them. For a man like Daniel to have come out and admitted such was nothing short of a miracle. He was intensely private. Kept things inside. She'd watched him rage, as it showed on his face and in the storm of his eyes, but he'd kept his thoughts to himself. He had an amazing control that rivaled all others. He was a master at keeping himself calm—and the only time she'd seen him lose that calm was with her. Why? Because she affected him.

Realizing all she did, left her breathless. But what stopped her heart was that she wanted it too. Wanted him to be her companion, her lover. Wanted to look across the table in the great hall of whoever's castle they ended up in and see his face, now and when he was more wrinkled than a crumpled linen shift at the bottom of her wardrobe.

"I want to, I do."

There, she'd said it. The heavy weight that had made her shoulders sag lifted some, but what lifted it completely was seeing the brilliant light that flashed inside his eyes.

"Ye do?"

The insecurity in his tone made her laugh. "Aye, Daniel. 'Twould be an honor."

"Nay, lass, the honor would be all mine." Daniel covered the space between them in long strides.

Air rushed around her as he moved to quickly stand within inches of her. The scent of him surrounded her, intoxicated her even more than all the wine or whisky. She could become drunk on just him. For a very brief moment, she thought he would kiss her. His lips were so close, his eyes heavily lidded. Every inch of her body leaned toward him, begging for him to touch her. But he didn't. Daniel kept that small distance, torturing her with how close they were, with how she couldn't take another step forward if she wanted to.

"Ye want to be my wife?"

"I already agreed by the burn."

"But ye didna know me then?"

"Nay. But does it matter?"

"Aye. I've spilled my heart to ye, tell me what's in yours."

Why was it so much harder for her to express how she felt than for her to hear him say the words?

"I didna recognize ye for ye, Daniel, but that doesna mean I wasn't drawn to ye. I know ye had the impression a few years ago that I left ye there, that I was not interested, but that was far beyond the truth. I went to get my handkerchief for ye. A token of my affection, hoping ye'd return my esteem. But then when I returned and ye were surrounded by ladies… I thought myself a fool. I watched ye. Stood behind the walls, peering through the cracks or eyeholes and saw ye brooding. Saw ye playing cards and making merry. Saw the distant look in your eyes while ye did it. If I'd been honest with myself, I would have recognized that ye…were waiting for me. That ye were hurting from my having left ye. And I admit, I did. I did run away. I was hiding. Because my feelings were hurt. I'd never felt so…"

"Drawn?"

"Aye, I was, from the moment I laid eyes on ye, I was compelled, and then when we danced… That's when I knew. 'Twas the same magic in your arms."

"I want to make magic with ye."

"Dinna make me wait, Daniel. Kiss me now."

Chapter Twenty-Two

Myra's mouth was hot, demanding and tasted of wine and desire. There had been desperation in her voice, but it matched his and it wasn't the type of desperation that turned him away, but exactly the opposite. A rampant need. A hunger, a burning. They'd been dancing around each other for nearly a week. Hell more like several years if his dreams counted for anything.

He wanted her. Outrageously so.

And he wasn't going to stop this time with a kiss. Or a mere lesson in the ways he could love her. Daniel wanted it all. He needed to show her how he felt about her. To worship her as she'd wished he'd done all those years ago. He wouldn't disappoint her now. If anything he would prove his worth. Right the wrongs of both their mistakes.

Threading his fingers into her long, glorious hair, Daniel massaged her scalp. Took in the scent of lemons that curled through his nose. Myra. She was all his and he was never going to let her go.

The heat of her body was a balm on his cold limbs, more so than the fire in the hearth because she had the power to heal him, soul and all. He swept his tongue inside to taste her, reveling in how she eagerly curled her tongue around his. One thing was for sure, she was damn better at kissing now than she had been in the woods. Hell, she was the best kisser he'd ever laid his lips upon—and there had been more than he could count. She was passionate, curious, sensual. The woman knew how to turn a man upside down. His damn toes were curling.

Myra wound her arms around his waist, her fingers digging into the muscles of his back and massaging upward. He resisted the urge to howl like a wild animal ready to pounce on his mate.

"Oh, Myra," he murmured against her wet, plush lips. "Ye take my breath away."

"Dinna stop, Daniel. I canna bear it if ye do."

"I willna. Not now, not ever."

He circled his arms around her, stroking along her spine. He loved how soft she was, so feminine. Daniel gripped her rear, feeling the muscles along with the feminine curve. She'd bared her body to him before, but he'd not had the chance to see her arse... And he so wanted to watch her walk, to touch each plush globe, massage her, kiss the soft flesh.

About ready to rip her gown off, Daniel had to force himself to calm. To remember that this was her first time to make love, even if he'd already introduced her to it when he placed his mouth along the silken folds of her sex. Calm. He needed to calm. Needed to think of her pleasure only. With that in mind, he kissed her deeper, harder, his hands exploring the length of her back, her belly, the sides of her breasts.

Myra sighed, whimpered, arched her back so that her breasts crushed against his chest. Turgid nipples pressed hard

The Highlander's Lady

against his chest, easy to feel through his leine shirt. Daniel growled, and rubbed his thumbs over each nipple. She gasped into his mouth, bit his lower lip hard.

"Och, lass, we must go slow…"

At that she leaned back a little, her eyes cloudy with desire. "Why, Daniel?"

Why? That was a good question. "Because, 'twill be your first time."

"Aye… But I canna wait too long. I…I…" She bit her lip, her face flushed a pretty pink and for a moment she looked away.

Daniel was sure she was going to say that if they didn't hurry through the act then she would regret it or change her mind. But then she looked back up at him, her eyes blazing.

"I dinna want to wait. I want ye to make love to me. Tonight."

Oh, dear sweet Heaven. Daniel never thought he'd hear those words come out of her mouth—well maybe he prayed they would down the line, but he'd certainly not expected to hear them from her so soon. Now.

His veins pumped with blood, surging through his limbs and especially to his cock. He was hard before, but now he was rock solid and his desire to make love to his wife was potent.

Daniel nodded. "Aye, lass. I want to make love to ye…all night."

Myra shivered, a smile curling her lips. "Then let us not wait."

Mesmerized, Daniel watched as Myra undid the gilded belt at her waist, and peeled away her soft woolen gown. Her chemise clung to her curves, outlined her breasts and vividly showed the hardened pink buds of her nipples.

"Lovely," Daniel murmured. He stroked the sides of her breasts, gripped them in his hands, weighing and measuring them. "Och, lass…the things I'm going to do to ye tonight…"

Myra's heart had never beaten so fast. Her breaths had never hitched the way they did now. Indeed, she'd never felt this way before in her life. Not even when Daniel had laid his head between her thighs and licked her *there*.

This was completely different. She was acting the bold temptress. Urging Daniel to make love to her, to touch her. And his promise...the things he would do... It only heightened her desire. She reached for the strings of her chemise. Tugged them slowly until the two sides fell open exposing most of her breasts on down to the middle of her belly. Daniel's eyes were riveted to the spot. His hands were hot on the outside of her chemise as he'd cupped her breasts. That heat was nothing compared to his fingers skimming inside the opening of her chemise, shifting the fabric until her breasts were fully exposed.

Myra's nipples tingled. She shivered. Wanted, ached for him to place his mouth on her breasts. She didn't have to wait too long. Daniel bent low, his hair brushing over her collarbones, her chest, and tickling her breasts. He too smelled clean, like soap, but also full man. A unique scent to him that drove her wild.

Hot breath caressed her sensitive flesh and then his tongue flicked over her nipple and she cried out. Myra raked her hands into Daniel's unruly hair, tugging him closer. Her nails dug into his scalp as he sucked a nipple into his mouth. Sparks shot from that spot and straight to the pulsing knot of flesh between her thighs. How could touching like this be so moving?

"Daniel... That feels so good."

"Mmm, lass, I only want to please ye."

The Highlander's Lady

But she didn't want to be the only one experiencing pleasure. Thinking back on the moments she'd taken to watch lovers at Foulis, she did recall seeing a woman doing to her lover what Daniel was doing now. Myra tugged on Daniel's shirt. "Take this off."

He grunted. Unpinned his plaid from his shirt and untied the ribbons at his throat without removing his mouth from her breasts. She couldn't wait for him to finish. Myra tugged his shirt from where it was tucked inside his plaid, splaying her fingers on the solid ridges of his abdomen. She slid her hands up, marveling at the different textures of their skin. He was all hard muscle, taut skin, crisp hairs tickling her fingertips. Completely the opposite of her softer, more supple skin. She continued her exploration upward until her hands stroked over his chest, the tight hardness of his smaller nipples scraping over her palms.

Daniel sucked in his breath, a ragged gasp that puffed against her own nipple as she played with his. She liked to hear him gasp, knowing that it was because of something she was doing. Knowing that she was giving him pleasure. But touching him wasn't all she wanted to do. Myra wanted to lick him.

She tugged his shirt upward, until he had to pull away from her breasts. The cold air hit her wet skin sending shivers to wrack over her, but she didn't mind. Her mission was to strip this brawny Highlander from his shirt. Daniel smiled wickedly at her.

"In a hurry, I see."

"Aye," she said with a little laugh.

Daniel pulled his shirt all the way off, tossing it to the floor. Myra didn't know where it landed. Didn't care. She was completely mesmerized by the vision before her. Bronzed chest, crisp dark hair, muscles that bespoke of hours and hours of physical training every day. He was pure strength. Myra licked her lips, hungry to touch him. She reached out her hands, stroking from his shoulders down to his belly, watching his belly suck in as he gasped.

She stroked back upward, pinching his nipples lightly between two fingers. Myra took a step forward, glancing up at Daniel, to see that his eyes were heavily lidded. He watched her, the intensity of his gaze giving her the last bit of courage she needed to keep going forward.

Leaning in, she nuzzled his flesh, breathing in his masculine scent, then slid upward, scraping her lips over his chest until she reached a hardened nipple. Daniel let out a breath, the air whooshing in her hair. He stroked over the back of her head lightly, holding the base of her skull.

"Lass..." he breathed out low and gruff.

"Aye, Daniel?" she said in a voice she'd not heard before. 'Twas husky, sultry, utterly sensual and hard to imagine that it was her own. Myra flicked her tongue over his nipple before he could answer. "Do ye like it when I do this?" she asked.

"Oh, aye."

Myra smiled against his skin, stroking her tongue in lazy circles around his nipple before sucking on it gently. He jerked against her.

"Och, lass. Enough of that or this will be over before—"

"Shh..." she said, cutting him off. She was far from done with him. Oh, where had this wanton boldness come from? 'Twas like she'd been lying dormant for years on end, waiting just for this moment to occur so she could ravish Daniel. She wasn't a bit ashamed about it. In fact she fully reveled in this new powerful role.

"The things I'm going to do to ye, my laird," she said with a teasing smile, even though her cheeks heated to burning. Appeared there was still a bit of the virgin inside her, but she wasn't going to let that stop her.

Myra gripped the leather of Daniel's belt, wrenched it free and watched with fascination as his plaid unwhirled to land in a pool of colors at his feet. From there she glanced up over his muscled calves, knees, sinewy thighs and… Well, the vulgar men of Foulis were not wrong about large feet. Daniel's manhood was long, thick and stood upright, pointed toward her, like it was waiting for her. Her face heated even more. She wasn't embarrassed per se, but felt almost as though she'd bit off more than she could chew. That thing was certainly not going to fit inside her. None of the lovers she'd watched had a length or breadth like his. Daniel was a giant in every way. She glanced up at him, about to ask him if it would work.

"Ye look frightened, lass." He gripped her hand in his and pulled her close so that his shaft brushed against her belly, the chemise so thin it hid nothing. She shivered. "Dinna be afraid. I promise to be gentle."

She licked her lips, shook her head. "'Tis not that. I but worry that…ye willna fit."

Daniel chuckled. "I promise it will work just fine."

"Truly?"

"Aye." He moved her hand toward his thickness, pressing her fingers around him.

His silky flesh pulsed in her grip. Daniel guided her hand back and forth from the base to the tip. His breaths increased, and his hand covering hers trembled. He liked this stroking. She tightened her grip a little, growing bolder, and explored the soft tip with her fingers.

When he'd put his mouth between her thighs, she'd wondered if he'd enjoy that. Judging from how he was reacting from her hand, Myra was pretty sure he would. Without asking, she knelt before him. Daniel's hand still covered hers, but she stilled her movements.

"What are ye doing?" he rasped.

"This." She leaned forward, licked the tip.

Daniel groaned loud, enticing her to lick him again. She licked around the tip, then up and down the length, kissing his shaft as she went.

"Lass…"

"Aye?" She glanced up at him, seeing the veins in his neck bulging as though he held himself back.

"That feels good."

Myra smiled, licking the tip again.

"Can ye…" he asked through a moan.

"Aye?"

His jaw tightened and he looked as if he was trying to work to find the right words. "I want ye to put my cock in your mouth."

Her eyes widened. Now this she hadn't seen… Kissing was the extent of it. But she admitted the idea of putting his shaft in her mouth was extremely tantalizing. Not wanting to wait until her nerves took over, Myra wrapped her lips around his flesh and sucked. Daniel let out a feral growl that had every inch of her body tingling. He liked this. And she liked it too. Instinctively, she moved her mouth up and down the length of him, taking in the sensual scent and taste of his salty flesh.

Several strokes later, Daniel yanked back, gripped her about the waist and lifted her into the air.

"What—"

"'Tis too much for me, lass… I'm about to come undone in your sweet little mouth."

The way he growled the words made her shiver. She wrapped her arms around his neck and her legs around his hips as he carried her to the bed. Daniel laid her down gently, covering her with his body. They stared at one another for several moments, their eyes locked in a heated stare, forehead to forehead, nose to nose.

"Are ye sure?"

"Aye," she said. "I know I said I wanted to wait until we reached your home, but…"

"Ye didna have any plans to make it there."

Myra smiled through her haze of desire. "Ye know me too well."

Daniel chuckled, then turned serious. "And now? Ye said ye'd be my wife."

"Without a doubt. I aim to stay by your side."

Daniel's shoulders relaxed, as though he'd fully expected her to shun him. She wanted to tell him how much he meant to her. But while she was willing to share the intimacy of her body with him, she wasn't quite ready to share her innermost feelings.

"Make love to me, Daniel."

"'Tis the second time ye've asked me that tonight. I'm not making ye a verra good husband."

Myra stroked his cheek, kissed him, sucking on his lip and slipping her tongue inside his mouth to tease him for several strokes. "Ye are the best of husbands."

Daniel laughed. "And ye've had so many." He nuzzled her neck, nipping at the skin where her heart raced.

"I've seen many," she whispered, tilting her head to the side to give him better access.

"Ah, I'd forgotten, my little secret watcher."

"I…" Her voice faltered and shame filled her cheeks.

Daniel laughed, and nuzzled her breasts. "Dinna be embarrassed. I say, we go to Foulis and spy ourselves… Make love behind the walls."

"I will hold ye to that promise."

Daniel settled himself between her thighs, his large shaft probing at the space that was slick and quivering. But he didn't surge forward as she expected. He slid his fingers between the folds, stroking over the knot of flesh that fired potent sensation throughout her body, making her legs shake and her toes curl. She cried out when he slid a finger inside her and then pulled out. He repeated the move with two fingers, all while stroking over her sensitive nub. Myra panted, feeling her body vibrate, recognizing the sensations that had held her captive before. Her breath caught, back arched and legs instinctively bent upward, hips tilting up. Daniel continued to work her until spasms of pleasure gripped her tight then tossed her to the wind.

Before her body had a chance to come down from the high of her climax, Daniel surged forward. His length was a thick, painful invasion as he broke through her barrier and filled her completely. Myra cried out more from the shock of his plunge than from the pain. He settled all the way to the hilt, his pelvis pressed tightly to hers. Her insides quivered, pulsed and while she wanted him to pull out of her body, she wanted him to plunge deeper.

'Twas an odd sensation of wanting but not wanting. Myra shifted beneath him, about to ask him if he could stop now when doing so had her gasping with pleasure. How quickly her body recovered from the last shattering of sensation, wanting more.

"Are ye all right, love?" Daniel asked.

Myra took a chance to glance up at his face, unsure of when she'd squeezed her eyes tight. Daniel looked strained once more, his eyes cloudy with pleasure and concern.

"Aye."

"What about now?" He slowly pulled out, then gently slid back inside.

"Oh, aye," Myra sighed.

Daniel repeated the motion, slowly increasing the pace until she met him thrust for thrust.

"Oh, Daniel..." Myra panted, hardly able to catch a breath. She held on tight to his shoulders, bringing her legs up around his hips which only increased the pleasure of his

The Highlander's Lady

movements. Myra could no longer think, breathe. All she could do was feel, react.

Her body trembled, wanting desperately to reach that point again where she saw stars. To think earlier in the day she'd been planning on leaving him, never looking back. Sharing her body, some of herself with him…'twas life changing.

"Myra, lass, God I…" Daniel trembled above her, sweat trickling over his temple.

But Myra couldn't concentrate on the words he said. Blood rushed in her ears, loud as water crashing from a tall fall as it landed inside a loch. Every inch of her sang in crippling pleasure. Two more steady strokes of his body and she was crying out his name, clinging to his sweat-slick back and afraid she'd faint from the sheer magic of it.

Daniel groaned loud, shuddering, his thick length pulsing inside her. They lay unmoving save for the trembling of their limbs.

Myra wasn't aware she'd fallen asleep until a sharp knock on the door woke her. Daniel mumbled from behind where he cradled her. He ignored the knock, instead kissing her on the nape of her neck, his hand exploring the length of her ribs.

"Morning, love," he whispered in her ear.

"Daniel! Come out! The Bruce has returned and wants a word with ye in the great hall." The voice of his cousin, Ronan, was a bitter-sweet reminder of where they were and that they had to now return to reality—a world fraught with unrest and the entire country's fate hanging in the balance.

Chapter Twenty-Three

Although Daniel took his time leaving their chamber, making sure to kiss Myra leisurely and thoroughly, inside he was eager to get down to the great hall. Ronan wouldn't have woken him unless the Bruce's need was urgent.

Whipping on his plaid he left the comfort of their chamber behind. In the great hall, the Bruce sat at the head of a trestle table, Wallace by his side. Their leader looked worse for wear. His eyes had more wrinkles gripping the corners and several more streaks of grey in his hair than he'd had last time Daniel saw him. Surrounding the rest of the table were Ronan and several other key players in the Bruce's court. Daniel looked from the various earls, chieftains and warriors wondering if any of them were going to betray their leader as Ross had.

Daniel settled onto the bench in a spot Ronan had left open for him. Julianna sauntered into the room carrying a tray of food and set it in front of the Bruce. She whispered

The Highlander's Lady

something in his ear and he nodded. The room was very obviously devoid of other servants—testament to the nature of Bruce's need for counsel. Julianna stood several feet away, fully within hearing distance of everything that would be said. Myra and Ronan trusted her, but Daniel wasn't sure he could. There was something odd about her.

"Murray," the Bruce's voice boomed down the length of the table. "I hear ye came with a lass to deliver me a message."

Daniel nodded. "Aye, but 'twas not my message to relay."

"Your woman's?" the Bruce asked.

Daniel again nodded.

"Who is she?" he asked.

"I am Myra Munro, Chief of the Munro clan."

The men fell silent, pushing back their benches to stand. Daniel had to keep his mouth from dropping. He turned slowly to see that Myra stood in the doorway, head held high. She looked every bit the laird with her rigid stance, the stubborn set in her jaw, fire in her eyes. He waited for her to catch his gaze, but she didn't. The woman stared straight at the Bruce, the silence in the room thick enough to drive an axe through.

"Chief Munro?" Robert the Bruce finally said.

"Aye. My brother was murdered a fortnight ago. His heir has yet to be born and until that time, I am Laird."

Daniel had not truly thought of her as a leader before now, but the way she stood proudly telling all her place in the world, it became clear she was exactly that. The perfect wife for him. A woman who could stand beside him. He was proud of the strength in her voice. That was *his* woman. He smiled, fully aware that such an image would not go unnoticed by others.

"I am sorry for your loss. I suspect the message ye brought was not only about that. Indeed, I have been made aware of who took your brother's life and what your message was." He nodded his head toward Wallace. "When Will found me, he informed me of your urgent need to see me."

Myra inclined her head like a queen. "My thanks, Sir Wallace, for your help in my matter."

"Ye need not give thanks, my lady. 'Tis all of us who should be thanking ye." Wallace bowed slightly as did the rest of the men at the table.

"I dinna understand." Myra genuinely looked confused and Daniel wished to go to her.

The Bruce stood and came around the table, walking until he stood beside Myra. "My lady, I knew that Ross had switched sides. I thought to show him a certain amount of respect—perhaps more than ye'd give a rabid dog—by going to him, offering him something more to keep him on our side. Often times with these wayward earls, 'tis money. There's no doubt that Longshanks has more of it than I do. I'm not inclined to tax the people more than they are already being taxed. The entire country is drowning from the pressures of war and fighting the English. I'm their protector, their future king."

Myra nodded as she studied him. Daniel was surprised to see that her expression was unreadable. Whenever they were together he could guess everything that she was thinking. Now here, with strangers, with Robert the Bruce, with Wallace, she was able to hide everything going on inside her mind. He couldn't help but think that it was because she was comfortable with him that she let down her guard—not so with these other men. Another source of pride for Daniel.

"I'm not sure I understand what that has to do with me," she said evenly.

The Bruce chuckled. "Allow me to further tell it then. Wallace caught up to me before I met with Ross. I will be eternally grateful for ye passing your message along. Ross is far beyond negotiating with."

The Highlander's Lady

Myra smiled slightly and curtseyed. "'Twas my honor."

The Bruce held out his hand and helped her stand. "Ye are forever welcome at my court. And I welcome your input as a fellow leader among the Scots."

"My thanks, but 'tis my hope that I rule beside my husband, Laird Murray."

The Bruce whirled around to face Daniel. "Aye... This news was not relayed to me — that ye were to marry."

Daniel stood, kneeled in front of the Bruce. "Apologies, my lord. 'Twas necessary for Lady Myra's safety that we handfast."

The Bruce looked to them both. "I'd heard of the lady's betrothal to the Ross, is this the reason? I wouldna have allowed the marriage to take place."

A noble thought, but Ross would have forced her in any case. "Nay, my lord. The lass was in danger when we met upon the road. She was alone on her way to your holding. I offered her my protection and my name."

"Very gallant of ye, Murray."

Daniel inclined his head, his eyes catching Myra's which for a moment flashed gratefulness. He supposed she was thankful he didn't mention the man she killed in the woods. She didn't need to be ashamed of it, but all the same, it was most likely not an event she wished to rehash.

"My lord," she said, drawing the Bruce's attention. "If I may..."

"Of course, my lady."

"I met Laird Murray several years ago at Foulis. I had hopes then that he'd ask for my hand, but then the arrangement with Ross was made. I am more than pleased with our recent joining."

Talk of a joining reminded Daniel of just how well they'd *joined* the night before. He shifted his stance, hoping his body's reaction was not visible to anyone else. But the gleam in Myra's eyes told him she noticed, and that she returned his desire.

"Well, I am not one to stand in the way of both a love match and a political one. Joining your two clans will indeed be a powerful ally. Any word on how your holding fares?"

Myra shook her head. "Nay, my lord. When I left 'twas in a hurry and with smoke curling at my back. I hoped to return there as soon as I relayed my message to ye."

The Bruce nodded. "Aye, ye should afore another storm like the one we had returns."

Which could be any day. Daniel couldn't allow Myra to get stuck inside another storm. The risk was too great. "I will go. Ye stay here where ye'll be safe," he offered.

Fire sparked in her eyes, which she quickly quelled with many watching. When she did speak it was softly, "Foulis is my responsibility, my laird. I'd not wish to burden ye with it."

"Foulis became my responsibility as well the moment we joined hands. I'll not have ye exposed to more of this frigid weather."

Myra's lips thinned and he could practically hear her cursing his name from inside her mind. "We shall discuss who goes and when at a later time."

He knew a dismissal when he got one and could see his wife meant to do just that. Daniel wasn't of a mind to argue with her, especially not in front of everyone. "Verra well."

"My lady, ye are welcome to join us at the table, but 'tis not necessary. I wish to discuss the training of the men and what news I have of the English's planned attack come spring."

Myra nodded. "I would listen all the same."

The Bruce nodded and turned to sit at his chair at the head of the trestle table. His arse had barely hit the seat when a loud boom cracked the air, the very walls seeming to

The Highlander's Lady

shudder from it. Everyone at the table jumped and Myra who'd been prepared to sit beside Daniel grabbed his arm tight. He glanced down at her, eyes widened, she looked frightened, and he could only imagine what was going through her mind.

"The Ross clan," someone muttered.

Daniel watched as Julianna hurried from the room. He opened his mouth to call out to her but then another loud boom rent the air.

"They are coming now," the Bruce said.

"What do ye mean, now?" Daniel asked

"All the others were just threats. This is the real thing. The Ross will have noted I didna join him. The bastard thinks he's more powerful than all of us because he's sided with Longshanks. No pride in his own people or country. To your stations!" the Bruce shouted.

Men all around them ran to and fro, emptying the room. Daniel stood frozen for a moment, then turned to Myra. "Ye must go to our chamber. Bar the door."

She shook her head vehemently. "Nay, Daniel. Dinna leave me."

"I'm not leaving ye, lass, but I've got to help. Come. I will see ye to our chamber."

He lifted her in his arms, praying this wasn't the last time he held her close. Taking the steps two at a time, Daniel ran up the circular stair and down the hall until he reached their chamber.

Myra clung to him, her arms wound around his neck, face buried on his shoulder. "Daniel... Ross is ruthless."

"I know it, love," he said softly. "I promise, I will come back for ye."

Myra nodded, bit her lip. Daniel pressed his lips to hers, kissing her tenderly. He'd take the thought of her soft kiss and passionate nature with him while he fought the bastards.

"Daniel, I—" She clamped her lips closed.

"'Twill be all right, love. I swear it." Unable to look at her any longer for fear he'd grab hold and never let go—not good considering his help was needed in fending off the enemy—Daniel rushed from the room.

Halfway down the hall he heard the distinct sound of the bar being put in place. Good. At least he could rush into the fray knowing Myra was safe.

Myra stared at the barred door. Counted the lines in the wood. Refused to let her mind take her back to that day a fortnight prior when the sounds of crashing had forever changed her world. She placed her hands on the door, feeling the hard wood beneath, a few splinters threatening to sink into her flesh. Leaning her forehead against the panels, she forced herself to take deep, even breaths.

Today would not end the way the battle at Foulis had. Today would be different.

Had to be different.

Swallowing back her tears of fear, she sent up a prayer to God. Something she hadn't done in a while, odd enough since praying had been nearly an hourly thing for her at Foulis.

"Please, God, please dinna let the Ross win. Dinna let Daniel be hurt." She repeated every prayer she'd ever learned with Father Holden. Promised all manners of things, including that she'd give herself over to the church if he would only see Daniel to safety.

Outside the window, battle cries and shouts of pain filled the air and seeped through the gaps of the fur covering. Myra wanted to pull back that covering, to see what was happening, but if she did so… She may see something she didn't want to see. Oh, God…

The Highlander's Lady

Her heart beat so fast she feared it would stop all together. Her hands trembled as she ran them over her perfect coiffure. She'd made sure to look the part when she'd entered the Bruce's great hall. Little good it did now that they were under attack. She couldn't help feeling that somehow this attack was her fault. If only she'd gotten here sooner, or if only she'd convinced her brother to fortify Foulis, they could have contained Ross there.

And yet there had been no other choice in the situation she was given. She had to warn the Bruce about Ross. If she hadn't then he would have walked into certain death.

The lesser of two evils was a battle—here where the Bruce might have the upper hand.

Pacing the room, Myra contemplated what she could do to help. She couldn't just wait in here for news of doom and gloom. There had to be something she could do. With no walls to hide behind, she'd have to use her skills to appear invisible even out in the open.

Decision made, Myra walked with steady steps toward the door. She pulled off the bar and opened it—only to be faced by two burly-looking warriors. She recognized them immediately from the great hall. Problem was, she didn't feel at all safe. The hair on the back of her neck rose and alarm bells rang with ear-piercing clarity inside her ears. More enemies within the Bruce's camp.

"Well, lass. I see ye were expecting us. We didna even have to knock."

Myra slammed the door, but one of the bastards put his foot in the way at the last minute and the heavy wood bounced back hitting her square in the face. She stumbled backward, pain from the hit and dizziness taking over her mind.

"Stay...stay back," she muttered, her lips feeling fuzzy and numb. Blood trickled from her nose onto her lips.

They laughed, but she didn't let that discourage her. She'd not be a victim. Never. No one could make her. She'd not live the life her mother had. Myra pulled her dirk from its strap at her hip and prepared to defend herself. History was about to repeat itself in all its hideous glory. Fear made her throat close, her screams silent.

Her feet would not cooperate with her as she desperately tried to gain her footing. But walking backward while waving a weapon and seeing double did not make for good balance. Why hadn't she listened to Daniel? Heeded his warnings to stay within the safety of their chamber?

It didn't matter. These men would have figured out a way in. They would have told her that Daniel was hurt, anything to get her to open the door. The men advanced on her. Stomach flipping and vision blurred, she cut through the air with her dagger hoping to scare them back. Serious in their pursuit of her, they wasted no time in disarming her of her weapon. How it happened she wasn't even sure. One moment she was waving it front of her, shouting obscenities as she tried to slice through their reaching hands—the next her dirk clattered to the floor. Before she knew what happened, she was bound tight. The rope they used was thin and bit painfully into her wrists and ankles. The shorter of the men shoved a putrid rag into her mouth, tying a bind around her head to keep the gag in place. The other man hoisted her onto his shoulder.

"Good night, princess," Shorty said.

Myra shook her head desperately, trying to talk but only gagging on the rag as Shorty raised his hand and the brunt of a hard object crashed against her skull.

The Highlander's Lady

Myra woke to the feel of someone stroking a cool cloth on her forehead. She blinked open her eyes to see Julianna and an unfamiliar room.

"Traitor!" Myra shouted, shoving at the cloth and trying to scramble away without success.

"Shh... Dinna alert them that ye are awake." Julianna held two fingers to Myra's lips.

Confusion struck along with the pain in her head from her injuries. "What?"

Julianna shook her head. "I am no traitor. I offered myself in exchange for ye. They did not agree and took us both. Ye, the Ross wants for dead, I on the other hand have a lot more to offer him."

Myra swallowed hard, her throat dry. "Ye tried to save me?"

"Aye. Ye saved Robert. 'Twas only fitting that I should save the one who saved him."

Myra was so confused. "Ye are not a traitor?"

Julianna laughed bitterly. "I am the Bruce's biggest supporter."

"I'm sorry."

Julianna shook her head. "Dinna apologize. In fact, dinna say anything. The longer they think ye're asleep the better."

Myra did as Julianna instructed even though she desperately wanted to speak. Her injuries overtook her once more and she fell into unconsciousness. She woke some time later, her stomach growling and a headache that rivaled the worst of pains searing through her forehead.

"Good, ye're awake..." Julianna got up and glanced out of what looked like a flap of sorts, at least the bright light made it seem so.

"Where are we?"

"The Ross camp. They didna take my pin away." She pulled a dagger-like object from her hair and smiled widely. "I cut the tent. Ye must run. Can ye get up?"

Myra shook her head slowly, then tried to lift herself. Her arms and legs gave out and she landed, face in the dirt. After several tries she was finally able to stand. The world around her spun and she sank back to her knees before she fell on her face again.

"Well, this willna do," Julianna said sternly. "Ye must get up. Ye must escape and get word back to Robert. He needs to know that Alisdair and Colin are with the Ross' camp. He needs to know that I'm here."

"Ye are not coming with me?" Myra tried once more to stand, this time with her eyes closed, to ward off her dizziness.

"Nay, I canna. They will come right after us. If 'tis only ye, I can convince them ye're worth nothing to them. If 'tis only me that escapes, they will simply kill ye and then come after me." Julianna shrugged and stuck the pin back in her hair. "Besides, I could kill the brutes outside the tent if there were not another score ready to take their place."

Myra opened her eyes. Blinked several times. The pain in her head was bad and she could feel that it was swollen where the door had hit her in the face. Her nose didn't feel broken even if it had bled. And thank goodness, she was no longer dizzy.

Julianna shoved a sharp object in her hand. "I broke the mug of ale they gave us. Use this piece as a weapon if ye need it."

Myra nodded. "Why are ye doing this?"

"I told ye. 'Twas only fitting that I should save the one that saved Robert, Scotland's future king."

"I canna ever repay ye."

Julianna tilted her head, a vibrant smile filling her face, odd in this place. "Nay, my lady, ye already have."

"Aye, I saved the Bruce, but—"

The Highlander's Lady

Julianna shook her head and waved her hand in the air. "Aye, there's that, but there is also the rescuing."

She wasn't making any sense and Myra didn't feel like she had her wits about her enough quite yet to figure the woman out.

"Send Ronan my regards." Julianna gripped Myra's shoulders and thrust her through the cut in the tent. "Godspeed!"

Myra stilled, her body tense as she listened for the sound of footsteps. Their tent was almost to the edge of the woods, lined up with a half dozen others. There was no one in sight. She'd been able to escape Foulis. This would be just as easy. Suppressing a shiver, Myra willed her limbs to work the way she needed in order to get out of this alive.

One foot in front of the other, she crept the two dozen feet to the edge of the wood, turning to brush away each footprint in the newly fallen snow with her hands so no one would know to follow. Every step was excruciating. She counted her breaths, her heartbeat, the only thing she could concentrate on without going mad with fear.

The moment her feet hit the forest floor, Myra took off at a run, expecting to hear the sounds of someone alerting of her escape. Waiting for the arrow of a scout who saw her running away. But there was none of that. Only the long, treacherous road to freedom.

Chapter Twenty-Four

The battle was a hard-fought, blood-thirsty affair that left Daniel in need of Myra. Only her warm touch could soothe his soul. The Ross men rushed headlong into killing anyone in their path and it had taken much to subdue them—and many lives. But they'd been defeated and Eilean Donan and its inhabitants reigned supreme. The wounded were taken into the castle where healers began the ministrations and those able to walk went about seeing to the dead. Daniel himself had dug three or four graves, he couldn't remember now.

Ronan, Wallace and the Bruce, like Daniel, left with only a few cuts and bruises, testament to their own vicious skills. The Earl of Ross, coward that he was, did not show his face. Daniel found it odd that the man would orchestrate an attack but not take part. Ross may be a weasel, but he didn't shy from fighting. Nay, there was something else afoot.

The Highlander's Lady

Daniel climbed the stairs, intent on locking himself in his chamber with Myra until they were forced to come out, which he hoped wasn't at least until morning.

The chamber door was ajar. Alarm ricocheted through Daniel, landing in the pit of his gut. Myra would not have left the safety of the barred door… Not when there was a battle. Not when he'd ordered her to stay put.

Damn… He'd ordered her to. That meant she would directly defy him. Daniel pushed the door open, just to make sure she wasn't in attendance, but what greeted him left a cold knot of fear in his belly. The room was in disarray. A chair overturned, the water basin spilled, the rug in tangles. A struggle happened here. Now it all made sense.

This was why Ross hadn't joined in the battle. He'd another agenda. The fight was merely a distraction. Mayhap she'd gotten away… Mayhap she was somewhere else in the castle. Daniel rushed from the room, intent on finding her. He searched every room twice and circled the inner bailey three times. Atop the battlements he let out a roar that made the dogs howl.

In that singular moment of anguish, Daniel realized why his heart felt as though it had been ripped from his chest—he loved her. A feeling he'd thought never to have. She was everything he wanted in a wife, but he'd never thought to feel more for her than he already had before. Except, he did. He loved her so much he felt it in every inch of his bones. Myra was his other half, the completion of his soul.

Yet…she was gone.

A soul-wrenching cry split the air, coming from the direction of the castle. The chilling sound set Myra's nerves on edge—more so than they already were. She knew at once that it was Daniel. He must have only now found her missing. But she wasn't! She was here, just inside the forest, huddled beneath a holly bush that scraped the skin along her arms. Cold, without a cloak, she shivered. Twirling the gold and onyx Munro ring on the leather thong about her neck, she prayed that it had some connection to her brother, father, mother, that from beyond the grave they'd watch over her.

Leaving this spot was not an option. Too many of the Ross men had already passed by, their boots leaving deep tracks in the snow. From covering her tracks, her palms stung, her fingers had long since gone numb from cold. If only she had Daniel's gloves now.

There was nothing for it. This little hiding spot was hers for now. She'd have to wait until dark to move. Hopefully by then she wouldn't have frozen in place. Myra had yet to tell Daniel how much she loved him. Even if he didn't realize he returned her feelings, she'd make him see that he did. No man howled so painfully who didn't lose the one he loved.

Her soul howled right back.

Daniel would not listen to reason. He had Demon saddled and left Eilean Donan's newly repaired gates. He was not more than twenty yards from the gate when a thundering from behind made him turn.

His men.

Leo pulled up alongside him. The bastard would try to pull him back. Rage filled Daniel and he prepared to rip Leo a new arsehole.

"Ye weren't going to find your lady without us were ye? Too many Ross men left untouched by our blades. We need our laird and lady alive."

The rest of the men concurred, fists pumped in the air and the word, "Aye!" shouted from their lips.

The Highlander's Lady

Daniel's chest swelled. They weren't here to persuade him from his task? This was what he'd been waiting for all along. His men, finally on his side—for good.

"Let us not waste another moment then." Daniel turned back toward the woods that lay ahead. His gut told him that was the right direction. The bloody Ross clan had been camped in there, most likely they still were. Somewhere out in this cold was his wife, and he aimed to get her back, killing anyone who stood in his way.

The men thundered down the road, their horses' nearly flying their feet so rarely touched the ground. Daniel raised his hand for them to halt outside the forest. In the dead of winter, the only sounds were an occasional screech of an owl or the scurrying steps of a foraging animal. No insects, no birds. The horses huffed their breaths, snorting as they waited for their masters to push them forward.

"Form a line. We'll enter the forest thusly." Daniel scanned the dark, seeing more shadows that anything else. Dusk would be upon them soon and his search for Myra would be made ever more difficult, but he refused to give up.

The men formed a line and Daniel signaled for them to step into the forest. They did so slowly, stopping every couple of yards to listen. Silence reigned here.

"The Ross camp was to the left," Daniel said, trying to recall where exactly his men had passed it before.

Leo nodded. "They may have moved now though, if they've taken Lady Myra."

A sound coming from the right had the hair on Daniel's arms rising in alarm. He held up his hand for them all to stop. There it was again. A scuffling, and…a curse.

"Myra?" Daniel called out.

Silence.

He dismounted from Demon and handed his reigns to Leo. "Stay here, I could have sworn I heard something."

Leo nodded his understanding. Daniel took careful steps in the direction from which he was sure he'd heard his pretty little wife's muffled curse.

"Damn thorns." Definitely a woman's voice, and a familiar, comforting voice. 'Twas Myra.

"Myra!" he called out again, this time his call was answered with a gasp.

"Daniel?"

He would have missed her if he didn't look down. Myra crawled from beneath a holly bush, the frown on her face enough to ignite said bush into flames.

"Och, thank God!" he knelt in the snow and pulled her into his embrace.

Myra swung her arms around his neck and clung to him.

"Ye're freezing," Daniel said into her hair, taking in the familiar scent.

"Aye."

"Come, I will warm ye." He lifted her into his arms and ran effortlessly back toward his horse, refusing to let her go. "I thought ye were lost to me."

"Nay, never, I would have found my way back. I was just on my way to ye now."

"Ye should never have been taken. I should have stayed with ye, protected ye. I've failed." He put her on top of her horse and prepared to climb, but Myra stopped him with her tiny boot upon his chest. She shivered uncontrollably, her lips blue.

"Ye've not failed, Daniel. Ye have a duty to Scotland. 'Tis my fault." She glanced away for a moment, teeth chattering. "I wanted to help ye. I opened the door and there they stood."

"Who?"

She gasped, her angry-red hands coming to her mouth. "I almost forgot. Two men that were loyal to the Bruce—or so he thought."

The Highlander's Lady

Daniel climbed up behind her and wrapped his plaid around her. He took her hands between his and rubbed furiously in an attempt to warm them. "What men?" he asked.

"Colin and Alisdair."

"Damn." He turned his horse back toward Eilean Donan, his men following. "They've already made it back to our camp."

"Then the Bruce is once more in danger."

They reached the castle moments later to find both Colin and Alisdair in the courtyard, flat on their bellies and trussed up like pigs. Wallace grinned, his foot on Colin's back as a light snow fell on their heads.

"How did ye get her out of the camp?" snarled Colin.

"I wasn't in the camp, ye horse's arse. I escaped."

Daniel grinned widely at his wife's tongue. Many of the men snickered. He rode his horse right up to the stairs of the keep and dismounted, pulling Myra into his arms.

"Seems all is well here, Wallace," he shouted.

"For the moment. We've scouts looking for Ross. Ronan's gone out with them."

Daniel nodded.

"Oh!" Myra shouted through her chattering teeth, and clambered to get down, but Daniel held her tight. "I forgot! They have Julianna!"

Wallace's face fell and Daniel's stomach flipped.

"She saved me."

He'd never have believed it if it didn't come from Myra herself.

"*Mo creach!*" Wallace cursed and kicked Colin in the ribs. "Ronan is going to murder Ross when he finds out... The Bruce will be verra displeased."

Daniel nodded grimly. He'd had a feeling about the same thing. "Ronan will find her," he said with confidence. "I think he's...taken with her."

Wallace grinned. "Aye, there's no doubt of that."

Myra nodded. "That makes sense then."

"What?"

"When she shoved me from the tent she said, 'Send Ronan my regards.'"

Daniel had no doubt his cousin would find his lady, but he no longer wished to think on it. Right now, all he wanted to do was rush up to his chamber and make sweet, passionate love to Myra, the best way he knew how to warm her, and the best way he knew how to tell her how much he loved her.

"A hot bath!" he shouted to Marta as he rushed inside the castle.

"Oh, I dinna need that," Myra protested.

"Ye are shivering, love, and I'll not have ye freeze to death." He held her tighter, trying to encompass her as much as he could in his heat.

"I suppose a hot bath would be nice."

"Aye, love." He kicked open the door to their chamber and stomped inside.

Setting her down in a chair, Daniel turned to the fire, piling wood high until it blazed. When he turned back to her, she still shivered violently.

"I feel like my body is made of snow," she mumbled.

Daniel scooped her up once more, settling her on his lap. He brought her hands to his mouth, cupping his own around them and blowing hotly on her frozen fingers.

Myra sighed. "That feels wonderful and like pins are poking me."

Daniel smiled. "Aye, I'm thawing ye out."

She nodded and he continued to blow on her hands, kissing her frozen skin. The room was soon sweltering with the blazing fire, and added to it, the steam of the hot water as the servants filled a bath for Myra. Daniel dismissed them all and barred the door.

"What are ye doing? I plan on getting in that bath," Myra said, a stubborn brow arching. "And I canna do it with ye in the room. Go ahead and take that board off and be on your way."

Daniel grinned devilishly. "And I plan to join ye."

Her mouth fell open, but surprisingly no words came out.

"'Twill help to warm ye."

Myra smiled wickedly. "Among other things."

"Did ye see lovers bathe together when ye were spying?"

She shook her head and stood. As strong as she appeared, he still was concerned for her well-being and rushed toward her. The bruises marring her tender flesh were enough to make him want to murder each and every Ross warrior.

"I am not a bairn, Daniel."

"I know it. But I can still worry over ye." He tipped her chin up, their eyes locking. "I'm glad to still have ye to worry over."

Myra leaned against him, her cold cheek resting on his chest. "I was so scared. But I knew I had to get back here. Not only to warn the Bruce, but because...because I needed to tell ye something."

Daniel wrapped his arms around her, slowly stroking up and down her spine. "Ye can tell me anything."

She leaned her head back so she could gaze once more into his eyes. She had the most beautiful brown eyes. Like what he imagined a faery's eyes would look like.

"I love ye."

His heart stopped beating. Had he heard right? She loved him? He could honestly say that no one had ever told him that. Maybe his mother when he was a lad, but he couldn't recall. Daniel swallowed, taking in the sentiment with powerful emotion. He wasn't sure he could even speak.

"Did ye hear what I said?" Myra frowned, pinched his back.

That was his woman. Fiery to the very end.

"Aye, lass." His voice sounded choked and he didn't trust himself to speak further.

"And..." she prompted.

Daniel grinned wide, ready to tease his spirited wife. "And thank ye."

Myra shoved him away and let out a disgusted noise. "Brute! Get out. I'm taking my bath."

She stomped toward the bath, wrenching off her clothes as she went. Daniel was caught between being spell-bound by the pink flesh she revealed and laughing at her ire. In two steps, he was upon her. Arms around her waist, he yanked her toward him so that her naked back was flush against his fully clothed chest. He laughed and bit her ear.

"Ye little tease," he whispered. "Ye've made me realize the man I was meant to be. I love ye too."

Myra whirled full around, her soft, cold breasts pressed to his chest. "I knew ye did."

"Arrogant wench."

"Overconfident beast."

Daniel gripped her arse in his hands and pulled her even more tightly against him. His mouth crashed on hers in a demanding, carnal kiss. One filled with passion, fear, love, every single emotion he'd felt this day. He let it all flow into her mouth and she pushed it right back at him.

Myra switched from clinging to him to ripping at his clothes to clinging to him once more.

"I need ye inside me," she said. "Now."

Daniel growled and wrenched open his belt, flinging it behind him. His plaid and sporran fell in a heap on the floor, his ripped shirt long since flung away by Myra. He lifted her into the air, her legs wrapped around him, his shaft pressing hotly on the wet center of her. The only place that appeared hot on her whole body. He needed to get her into that warm water.

The Highlander's Lady

Daniel carried Myra to the tub, effortlessly climbing in with her wrapped around him. He sat down with her straddling his lap.

"Daniel..." she moaned, her lips grazing his stubbled cheek and neck. "Not a bath... I want to make love."

"We will..." He snaked his hand between their bodies, finding her little bead of pleasure, listening to her cry out. Sliding two fingers inside her, he said, "We are."

The water was hot and surrounding them both in a steamy cocoon.

"I...oh!" Myra found his lips once more, tenderly nibbling and then swiping her tongue inside to meet his. She'd become a master at kissing since that first one.

And a master at other things...

Myra gripped his length between their bodies, stroking up and down. She wanted him inside her, desperately. If he wasn't going to listen to her, then she was going to torture him as he did to her. But Daniel only upped the stakes, nuzzling her breasts, laving her nipples, sucking one and then the other. Her body coiled inside, pressure mounting and a humming sound filled her ears.

The cold had left her. Now all she felt was heat and glorious pleasure.

"Och, lass, I canna wait."

She grinned and pressed her forehead to his. When she spoke, her voice was husky, sensual and still shocking that it could come from her. "I was hoping ye'd say that."

Daniel took her bottom lip into his mouth, sucking gently as he probed her opening with his shaft. Myra had seen lovers in this position before, knew it could be done...but had never fathomed the logistics of it or how wonderful it would feel. She arched her back, head thrown back with pleasure as Daniel thrust upward, filling her completely.

He gripped her hips, gently guiding her to rock back and forth. Water sloshed over the sides of the bath, but neither of them cared. They only had a mind for each other and the pleasure they both gave and received.

Myra increased her pace, rolling her hips back and forth, rising up and down, the entire experience ethereal. She wanted to go faster and faster, racing toward that ultimate climax. She was so close… Daniel tried to slow her down, but she'd not hear it. Myra gripped his hands in hers and tucked them behind his head as she took over their love-making.

"Love…" he groaned.

"Aye, love, 'tis what we have."

The room echoed with the sounds of their moans and the splashing of the heated bath water. There was no stopping now, no slowing. Myra took Daniel's mouth in a heated kiss, claiming him as he often did her.

They'd chosen each other years ago, both too stubborn to see it through until they'd been tossed into hell. But they'd climbed out on top, and they'd keep climbing. Together the sky was the limit.

At last, sensation ripped through Myra's body with the force of a gale wind. She cried out, shouting Daniel's name as her body shuddered violently. Daniel clenched her hips hard as he thrust upward again and again.

"Myra!" he roared with a final thrust.

She collapsed against him, her head on his shoulder, lips on his neck. Sated to say the least. Myra twirled his hair around her fingers, felt him doing the same to her.

"I love ye," she whispered.

"I love ye, too."

They stayed like that until their skin pruned and the water grew tepid. Daniel pulled her from the bath, dried her, tucked her into bed naked with a cup of wine and a hunk of mutton.

"Now eat and drink."

"In bed?"

The Highlander's Lady

"Why not?" He climbed in beside her. "I've a mind to lick wine from your breasts…"

"Wicked, husband!"

Daniel winked up at her. "Only for ye."

After feasting on each other, Myra and Daniel collapsed into the warm nest of blankets. Myra rested her head on his love-slick chest and scraped her nails gently over his ribs.

"I dinna care what my cousins say, ye are indeed the most proper wife for me."

Leaning up on her elbow, brows raised, she asked, "What do ye mean by that?"

Daniel chuckled. "'Tis a long story, that's bound to get me a lot of ribbing when we visit Dunrobin. Let me just say, I told my cousins I would only marry a proper wife who listened and obeyed."

Myra laughed aloud and climbed atop her husband. "As long as I get my way first."

Epilogue

Early Spring...

Blair Castle loomed ahead. Myra was both frightened and fascinated by it. Daniel warned her of his mother's overbearing nature, and since Myra had grown up without her mother, she really hoped to be close to Fiona.

As they entered through the gates, the clan members cheered and children threw newly bloomed flowers at their horse's hooves. Myra waved and smiled and called her thanks for the warm welcome. This would be her new home.

And oddly enough, it felt like home.

Daniel had sent word to Magnus after the Ross warriors had disbanded—although no one was sure where to as Ronan was still on their trail—that he had found Myra and they'd wed. Another missive was sent to his mother informing her of his nuptials. They'd not been able to wait until spring, when the Bruce insisted the deed be done. A tearful letter had

The Highlander's Lady

arrived from Fiona at having missed the affair. A returned letter from Magnus detailed that Rose had given birth to a boy — Byron Munro the II — the perfect Yuletide gift. But what was more, Rose also agreed to rule Foulis along with the elders until young Byron was able to do so himself. Much to Myra's relief, most of the clan survived as they hid within the walls — Byron's last order before he took up his sword to the enemy. Apparently not an order his wife had followed, but Myra could understand the woman was distraught.

The clan would rebuild. Plans were made for the summer for Myra and Daniel to visit Foulis. She could not wait to bestow a kiss upon the soft head of her nephew and give him the ring of his legacy. There was also the need to visit her brother's final resting spot. The clan had found his body and laid him to rest within the family crypt. 'Twould be painful to kneel before those of her family who passed before her. But at least the line would go on. Little Byron and now… She rested her hand on her belly which was still flat, only the slightest swell. The biggest change to her newfound situation was the nearly doubled in size breasts she carried with pride — and which Daniel gleefully enjoyed.

Happiness fell over her in warm spring-time waves. She'd literally taken the boar by its tusks and beat it — well Daniel had. But she'd survived! Life was forever changed, aye, but only for the better. How ironic that Father Holden had drilled that mindset into her, and she'd had to do just that. She was stronger for it. With Daniel, she could face down any enemy. Any situation.

In the meantime, however, she aimed to make a lot of love to her warrior husband. The man she vowed would be her first and last kiss. How true those words had been. And of course, she wanted to dance every day.

"The End"

If you enjoyed **THE HIGHLANDER'S LADY**, *please spread the word by leaving a review on the site where you purchased your copy, or a reader site such as Goodreads or Shelfari! I love to hear from readers too, so drop me a line at* authorelizaknight@gmail.com *OR visit me on Facebook:* https://www.facebook.com/elizaknightauthor. *I'm also on Twitter:* @ElizaKnight *Many thanks!*

AUTHOR'S NOTE

A note on curse words. As you may have noticed, Myra has a bit of a foul mouth! In deciding that I wanted her to use this type of language I had to do a bit of research. Readers usually think that expletives are more modern, but they are in fact, quite old. Now, some of the words I've used aren't in written documents until the later medieval days, and there is no way to know just how long they were used before recorded. A couple of examples:

~F-word—first written documentation in the 1400's, so in essence could be much older than that.
~Shite – this is where the word shit comes from. It actually means excrement. Has been around since before 1508 when it was first documented to be used. Seen as a very taboo word however.
~Zounds – Actually a variation of God's Wounds.
~Damn – from the late 13th century.
~Mo creach – a Gaelic exclamation, meaning Good Heavens.

A note on hidden walls in Foulis. Foulis stands today with only shadows of its original self still in existence. The motte is still present, and a few stone structures such as arrow slit windows and a stone archway. The majority of the castle as it stands today was rebuilt in the middle of the 18th century. The hidden passageways were entirely my own creation—however, you never know.

A note on Murray's holding Blair. Not until several hundred years later did clan Murray hold Blair Castle. For the purposes of this story, I used creative license to move up the date, particularly because of location.

The Highlander's Lady
A note on the song Myra's mother used to sing to her. This is from the Scottish lullaby, Loch Lomond.

The saga continues! Look for more books in The Stolen Bride Series coming soon!

Book Four– *The Highlander's Warrior Bride*– March 15, 2013

Their greatest opponent won't be battled with a sword…
But with their hearts…

Ronan Sutherland is a fierce warrior. Swearing off all else, he thrives on his powerful position within William Wallace's army. Freedom for the Scots is his mission—until he meets fair Julianna. She captivates him, intoxicates him…makes him want more out of life than what harsh dangers he's accustomed to.

Lady Julianna is no meek maiden. She's trained in the art of war, sister to one of Scotland's most powerful men, and tasked with keeping the future king safe. Until she's kidnapped by a rivaling clan. Now her only hope is for the one man she trusts—and desires—to save her.

Together, they'll have to face down one of Scotland's most treacherous foes… And keep from falling victim to the one thing they've both eluded thus far—love.

There are six books total in The Stolen Bride Series! If you haven't read Book One or Book Two, look for THE HIGHLANDER'S REWARD & THE HIGHLANDER'S CONQUEST at most e-tailers. Check out my website, for information on future releases www.elizaknight.com.

ABOUT THE AUTHOR

Eliza Knight is the multi-published, award-winning, Amazon best-selling author of sizzling historical romance and erotic romance. While not reading, writing or researching for her latest book, she chases after her three children. In her spare time (if there is such a thing...) she likes daydreaming, wine-tasting, traveling, hiking, staring at the stars, watching movies, shopping and visiting with family and friends. She lives atop a small mountain, and enjoys cold winter nights when she can curl up in front of a roaring fire with her own knight in shining armor. Visit Eliza at www.elizaknight.com or her historical blog History Undressed: www.historyundressed.com

Made in the USA
Monee, IL
28 July 2020